Mystic Place

Mystic Place

A NOVEL

Tanya Mardirossian

This book is a work of fiction. Names, characters, places, and incidents are either products of the author's imagination or are used fictitiously. Any resemblance to actual persons, living or dead, business establishments, events, or locales is entirely coincidental.

ISBN-13: 978-0692174296

ISBN-10: 069217429X

Printed in the U.S.A.

.

Prologue

The casket was open. He had requested to see her this way. He stood over it silently, in his head the haunting realization that this would be the last time he'd ever see her in the flesh; in her helpless, timeless, beautifully made-up state.

This wasn't the first time he'd stood over a dead body. He'd worked in Homicide for what should have been the prime of his life—the time his friends took to pursue spontaneous vacations, careers, and relationships.

The only difference in this instance was that there was a type of grace in death, something murder didn't have.

Yet, he thought, *they worked all night cutting her open, gutting her insides, sewing her back up, and applying makeup.*

He looked around the room, saw he was the only thing breathing except for the flowers. He watched her in the casket again. This time, the silence felt heavy on his shoulders. Now he saw a pale corpse and missed opportunities.

Then the funeral came. He hadn't made any announcements—not in the papers, social media, or so little as a text message to people he considered dear. But it was a crowded room, with people full of love and grief. Still, all he felt was the absence and some type of relief, mostly for her eternal rest.

The open casket wasn't presented to anyone else. No one was allowed to see what had become of her. He wasn't sure if he wanted it this way out of guilt for not spending much time with his late mother, not wanting anyone to see how much he failed her, or maybe he just wanted her to himself one last time before she went six feet under.

Little did he know that the changes were here and now, and more were coming. They'd come so slickly that they wouldn't be noticeable to the naked eye until it was too late to alter the path taken. It was new territory for him, feeling a stir of contradictions, because changes were abundant in his lifestyle. Being a detective depended on change, heavily. And this wasn't the first time he'd lost someone to the Reaper. But now he was a grown man, no one else around to take care of this for him. There was time spent, effort executed, both love and frustration felt. Grief could come and go, and he would too. He had to move on, and briskly. He wanted to skip past the things that would truly matter once the hurt would wear off.

The wedding he had been planning with The One was called off. The caterer, planner, and venue had to be notified at once before the calendar unexpectedly flipped on him and it was too late to be refunded. The One would understand, he wanted to believe. And she did, until they both realized picking up where they left off with the arrangements wasn't going to happen any time soon, and maybe, not at all.

He drank. He always did, and even he knew it could be excessive at times. But this act had a different twist to it, because now he drank with breakfast, lunch, and dinner. He never had a standard time to get out of bed; no alarms set on the clock as an excuse. He'd wake up at 5 p.m., 3 a.m., or any time before and after. No one told him not to, including the little voice in his head: Reason.

Not even a full month of grieving and he was moving on to his new life, those inevitable changes taking control of the present he eventually became oblivious to. He hadn't always been so vain—cocky, maybe, but not vain. He didn't let out any tears, and he didn't call anyone afar who he knew and loved to express any kinds of sentiments or problems. He didn't look back, ignoring the answers that might've laid there.

No more regrets, he thought.

Regret found Reason somewhere in the dark.

1

Homecoming

Freddie McAllister was just short of stubborn. He was tenacious but charismatic. He could make conversation with anyone, anywhere, at any time. On this particular late Friday morning, he was cool, relaxed, not conflicted. Mostly.

His realtor had said she would meet him at his hotel bar. He waited there, twenty minutes early, so that he could sneak a drink before she arrived. Rum on the rocks. The bartender asked if he wanted to make it a mixed drink, something smooth to have before noon. Freddie internally argued that a good scotch could be smooth. He refused the bartender's offer and restated his order.

He had his drink but shook his leg irritably anyway. He checked his watch. She wasn't late, but he felt the time drag.

As she entered the lobby, it made Freddie feel like he was a soul entering the gates of heaven: She brought him promise, delight, and paradise. She was right on time, wearing a light, gray turtleneck with a black pencil skirt and matching heels. He didn't know why she dressed up to show him a house, but maybe it was strategic. Her long, dark hair flowed with the outside breeze as she made her way in, and her modish sunglasses hid her green eyes. He kept shaking his leg, more aware of it now. If only she was the only reason to get him this excited. But it wasn't that long ago when he was sitting in his room, pre-booze, feeling his heart race, blood churning and flowing to his head and shaky, red hands. He needed another drink, but she was there now, and he wanted to spare himself of judgment—hers and the bartender's.

He had a right to think about her a little too much; he came to that conclusion before feeling like an obsessive stalker for staying informed about her life over the years. It was easy to do as a detective. And she wasn't just somebody. Veronica Dorian: the person in undergrad he thought he would never see again after the semester concluded.

She was there to pick him up from his five-star hotel on Sunset Boulevard to drive him through surface streets that would eventually meet Pacific Coast Highway from Santa Monica to Malibu. He could've picked a place to lodge that was closer to the water, but he figured he was going to live there soon anyway, so why not see Hollywood before taking it for granted—the people in flip-flops, rain or shine; the punk haircuts; ladies of the night working the streets—all soon-to-be memories of a tourist.

Thank God Veronica smiled; he needed to see that, to turn his mind off.

She followed with "Hey, Fred," (not as enthusiastically as he'd hoped) and a hug. After a few moments of embrace, she pushed him away gently to take a good look at him. "You look..." She tried hard for the right word to avoid being offensive. Freddie silently gave her credit for it. She had expected to see him now, nearly ten years later, skinnier or heavier, with his hair longer or shorter, and even with the premature spurts of grays he had amid his thick brown hair. "...well," she finally said.

"I see your bullshitting skills still need some work."

But her authenticity was just one reason he loved her so much. Had he messed up, telling her a sarcastic but true insult so soon?

"I see you're still an idiot."

One of the few things she had said to him since his mother's passing. They kept their smiles. Some habits were too tough to break. So, there they were, in their old rhythms.

He adjusted the passenger seat in Veronica's car, leaning back to focus on her. He wasn't as sly as he thought he was. She could feel him staring but didn't comment on it until she was well on the road and annoyed at him for ignoring her questions; *How's your stay? blah blah blah.* He had stopped listening.

So, he looked unwell, apparently, but how did she look different but the same, in the best of ways?

When he wasn't watching her, he was watching the hills passing by at 40 miles per hour as they rode on PCH. The hills were browning, but what else would one expect in Southern California? It was what it was, not pretending to be anything else. Being with Veronica was better than walking on the Sunset Strip, and he couldn't handle much more of the things he had been doing alone in the hotel room—sleeping, drinking, acting on impure thoughts to satisfy an appetite that hadn't been met in a while; even helping the maids clean up after waking up at noon thinking, *How did it come to this?* He would've been ready for a part-time job there, if he wanted, but it was time for another change in scenery, another home.

He was still staring.

When it came to Veronica, it was easy for anyone else to notice that Freddie was always too late. Freddie had heard she was ready to move back to the East Coast, making him wonder why their friendzoned relationship never became anything more, possibly because of timing. But this coincidence—of him moving west and her ready to move to where he'd left—seemed to be something other than pure coincidence. It was bad luck or some type of fucked-up karma.

Suddenly, Freddie could feel the air in the car thinning. His leg-shaking escalated to fidgeting in his seat. He was about to lose his cool.

Not now, he kept thinking, until he eventually said it aloud, lowly.

"What is it?"

He could blame his irrational behavior on Veronica being far too calm for someone driving in L.A.

He failed at suppressing this feeling—generally what therapists had said to likely be part of his PTSD—a little while longer. Yes, he had attended therapy sessions, which he had stopped going to. According to Freddie, there wasn't anything that alcohol couldn't fix, and, all in all, it was a much cheaper and quicker solution than therapy.

But the luxurious bar was in another town now.

"Stop the car," he commanded out of silence.

"We're almost there, Fred," Veronica said, a little thrown off by his tone. "Are you carsick? The house is—"

"Stop the fucking car!"

She made a sharp U-turn (illegally but safely; luckily there was no motorcycle cop around to ticket her for it) and pulled over into an empty dirt parking spot alongside PCH. Freddie threw the door open while Veronica left the engine running and remained seated silently in the car with an expression that said, What the hell?

It hadn't been a full hour of being together, and it was a swirl of chaos and emotions. Those old rhythms.

Freddie would have sprinted dramatically as far out to the cliff as he could before becoming broken remains like the sand below. But his long legs felt too heavy and wobbly for that.

Deep breaths.

Veronica put the gear in Park but left the engine on. She got out and slammed the door shut, and it took every ounce of Freddie's concentration not to break his meditation. She crossed her arms and waited.

A breaking wave that hit the rocks was a bullet that ripped from a gun, and it hit Freddie in the chest, causing him to flinch. *Keep looking straight ahead,* he tried to tune everything out. That was why he was there, which brought him to thinking about Veronica in that pencil skirt and hiding behind a pair of sunglasses despite the lack of sunshine.

At just thirty-three, he was too young to feel this tense all the time. Thirty-three and "retired," a former New York Police Department homicide detective done with the job so soon. He was one of the best young ones back home, and he knew it. He was loved and hated for it before he could sucker himself into accepting a major government position. He'd seen enough. Knowing that his father had died on duty aged him even faster, but he kept the job because it was something they had in common. And it was a distraction from thinking about his recently deceased mother. But why be around death by choice? He quit—retired, ready for a simple life like his father had taught him, but with his new inheritance from his mother. A balanced lifestyle to honor them both.

He kept his eyes on the murky, blue-green ocean until his heart stabilized. The view wasn't as rich as the area, but it was better than staring into the Hudson. He thought about Veronica again, how good she looked, standing at a short distance behind him by her car.

"Freddie," she called against the breeze. She didn't need to worry about the wind exposing her legs and more with such a fitted skirt. "We should get going."

Continuing their way to Mystic Place, a narrow street off PCH, Veronica began giving him an overview of the house they were scheduled to tour: a villa near the water, a bachelor pad. Maybe she kept narrating the details to avoid talking about his episode.

"How's the crime out here?" he asked, noticing the remoteness of the street. The houses on the left were built closely together, most of them classic beach bungalows. The houses on the right of the street varied in style and were more spaced out to accommodate private beach access.

Veronica shrugged, her hands on the wheel and eyes on the road as she pulled over in front of the villa. "Celebrities getting tickets for parking in red zones."

Perfect.

They walked past the grand staircase and formal living room with a bar and lounge area. "Perfect for entertaining new friends," Veronica said.

"What is it with realtors and their obsession with entertaining?"

She ignored him and showed him the open-concept, second living room. Across the floor was the kitchen, equipped with a full-functioning island. "There's also the three-hundred-and-sixty-degree patio—great views and the back doors lead to the pool and beach."

It was enough to capture Freddie's interest now that he had a bountiful inheritance, easy money for easy spending. But he couldn't help but think L.A. was just a little wacky.

"A villa, huh? This is all I get for a villa?"

"Welcome to L.A.," Veronica said. "It's not a tech billionaire or Hollywood man's lair, but it's a quiet street with easy beach access, and you have an updated property people would die for. This is what your money gets you."

Veronica's voice echoed in his head as she spoke, taking him back to the day they met in an anthropology class about ancestry and immigration. They bonded over their Gaelic roots: Scottish for Freddie and Irish for Veronica. She never knew for certain if her last name was from her Irish or Armenian heritage; her dad was both. Freddie talked about how he was glad he didn't come into the world as a ginger, though some patches of his facial hair would be a reddish-brown amid premature grays. He had dark features except for his pre-tanned skin. His hair was thick, wavy, medium-dark brown, his eyes also brown but variable in the sun. In other words, he was well aware that the beach would compliment his features, if not enhance them.

Freddie stationed himself at the kitchen sink. He admired the ocean from the window, the dark blue water, the waves unpredictable but perfect—his very own live piece of art. They stepped outside to the backyard. Freddie looked around, took his time at it, but didn't really pay attention to anything specific. He took it as a good sign, like he'd been there before, and this was his homecoming.

Veronica interrupted with, "You're lucky I found this place for you."

Her words weren't to be taken lightly. The houses in the area were known for their changing owners and renters. The house on Mystic Place she was showing Freddie was known for its changing men, so much so that local realtors had notoriously known it as Dead Man's House. To this Freddie said, "Don't make my shopping day morbid."

Morbid. A thought came and left like a flash of lightning, one about his parents. What would they think about his move, his new abode?

"It'll do," he said.

"You haven't even seen the best part. It's upstairs."

Was she toying with him, trying to seduce him? He wiped the thought clean before he would get hung up on some idea of anything more than flirtation with her, a friend. He'd gone through a lot in the last few months after his mother's death, and alone.

"Right," he said. "More views."

"A house like this has several perks, Fred, but it's only the second one you've seen."

"No mountain lions," he said approvingly.

"No, but you may see some dead marine life washed up on the shore." His eyes scolded her for the negative remark. "What, they don't talk about climate change on the East Coast?"

His eyes clung to the view. "This is it. I'm sure."

"It's a lot of money just to settle."

"I'm sure," he said again.

"This is the problem with you rich folk. You have the money and just toss it. If I had millions to give up just like that?" She snapped her fingers by his ear, making him flinch. He didn't know why; he'd heard worse. "I'd take my time, see what feels right."

"Negotiate however you need to. This is it."

As Freddie followed the stretch of the ocean, he noticed the modern Tudor next door, not too distant on the downward curve of the beach. It was closer to the water than the villa was, making him grateful for the spacious backyard he was ready to call his own. But he also liked that this home was closer to the street, closer to life. Not so isolated. He had a decent view into the Tudor's living room at the side of the villa. As his eyes coasted, he saw a woman—in her late twenties or early thirties, he quickly profiled—sitting on a large outdoor sofa. Her hair was tied back and she wore an oversized beige sweater with denim shorts and knee-high socks as she rested beneath her sheltered deck with a book.

She didn't read. She tried, flipping a few pages here and there, but she was preoccupied by the ocean waves the same way Freddie was.

"Who's that?"

Veronica followed his stare and chuckled. "You move fast."

Was it a hint of jealousy he detected? And he was usually good at detecting things.

"Just want to be neighborly."

"You'll have others—if your offer's accepted—like an eighty-year-old, *actual* retired man to your other side. You asked about the quirks to the house, there it is. You're looking at it."

"She's no mountain lion."

"No. More like a slimy fish on the shore." And after another scolding look from Freddie: "People talk, Fred."

"You believe everything you hear?"

"I'm more concerned about what happened in the car earlier."

Freddie wished she hadn't been so candid. "I'm fine." He didn't sound convinced himself.

"I know you've been through a lot and seen things I can't imagine, but you're still having these—"

"I'm fine," he said again, his voice tighter.

"Find a therapist out here?"

"No more shrinks, Veronica. The beach is all the therapy I need."

She let it go.

"You were saying about the neighbor…"

Veronica took a deep breath then let it out slowly. Could his tension be contagious? "This house has been on the market since she moved into that Tudor. Figure that one out, Detective."

"Bull," he said, ready to bet on it. "I never pegged you for the superstitious type. Or jealous, for that matter."

"Don't flatter yourself." She took a moment to stare out to the water. She noticed Freddie silently counting the seconds, the tides; meditating, he called it. She said, "Why do you want to make such a rash decision? With the house."

He thought about it for a moment and said, "I've been gone, and in my life people have been gone. I just need a place to settle into, and this place is perfect."

She couldn't argue with him about the property. "Just think about it," she said, then left him to do just that.

The cloudy skies still hadn't given any rain. A more violent breeze made one of the French doors push back into its frame; the others moved along with the wind, shutters rattling against the windows. These sounds didn't make him flinch. Before heading upstairs to complete the tour, he kept his gaze on the view then closed his eyes. He felt a chill move through him—a good kind.

Homecoming.

2

Jealous Sea

Veronica pulled through with Freddie's offer for the villa, a job well done as always.

Shortly after retirement, Freddie had tried the Hamptons, but found them overhyped and too close to home. Next was Miami, but the mosquitos made his New-York-City-pale skin look like he'd caught some disease. There went his chances at picking up women. L.A. seemed right; he'd get an olive glow, and everything seemed calmer, laid-back, that California living. If he ever missed home, he'd remind himself that the air was as polluted as in Manhattan, (but less so by the beach). Before touring the canyons, Veronica had warned him about mountain lions. He remembered thinking, *No more guns*.

He was happy with his choice. A week after seeing the villa, Freddie moved his boxes out of his four-wheel drive sedan to the entrance before he could even visualize what went in each room. But he was a simple man and didn't have much to unpack. It didn't matter. The villa was more than a step up from living in his car or at a hotel while house hunting. He was happy to be a drifter no more. The houses on the street had decent-sized front lawns and were well kept. This suburban view pressured Freddie to continue tending to his clutter, his maroon T-shirt becoming more plum at his non-existent V-neck, sweaty as he worked.

Veronica arrived earlier than expected to give him an extra set of keys, and he resisted telling her to keep it for visits. They weren't in college anymore. What were the lines now? The way she looked around, Freddie knew she was thinking about the property value going down if he kept the place a mess. He set a heavier box down in the middle of the doorway and dusted his hands off. "Come by for a drink later to celebrate my move-in day. I'll have all the boxes put away, promise."

Why the reassurance of a promise, like he needed to answer to her? He instantly regretted extending the invitation.

"Can't," she said.

After a moment: "Not because of what happened in the car the other day."

She gave him a shrug and look that said, What am I supposed to think?

"A drink, Fred? Really? I mean, when I met you at the bar, seeing you so, so—" She couldn't find a politically correct alternative for fucking psycho. He would have settled for disheveled.

"We didn't meet at the bar." Him and his technicalities.

"You're right. I met you coming into the bar. You were already there for who knows how long."

"I had *one* drink, all ice. You know those hotels; they charge you twenty-five dollars for a washed-down beverage."

She wanted to believe him, she did. At least she had a valid excuse to reject him. "I can't. I'm having my first ever yard sale tomorrow, if you can believe it. Need to organize."

He couldn't believe it. Veronica wasn't on the people-person list he kept in his head, yet she dealt with pleasing people, making their lives full in their new, grand residences. He loved the irony.

"You seem more relaxed today," she admitted.

"Yeah?"

"Yeah. Happy."

"Then I must be."

Maybe it was true. He had the same floaty feeling through him, like he was in grade school with an instant crush. The crush now was, as Veronica would say, "location, location, location."

She gave him a tight smile and left.

He'd might as well start getting used to it.

It was his first night in the house. He popped open a bottle of beer, a summer lager he pulled out of a cooler he had used during camping trips driving to Utah or Arizona from New York. It was always after a big case, boxes of evidence stored in the basement to collect dust. None of his trips ever required much planning; just a man and the open road, which reminded him of the days spent camping with his dad.

Freddie didn't take vacations otherwise. A homicide detective couldn't just pick up and go; murder didn't decide to take a nap or turn off. Neither could Freddie. No one ever wanted him gone. Between his annoyingly meticulous personality—on the job, that is—and his brain that could never shut off, he was a workaholic and tough case cracker. But even he knew when to stop, to leave things alone. He had the financial freedom to quit, and no one ever dared to can him. They wished they had, though, after he quit. Not because they wanted to, but because they wished they'd had the satisfaction.

Freddie unloaded an old beach chair from his car and carried it to the side of the house. He set it down where he had a view of the Tudor to the left, Mystic Place behind him. He went inside for the cooler and carried it outside with its handle over his wrist, and a bottle of beer in his hand. Maybe bringing the cooler was excessive. He wasn't camping, but this was supposed to be an endless vacation. He intended to watch nothing but the beach just past his backyard.

As the evening went on, that changed. It was a night of lonesome celebration. In other words, Freddie was going to get shitfaced by the shore. A snazzy title for an autobiography. *Shitfaced By the Shore*. He thought about giving writing a try for once in his life, for the sake of therapy. In addition to seeing a shrink, he'd been to group therapy, like AA but for detectives and their trauma. He'd been to AA too. He felt pathetic for all of them, but it made for a good chapter in this make-believe book he was suddenly aspiring to write. *Shitfaced By the Shore: Life After Homicide*. He liked it. He even got up, ready to fetch a notepad and fancy, probably overly expensive pen. One of his mother's.

But from the corner of his eye, he noticed a light turn on from the only window visible within the darkened slope that hid from the gorgeous, orange-purple sunset. For a moment, all he could see was the inside of the Tudor, admiring the exposed rich brick wall and a Victorian fireplace. He liked this too. He missed the Queen Anne townhouse that held most of his childhood memories, the happy ones. The Tudor was clean, neat, well furnished. The living room had two modern white Victorian couches, a matching deep purple ottoman, and a glass table in the middle of the room to separate it all. Freddie was envious of the aesthetics, but it was only his first day in his new place, and he'd have plenty of time to customize things. Besides, the Tudor's interior was feminine, or maybe it just had the touch of care to it. Spending time with Veronica again would make him think this way. He admired the setup of a wooden table against the wall that separated the entryway from the kitchen and living room. On it were a few candlesticks and, what he made out to be from the distance, a bowl of seashells. He could see too much. How were people so careless about what they decided to show to the world?

I should ask her over to decorate for me. It would be an ice-breaker.

Then he realized how quickly that would go south.

I love what you've done with the place. The TV and the pictures of your family and friends are all great.

He shook his head and sipped his beer, listening to it fizzle as he moved the bottle away from his lips. Fizzes of beer and swooshes of waves. A title for another chapter.

His eyes went back to the illuminated window, almost thoughtless in his frozen ecstasy, until he was rudely interrupted by a figure moving inside the Tudor. It woke him up. He leaned forward, sitting at the edge of his seat with his eyes still fixed, watching with intent now.

It was her. He looked her up and down, what he could see. Her tan arms just right against her white lace blouse.

It had to be lace.

Freddie had an affinity for women in lace, naturally. It was ruined, though, when he'd seen his mother in her casket, her face covered by a black lace veil. But the feeling was warming him again.

The woman threw her keys into the empty bowl and placed her purse on the lower shelf of the table. She kicked off her low-top boots and put up her wavy hair, then leaned back on the couch like she was relieved to be done for the day.

That was it. That was everything he'd seen that evening and it was oddly satisfying for him. In fact, it made him want to see more. More of nothing spectacular, but he was very interested for reasons he couldn't comprehend. He'd heard of the high tide's effects on the mental state, or how the ocean could lure people in during the night, its currents taking people far off to places they shouldn't be. That's how he felt watching her from his chair, still in the dim sunlight, without drawing attention to himself. He wanted to go to her, to say anything, but what would it be?

Want a beer?

No.

Tomorrow, he thought. *Tomorrow is a new day.*

The idea that no one knew where to find Freddie should've let him sleep in peace, tune out like he wanted to.

But he realized: *No one knows where to find me.*

It was going to be a sleepless night.

A sleepless night wasn't anything out of the ordinary for Detective McAllister. His days had consisted of sleeping on the couch and occasionally waking up to the sound of the landline phone ringing in the apartment he hardly spent time in. Relaxing by the sea was the last place anyone would think to find him, because everyone knew he didn't know how to relax. This was the man who left his then-girlfriend on a romance and relaxation trip, constantly checking his phone until he eventually drove back to the city. Now, his cell phone could ring, but he figured he had the ocean to throw it in, though he liked the ocean too much to trash it. Imagining tossing it would do.

He woke up to a new sun with a headache, still outside in the same spot he drank away the night, slouched in the beach chair, knowing he'd feel the effects later. Around him were half a dozen or so beer bottles, some tipped over, one broken. He stood a little too quickly, too hazy-headed to do the math on how much he had consumed per his blood alcohol concentration. He rubbed his eyes, the sounds of aggressive seagulls giving him another type of headache, and checked his watch.

Quarter to noon. And he still had boxes outside, overnight like he had been. Unpacking wasn't something he felt like dealing with, but he had to, especially if Veronica was to drop by unexpectedly. *This is why things could never work.* It was a promise to her broken, even if it was just a silly one.

He managed to get himself to clean. In both hands he carried two bottles by his index and middle fingers poked into them, another two under his arm. He threw the bottles into the recycling bin tucked away in a spacious kitchen drawer. Freddie had heard the lectures about recycling, climate change, pollution, all the L.A. preaching; not that he disagreed. He searched for the little duster he used to keep by the water heater in his apartment. It had to be somewhere in the many boxes he hadn't unpacked. He found it after an hour of digging through boxes. He swept the broken glass on the side patio and dumped the pieces into the recycling bin.

Having a cup of coffee in the chair outside seemed like an assuring way to make the headache go away, until a screeching seagull landed on the porch rail. Clearly, it had been waiting for Freddie to relax so it could annoy the shit out of him. He wished a piece of broken glass was still nearby so he could throw it at the bird; not to hurt it, just to piss it off. It was better that nothing sharp was around. The bird could fly away and bring back vengeful friends. Freddie was too tired to deal with something as trifling as that. But if some beach birds were his biggest concern in his new home, he had it okay. The seagull eventually flew away, but Freddie didn't follow its flight over the water; the ocean's spell didn't have him bound today.

His eyes were pulled toward the slope again, scanning Mystery Girl's deck. The table and two chairs were out of place like they had been used. But he hadn't heard anyone around. Then again, the waves were loud, and he was shit-faced by the shore. It bothered him that everything was left a mess. It seemed off, unless the woman next door was an utter slob. *Doubt it.* Based on what little he'd seen, she played by routine. It made him more curious, this one, basic similarity.

It's not your business anymore, he thought. *It's not your business at all.*

He was used to prying for the sake of safety. But he was done with work, the whole reason (that he admitted to himself) he moved to the other side of the country. L.A. had its crime, but he wouldn't take part in helping any of it. *Run loose, you criminals and crooks, wild like the fucking seagulls.* A seagull—the same one or its friend—was there again screaming. Now he wished he had a gun. He had wanted to avoid shooting mountain lions. But a seagull? He'd load, aim, and shoot from miles away.

Freddie turned away from the view. The seagull had been enough to convince him to stop thinking about the house and the woman who lived in it. He had his hand on the doorknob, ready to head back inside when he noticed a small rectangular notepad under the chair. How did that get there? He remembered the fake autobiography, but he hadn't left the chair all night, had he? He didn't remember unpacking office supplies for the upstairs study either, not even to get a pen to write his titles, which reminded him: he wanted to get all that written down before he'd forget. He deliberated inwardly for a moment on whether he wanted to pick up the notepad. He had better things to do, say, swimming, surfing, biking, or running alongside the low tide.

You'll feel addled until you reach for it and see for yourself.

He slid the notepad out from under the chair. He took a step toward the door again, ready to find a pen to record his creative ideas and change into new clothes, maybe swim trunks, but the writing on the pad got to him:

She's going to get you too.

His heart stopped cold, then gave a beat so hard that it felt like a punch to his chest.

It's probably Veronica playing a joke on you.

It could've been Freddie's handwriting. Then again, he and Veronica had forged one another's handwriting before, back when they completed the other's homework for subjects they didn't care for. He was bothered that he couldn't figure out who had written this, worried his skills were going askew because he'd moved. It couldn't be.

Someone—a she—is going to get me in Dead Man's House.

Too? Someone's already been gotten to.

It was a warning, an unwanted warning. A threat? Still, this was nothing as daunting as what he had dealt with: wearing a bulletproof vest, a wire, and carrying a gun (these were the more trivial things). But instinct told him to take this warning seriously, like he was going to put it in a plastic bag and store it away as evidence.

Fright became curiosity. He threw the notepad onto the chair and stepped toward the edge of the patio to look down at the empty chairs and table. He wouldn't be doing his due diligence, as a neighbor, if he didn't check out the scene. Before he could overthink it, he walked over to the short, steep wooden steps that led up to the Tudor's back.

The deck was practically an indoor space. It had a wood-panel ceiling with a fan, and retractable shades for shielding the ocean breeze, open now with a close view of the water. A coffee mug sat on the tall table. Next to it was a book, its pages riffling in the wind. Freddie closed it to see the front cover. He chuckled: crime fiction. She'd already earned points with him. He placed the mug on top of the book, mentally noting that the coffee wasn't warm, which meant no one had been there lately. *Or it's just a chilly morning that let it go cold.*

Standing around thinking about a cup of coffee wasn't going to matter if danger was around, and not after hearing a startling noise that came from the opposite end of the house. Freddie reached for his nonexistent holster, feeling stupid after he did. He let out an irritated sigh at his inanity. But the scene was suspicious to him, and for all he knew, Mystery Girl could be inside sound asleep…or dead on the floor. It was normal to think the worst. His entire career was based on what-ifs, hypotheses, and storytelling. It was also based on logic and facts. Science. But even science was founded on theories and hypotheticals.

He turned the corner ready to reprimand an intruder. A pair of eyes met his, wide and shaken. It was no intruder. Her. Just her. They stood motionless for a split second, measuring what the other would do.

When she saw he wasn't a threat, she set down her brown paper bags by the front door and said, "Can I help you?"

She's very polite. If it were someone on his property, he would've scared them off with a badge or worse. That was another thing about the job aging Freddie: it made him grumpy, almost like an old man who hated all other living organisms.

"I live next door," he pointed to the villa, "up there."

She noticed the chair before looking back at him. "Ah, I'd heard someone moved in. I began to think it wasn't true with the house so dark."

Freddie wondered if she'd watched him as much as he'd watched her. How tragically boring and disappointing that would be for her. He felt a spate of guilt and comfort all at once.

"Welcome to the neighborhood," she said more flatly than an enthusiastic welcome. "What brings you to the wrong house?" She said it calmly with a small curve to her lips, like she could say anything, even Fuck you, and still make it sound cute.

"I heard some noises. The cop in me had to investigate."

It could've passed as the truth. He couldn't help but peep into her grocery bags, as if seeing something like toothpaste or plastic wrap was going to give him more insight about who she was. He looked away, but it left him looking at her, taking in her facial features like recording paperwork on interviews. They were all nut comparisons, of all things: eyes, chestnut brown and almond-shaped; body build, like a peanut, almost hour-glassed, but petite. Her small size made him feel a sense of urgent protectiveness for her.

"You're a cop?" Her confusion became worry.

"I'm a detective," he corrected, but that wasn't right either. "Used to be."

"So, you could fight off some raccoons for me? That's probably the noise you heard. You can get rid of city life out here, but the city will find you. They go through garbage bins all the time. Keep yours sealed tight," she said, walking around back with a wave-like motion prompting him to follow. She showed him the bins. Untouched. Freddie couldn't see her face, but he knew she had to be confused if not suspicious of him. He'd better come up with an explanation for his skulking. There was really no better explanation than the truth of it: outright skulking. *At least I can blame it on old habits on the job.*

She made her way up the steps Freddie had welcomed himself to, probably wanting to check things out herself.

He said, "Your space out here looked like it was being used, but I didn't see anyone around for a while. I grew suspicious. Then I heard the noise and thought maybe something was up, and here we are."

"I must've ruined your beach view. And to have you worried. But, uh, for future reference, I'm a black belt and have no problem with the Second Amendment."

Why did he find that attractive? How she said it so humbly. He quickly got a mental picture of the two of them at a shooting range, blowing bullets into tin cans and paper silhouettes.

Stop it.

"Do neighborhood watch too?" he asked.

She smiled at him awkwardly, prompting him to nervously survey the deck. He took in what he could until his eyes stopped on the book again. She caught it and said, "It must be weird reading these kinds of books, spotting flaws or having it be so close to your life. Unless you've read it already?"

"I haven't," he said. "But if you tell me it's any good, I might read one like it. Retired life has given me some time."

"Retired? Shouldn't you have white hair and bad eyes?"

"I've gotten used to the word."

She let an awkward moment pass before saying, "You can take this one." She removed the mug from on top and handed him the book, then waited for the strange man who now lived next door to go away.

"Oh, no," he said, repelling from it like it was a snake or something else he hated…a seagull. "Looks like you're in the middle of it."

"I know where to find you when I want it back."

Freddie accepted the book and she moved on to unlock the back door with an easy turn of the key. Freddie was surprised by this simplicity; locks, including the ones to his new home, tended to have quirks.

"You can help me with the bags," she said, leaving the door open for him. Freddie raised a brow. "A small debt for trespassing," she added.

Maybe this was going better than he thought.

"I really am sorry about that. This." He looked as guilty as he felt. He hadn't had this wretched feeling since he was calling off his last engagement. It still weighed him down every now and then.

She made her way across the house to the front door, where her bags were waiting on the other side. He picked up a couple, giving himself a cover for working up a nervous sweat. He wished the house was new to him, but he had seen it before, the living room and parts of the kitchen area, anyway. "Nice setup," he said.

"Thanks. You can just put those on the island right there," she said, directing Freddie to the kitchen as she put her key in the same bowl Freddie had seen. "Thanks again for the help," she said, coming off as a hint for him to leave; he acknowledged it.

"No problem. Glad there's no intruder."

"There kind of is," she said with the same smile she gave him outside, one that was kind but malignant.

"Right," he said bashfully. But he recouped. "If you're free sometime, I could use a friendly face to show me around, give me the good list, bad list, that kind of thing," he said, peeking out to her view of his place.

Freddie usually liked chatting people up to distract them from something he had up his sleeve, like a magician, fooling them and not giving a damn about how it made either of them look. But the request wasn't entirely made up to coast them along. He was interested. He wanted her to show him around and give him those lists.

They stood in dead air until she said, "I'll see you around." Another hint.

He had gotten terribly sloppy at being Mr. Suave. But her tone was certain. He liked it at first, but then he thought how it was something he would say to give a firm vibe to a suspect.

He stepped out to her front porch, though he felt pushed out, and remained there with his back facing the door, looking down at the book in his hands until he heard the lock fasten behind him. Instead of going straight home, he decided to take Veronica's advice and visit his retired neighbor, Earl, to introduce himself.

When he did get home, the weekly paper—a subscription gift from his and Veronica's friend, Ben, a journalist in Philly—was on the mat. He knew it was coming, since Ben texted him letting him know to expect something small as a housewarming. Freddie placed the book under his arm and removed the plastic bag off the paper, and turned the pages until he found his preferred section. The key phrases stood out:

...missing locals...males in their thirties...outstanding community members...family and friends seeking answers...tip line...

Blood pumped through his body vigorously, the way it did each time he had gotten a new case.

I don't deal with it anymore, he needed to remind himself.

He tossed the newspaper back to the ground and stepped inside. How long had the door been unlocked for? Then back to the paper. He had journalist friends, ones who worked hard and felt proud seeing their names in print. Out of guilt or respect, he tossed the paper onto the granite top. He opened all the shutters, letting the natural light make its way inside, everything outside visible. He was still carrying the book. He placed it on the coffee table, thinking about that lager he liked so much. Then he remembered how he'd left some in the cooler, still outside. He stepped outside from the side door to retrieve it. His eyes naturally glanced at the Tudor again. The sea had to be jealous now, not having his full attention. The loud, jealous sea.

He turned away from the Tudor but did a double take. The second time he looked, Mystery Girl was gone; she wasn't in the kitchen chopping away, nor was she resting in her living space. He wondered about an intruder, a real one. A psycho on the loose in town. The paper validated some aspects. Now no one was on the beach, and Mystic Place was quiet except for the cars zooming on PCH.

What had he missed?

Back in the kitchen, he raised his head to the sound of the doorbell.

He left the cooler on the kitchen counter and made his way to the door, thinking, he'd conversed with her, he'd been in her home, he'd left with one of her belongings. He hadn't gotten her name.

3

Dark Times

The sounds of the doorbell became hard knocks. He was hesitant to answer, the vibrations echoing through the entryway. But Freddie was a big boy—a big boy who knew how to fight a man off and use a gun. He was tired, though, feeling the need for food, water, and some type of alcohol. Could he fend for himself if it was someone unexpected at the door? He had to man up, sharpen his blurred vision.

He walked across the wooden floor as lightly as he could so that he could open the front door quickly enough to try to startle whoever was on the other side. It worked, but it was wasted effort. It was only Veronica.

"What're you doing here?" he asked, showing some relief.

"I'm sorry," she didn't mean it, "were you expecting someone else?"

He ignored her, raising the paper in his hand. "Seen this?"

"You shouldn't wrap your head around the news too much," she said plainly.

"Subscription from Ben. He'd love to hear you say that, I'm sure."

"He does. He laughs when we're on the phone. Have you talked to him lately? He asks about you. Says you barely ever get back to him."

"No," Freddie said, almost regretfully, and closed the door behind her. "I haven't talked to him, but I appreciate his sentiments."

He didn't want to talk about Ben; it was just Freddie and Veronica now, and he never liked that Ben and Veronica had an unresolved relationship that was more than pure friendship.

"You said you had a busy day. Something about a garage sale rings a bell," he said.

"I felt bad for leaving you the way I did. My amends are in here," she pointed at the takeout bag. "I *know* you don't have food in your fridge."

He didn't like it at first, her showing up like he was so helpless. He was Freddie McAllister, the guy who wasn't fazed by the crazies. But when Veronica Dorian was around, Freddie was an odd mix of on-edge and comfortable, like he was now. Maybe too comfortable, the root of their problems. That, and something about her that made him feel like they were a divorced couple that tried to be friends like years of a bad marriage were never there. But any negative thoughts went away when she walked past him to the kitchen counter, comfortable like he was, like she belonged.

"You worry too much," he said.

"Yeah, but with my genes? I'd be a freak of nature if I didn't."

Veronica unloaded the bag then searched the cabinets for plates and glasses and everything else that went with them. She hated disorder, something she and Freddie usually had in common. "All the way to the right, by the fridge," he directed. He pulled a container closer to open it, feeling like a hungry boy after soccer practice, ready to eat anything and everything. Bonus that the container was full of fries. "I haven't eaten grease like this in years," he said.

"A strict beer diet will do great things for you."

"Trying to get me to put on a few pounds? Make me unable to run after bad guys?"

"You shouldn't be doing that anymore anyway," she said, adjusting her skirt as she sat at the breakfast bar.

"Thank you for this," he said. "And for that note you left me this morning." He sat next to her, but her expression was blank. They weren't on the same page. "I made detective without reaching the point of bothering the higher-ups about it," Freddie said, fries sticking out from the sides of his mouth.

"Are you going to tell me what you're talking about? I'm a little old for guessing games, don't you think? Unless you want to give me a million dollars for my try," she said with a sinister smile.

"This," he said, pointing his index finger up for her to wait while he got up and searched through the top drawer of the table by the couch. Then he smacked the notepad on the counter before her.

Veronica dragged it closer and read aloud, "'Shitfaced By the Shore'?"

"Fuck. No, not that. Flip it. Flip the page." He stretched his hand out to do it for her before she read any more, but she slapped his hand away. He wasn't used to feeling her flesh since being with her again, and now he did because of a slap. A motherly slap. A future with her wasn't promising.

She read again. "'She's going to get you too.' Why would you write that?" She tossed the notepad back on the counter and nibbled on a fry. "One too many last night, that's why."

He shook his head, picked up the notepad, and waited for her to break her poker face, to laugh like she'd lost a staring contest. He gave it a moment, saw she wasn't going to budge. He said, "I didn't write it," then he searched her eyes some more.

"And you think I did?"

"You didn't come by earlier today while I was sleeping?"

"I'm here with food apologizing for leaving you alone. Believe me, I'd rather see you sound asleep. Quiet."

Believe me. In Freddie's experience, anyone who said it at the beginning of a sentence was lying.

"Quit giving me bull. That's your handwriting trying to pull off my handwriting." He held the notepad too close to her face. She snatched it from him. "Are you the 'she'? I didn't know you had it in you, you sick fuck."

"Cut it out, Fred." She was using his big-boy name, a sign that she wasn't playing games. "That's not my handwriting. If it's not yours, I believe you, but it's not mine."

"So, someone else was on my property."

"I don't know, Fred. If you think someone was here earlier, make sure your doors are locked tonight and sleep with an eye open. You have a gun anyway, don't you?" She wasn't taking him seriously.

"Not even to leave a note?" He wouldn't let it go.

"Drop it, Fred," she said through her teeth. "You're the detective. Tell me, which makes more sense: the culprit being the drunken idiot writing about being shitfaced by the shore, or the sober friend who knocked on the door five minutes ago?"

He sat on the barstool again and let out a sigh. He gave up and she was getting irritated, and he didn't want that.

"I don't have a gun," he said, like he was puny for it. "Turned it in when I left."

"But one of your own?"

"Never owned my own."

"You're kidding."

He shook his head, his lips pouting at how he was sad about the fact. Mystery Girl made her way to his mind. Was it the fact that he didn't have her name that made him think about her more and more, or the fact that she was right there, accessible? "It's okay," he said. "Neighbor's got one."

"Earl has a gun?"

"Not Earl."

She showed a different type of concern. "Why do you know she has a gun?"

"I interviewed her." *Interview is a loose term.* "Her place looked like an amateur crime scene this morning. Just a little B and E. Nothing wrong, though. We got to talking and she mentioned she owns a gun. Knows how to use it too."

"You've had a history with crazy chicks, my friend. Why is that, given your former profession?"

"They're predictable," he said. "To me."

"Maybe you can ask her if she saw anything early this morning. She might've been able to see something from her place."

"She does have a good view."

"Why do you know that, Fred?"

He said, "What does it matter to you?"

"It doesn't. I just know you've been down a weird road before, getting into business you shouldn't be in. Your mom knew it too."

"I wouldn't call being engaged to my partner business I shouldn't be in."

"You forget the details about you being paranoid and possessive. Write that down on your notepad, Shitfaced."

Freddie rolled his eyes.

"Just be careful, is all I'm saying."

"Always am."

He always was.

He spent the evening sitting on the chair outside again. It was enough to serve as patio furniture for the foreseeable future. Buying furniture meant being stationed, and he didn't know if his villa was It. Malibu could be Miami; he was in Florida for only three months before he'd decided to move out west. Charleston could've been next—anywhere in one of the Carolinas. If California living wouldn't suffice, southern living would.

Like his days living out of a car, he ate a sub wrapped in its paper packaging, peeling away at it as his bites got farther to the bottom. At the moment, he didn't need television or a book. The water served as a sound machine. He was set.

The Tudor's lights had been off all evening. Once in a while, the motion-sensor light at the back of the house would flicker before going dark again. Freddie was concerned at first, on edge—literally; he sat on the edge of his seat the first few times he noticed the flashes, thinking something had to be out there to trigger the light's sensor. During the next set of flashes, he felt more relaxed, leaned back, seeing there wasn't a figure in sight except for the black palm trees in the distance swaying to the evening breeze under dark purple skies. It reminded him again of camping with his dad, a happy thought before submitting to sleep.

He couldn't be certain about how long he had actually been unconscious for; he hadn't checked his watch. The sounds next door brought him back. But no flicker. He could see two dark figures on the deck. They were people, he was certain, confirmed by the sound of the back door opening and slamming shut. He almost got out of his chair ready to pounce at the chance to help arrest two intruders. But he instantly relaxed again in his seat, recognizing one of the voices as his neighbor's. Hers. The other voice was a man's.

Date night.

He found entertainment for the night, perfect, considering he hadn't bothered setting up the TV in either one of the living rooms. He felt like a hermit, the way he spent his time. He must have looked unkempt. He ran his hand through his hair before it became a scruffy rub. He thought about sniffing his T-shirt but didn't want to; he knew what it would smell like. He ditched his phone, ready to walk straight into the pool fully clothed. He went to grab a towel from the shed next to the outdoor shower. He was sure to store one in there for spontaneous swims or jogs on the beach. He took the one out, leaving the shelf empty. He considered buying more towels, but why? It was just him now. He plopped into the pool, feeling refreshed and clean, and let himself go under, his clothes weighing him down.

With his head emerged, he noticed how dark the night had become, his yard nearly painted black, only able to see the outline of his house as a shadow. It was a clear night. He could see stars above and hear the sea shouting to mere mortals about how powerful it was.

Bullets ripped again.

Could they be real gunshots?

It was impossible for him to make out distinct sounds with the crashing waves, something good for anyone who valued their peace and quiet. But Freddie didn't like things too quiet. It never meant calmness; it meant something unpleasant was around the bend.

He floated on his back for a few minutes, water filling his ears, listening to the sounds of his stable breaths taking over. It was peaceful enough for him to fall asleep, but now wasn't the time for sweet slumber. He tried to think of something that would keep him awake, alert.

Work.

McKinney, one of the old-timers (he'd kill Freddie if he called him that), liked to ask, *What're the weekend plans?* McKinney was a guy in his late-sixties, but he'd never tell anyone his age even though everyone had their ways of figuring it out.

Camping here and looking through records, would be my guess, Freddie would say.

Give your eyes a break. Sometimes coming back to it Monday morning will give you all the answers you need, McKinney had said, unlocking his car door the turnkey way. It was a typical old-timer thing to say.

It's a computer, not a crystal ball, Freddie would think.

Old-timers thought they had all the answers because they thought they had seen it all. McKinney probably had, having been in Homicide since his twenties, close to Freddie's age when he had joined. Freddie thought he'd seen enough, so he could imagine what it was like for McKinney. Freddie missed him like a father. They even had the same initials. But with McKinney's old-timer status and Freddie's young skills, there was always a competitiveness. They bickered like family and it never got old. The days were incomplete without the dynamics and banter, because no one else cared about anyone in the precinct. What Freddie and McKinney had was friendship, brotherhood. Freddie had also come close to finding the partner of a lifetime.

Detective work could feel a lot like marriage. There were bickering partners, the partners who couldn't stand each other; the ones who tolerated each other; and the ones who were inseparable; the best friends. Freddie was lucky enough to have a partner who understood him on and off the clock. They were the newbies at the time, the two youngest in Homicide. After six months of good friendship and some flirtation, they began dating, something they had to disclose up front, making the whole thing feel more rushed than it was.

Freddie was convinced she was the love of his life, someone who understood the crazy work hours and better yet, knew what they consisted of. They could help each other at work and at home, knew the same people, had the same mind, and different minds. They were the perfect match, and their romantic lives didn't particularly concern anyone else on the force. But as the cases poured in, there was that competitiveness Freddie had felt with McKinney, and that was never meant to go home. Eventually, they terminated all things romantic—and eventually, platonic. They let plans go, like a cold case file: so much left unresolved but it was over. Freddie hadn't exactly rebounded or moved on since, not with a funeral to execute, and not with the big decision to move across the country.

As Freddie got out of the pool, his wet clothes made him sensitive to the cold air. The waves were still angry. It was almost a full moon, the only light visible anymore. He stripped, leaving the wet clothes on the ground near the shed. He wrapped the towel around him, felt its coldness that could've been mistaken for dampness. He flinched, not from the coldness, but from withdrawal jitters. All he wanted to do was drink again, drink and sleep on his beloved chair, but he didn't want to catch his death out there.

Before going inside, he glanced at his neighbor's house, something to do to keep from leaving little puddles of water on the floors, he quickly justified. He could see her and her guest lounging on the deck with drinks now. She was probably being an attentive host, their evening likely to roll into the next morning. Freddie could sit there and perform voice-overs for the two of them, but he thought warmth would be good, in his bed this time.

He turned on the light to the master bedroom and ut-
tered, "Fuck. Me." It was not an ideal view. Just a room
with a mattress in its rightful spot surrounded by boxes.
Sheets. Where are the goddamn sheets? He suddenly felt a draft
down below. "Clothes would be fine if I can't find sheets."

Oh, no. He was becoming one of those people who lived
alone and talked to themselves.

He went through each box, one by one, opening them
gruffly. Until, finally...*Clothes.* He took each item out, re-
folded, and placed them in the dresser across the bed or
hung them up in the closet. After moving around the room
for some time sorting through things, his towel dropped.
He worried for a moment, not intending to flash his neighbors. He figured any nighttime water adventurers wouldn't
see anything but a dark shadow from afar. His female
neighbor would maybe get a peek at something good, and
Earl was probably senile. Freddie took it as a sign to shower
now that he had clothes to change into when he would step
out. The sheets would have to wait until he was clean; salt,
sand, and depression down the drain.

He got out of the shower feeling clearheaded. He was
warm, comfortable, ready to take pride in inhabiting the
upstairs. He found the sheets a clean white T-shirt and set
of boxers later. He made the bed, not caring about the half-
assed job he did. Then he took some boxes to his walk-in
closet for temporary storage. Once he leveled all the boxes
next to each other so that there was no risk of a pile falling
in the middle of the night, he opened them up, just to get
an idea of their contents. He hesitated at the next one, having noticed the writing on the side. His dad's life, what was
left of it, shacked up in a box. Dad's Box.

He opened it with more interest. Inside were some old
CDs, even older LPs—Freddie put those aside for proper
storage downstairs—and one of his sweaters; and all the

way at the bottom, his dad's old revolver and its locked speedloader keeping .38 Specials in place. Freddie loaded the cylinder with the help of the speedloader and clicked it in. He aimed at the French doors that led out to the balcony. The revolver felt right in his grip—different from what he had used on the force, but good, because it was his dad's.

He locked the bullets back into the speedloader, all but one. One he placed back into the cylinder before storing the gun and all of his dad's other belongings in the last, empty dresser drawer. He closed the drawer somewhat doggedly, closing off all thoughts about his parents while he was at it.

He went back downstairs with an emptied stack of boxes and stored them in the garage.

Now to relax.

He flicked the switch to the electric teakettle. As he waited for the boil, he found one of few mugs he owned, remembering the orientation from when Veronica had searched the cabinets.

Click.

He slipped on the sneakers he kept by the door and took his tea to the chair. The spot. It really wasn't the best view he had. The pool entrance was better. It was a straight-on view of the water. But the chair was higher up with a perfect view of the Tudor next door near the water. Even in the dark, the scenery looked like one in a painting. He thought about standing out there with a blank canvas and paint palette instead of taking a notepad and pen. So, he settled in the chair.

The Tudor's living room lights were on. Freddie looked harder past the steam coming out of his mug. He lowered it, steam disappearing in the wind. He looked hard again. There they were, near the front door. The scene had changed a little since the last time Freddie's eyes rolled down. They were inside now, with emptied wine glasses in the kitchen. *I'll just leave it in the sink,* he could imagine hearing his neighbor say to her guest when he would offer to help clean up.

Freddie felt rude for watching. Rightfully. *Old habits die hard,* he told himself again. But he thought how he was on his property, in the dark, sitting in the chair he loved so much. He knew what the definition of crime was, and the forms it could come in. This—watching—wasn't one of them.

Her guest went in for a kiss, but she gave him her cheek. It made Freddie chuckle. But Mystery Girl grabbed her guest's hand on his way out. He looked down at his hand in hers and went in for a kiss again, this time successfully. Freddie was ready to quit for the night, but his eyes stayed glued to the living room. There was no way the guest was going home any time soon. His hands were on her hips, kissing her as he led her backwards. She knocked into the entry table Freddie had seen her put her keys on the other day. The man took the knock into the table as a sign of advancement, lifting her on.

Freddie was feeling heat and guilt. *This is what the hot seat under the lamp feels like.* Some of it was left over from the inexplicable anxiety thinking about his dad, McKinney, and work. Dark times. He got up, hoping no one noticed movements from where he pried. They didn't; they were too busy.

Freddie finally looked away. It wasn't his business. He was just glad her guest had closed the door before he took his second chance. An unattended open door would've been enticement for a trespasser. An invitation.

4

Seaside Rendezvous

His dreams that night weren't anything good, but dreaming was an improvement to his sleep cycle. Well, there was that one dream about *her*. Nothing special, but it was a dream, and a dream was a fantasy. Or premonition.

The two of them by his pool early morning waiting for the sunrise with a steaming mug in each of their hands. The contents of his mug had a little something extra, of course. Something to take that constant edge off. At least the dreams weren't about his parents, his work, or all the places he'd moved to and left. He didn't dream much about his ex either. She just dropped in to say, *What are you doing, Freddie?* in a patronizing tone. But he shifted his trance to something else in the good instance of being able to control a dream. Back to *her*.

Next was water—the tough sand near the frothy waves. No bullets fired, no nagging exes. It all felt real, probably climaxing in his head to the sound of crashing waves coming in from the bedroom's open balcony doors. He thought he'd wake up feeling like his lungs were taking in water, the current taking him under and away. But he was pleased, happy, in such a good mood that when he woke up, he made his bed to keep the upstairs clean, even if he didn't have anyone to share it with. There were no boxes to trip over, no ugly messes to be upset about. The mattress was comfortable, and he had rested better than expected. All a good start to the day.

First things first, he followed his coffee ritual. He could feel his happiness surge to the patter into the pot and the smell of fresh brew. It was too good of a morning to spend it indoors or in the usual chair.

After a cup, he had himself another—because it was just coffee, nothing to be shameful about; *just another cup of one of the most addictive drugs in America*—and stepped outside to the backyard.

The wind hit his bare chest and legs. He breathed in the salty morning dew, then took a step forward with his eyes closed to just listen. But he felt something slimy beneath his feet. He opened his eyes in disgust, only to find the crumpled-up, wet clothes from the night before. He hung them up to dry on his balcony rail, then changed into a pair of swim trunks.

Freddie walked down to the shore, leaving the doors unlocked, house unattended, not caring about recent crime excerpts he'd read. The water was calling him, ridding all other sounds in the world and his head. The waves smothered all other sounds too well, it seemed, for Freddie was so in peace that he was thrown off seeing another figure on the beach. A familiar face. Mystery Girl's. At first he wasn't sure if it was her. She looked different, not necessarily in a bad way. Her hair was darker, wet.

He wasn't going to say anything, determined to make it to the water to keep his good day uninterrupted. But she was walking past him—this was inescapable—her skin glazed by water before drying under the sun.

"Hey," they said simultaneously.

She looked up at him with a hand blocking her face from the sun and said, "You're a morning person too."

The amber in her light brown hair sparkled under the sun, the bottoms of her hair still dark and wet.

"Not by choice," he said.

There was always something keeping Freddie up: caffeine, an unsolved case, gruesome photos of a crime scene, or sometimes, not being put on a case. His mother. He needed to think of something else before his morning was ruined for good.

"You know," he said, "I feel like an idiot for not getting your name the other day."

There was a moment of no words between them, just the sound of waves. He was starting to think he would never get her name. Earl would live next door. Just Earl and that girl. Then he had mental images of what he had seen the night before. It made him rub his eyes, knowing it wouldn't be enough, to keep from thinking of her when she was right there.

"Charlotte. Charlotte Walker," she said. "But if you call me Charlie, I might have to kill you."

Charlotte, he told himself so he wouldn't forget.

"Oh, that's right." She nervously pulled back her hair over her shoulder. "I'm sorry, I shouldn't have said that, having left your job. It slipped my mind. It must be triggering or annoying to hear things like that."

"I can take a joke," he said, maybe too defensively. But how *did* she know work was a sensitive topic for him?

"I'm sure you can. It's just—" She gave him an awkward smile and looked at the water before looking back at him.

"What?"

"No, it's nothing."

"What?" he insisted.

"You kind of give off an aura that it's a delicate subject to you."

"An aura," he awkwardly repeated as he brushed his facial hair. "Okay, so you're one of those people."

She smiled. "I'm really not. I don't think I've ever said that to anyone before. But you do put something out there. Either way, I'm sorry. I forgot about your job. Being retired, you said. Right?"

Freddie was offended. He'd watched her from his house, seen things he shouldn't have had. They were private, personal things. Intimate. But she knew nothing about him. Actually, she had known and had forgotten; that was worse than not knowing anything at all.

"Don't be sorry," he said. "And I get it, about the name. As a kid by mom always used to say 'Ready, Freddie?' every time we were leaving the house. I couldn't stand it."

"'Sorry, Charlie' for me."

Freddie gave an apologetic smile and resisted to say the phrase she couldn't stand. "I need to get used to the fact that I can't say I'm part of law enforcement." A moment slipped away. "So...Charlotte."

She gave him her hand.

He shook. Detective McAllister had the puzzle piece now. "Charlotte's pretty," he said, then hated that he said it aloud. "The name. Your name." *Shut up.* "Fred McAllister. Or Freddie. I won't kill you for calling me either."

Their hands finally parted.

"Now I know you and what you do."

She made it sound implicative, making his heart skip a beat. Or was he just nervous around her because she was beautiful, sharp, and he was acting like a doofus? He had a sudden sense of sympathy for his past interviewees.

"What do *you* do?" he asked.

She smiled guiltily as she looked away to the water. Freddie knew what it meant. She was searching for a lie, but failed. She was going to tell the truth, even if she didn't want to. That was one of his best abilities as detective; he could make just about anyone crack. He could make anyone feel relaxed, comfortable. Or simply tired enough to give in. After a while, suspects would forget that they weren't opening their heart to a friend, but that they were on record confessing to their actions.

"Would it be awful if I said I'm an heiress?" She shook her head. "That sounded pretentious. I just mean that a turn of events has brought me out here permanently." She waited for a reaction, appearing to give a nervous smile, as if she was preparing to dodge the backlash.

He was taken aback. This was unexpected. He had made up stories about her life, but what she'd just revealed wasn't one of them. It was too easy. It made him wonder if that was why Veronica let him tour the house. Maybe it was a block full of inheritance collectors.

Earl too?

"Not pretentious. I guess I'm on the same track."

She seemed doubtful. "How so?"

"Dead parents." He sounded excited about it. "You?"

"Dead friend," she said more solemnly. "She was an older lady. She had kids and a grandkid, but it was either leaving proof of her life to me or her three cats. I got them too."

"By the water? Sucks for the cats."

"They're long gone," she said, still solemn.

Even for him, it was getting too gloomy for a sunny morning on the sand. But so far, she'd been the only person who didn't jump at the opportunity to say sorry for his loss. He found it refreshing.

"Do anything good with the money?"

Not your business.

"I'm a business owner. When I'm not tangled up in that, I volunteer and donate to nonprofits that provide mentorship to delinquent youths." She didn't seem upset by the question, and why would she with such a brag-worthy response?

"That's all great. What's your business?" *I know your business far too well.*

"I own a flower shop. I'm a florist. Charlie's Nursery. You might've seen it driving on PCH."

"Way to own the nickname," he said. "My mistake for picturing the owner of Charlie's Nursery to be an old man with another day job."

"I like to deal with problems head-on. And now you have a face to the business."

A pretty face to the business.

"Why a nursery?" he asked.

"It's my own weird idea of a family, I guess."

Freddie didn't see the connection, and it showed.

"Weddings, anniversaries, funerals, proms, birthdays, holidays…They're all occasions with flowers. Each order tells the clients' story."

"I can understand being drawn to stories," he said.

The job of a florist seemed just as intrusive as that of a detective, getting a glimpse into people's private lives. Freddie had PI friends who often questioned florists before taking the pivotal photographs of a cheating spouse.

Charlotte's outlook was far brighter than the shit he'd been through.

"Sounds like a full life," he said.

"I like to think so." She wore the same smile she greeted him with. "Well, I'll let you have your morning. See you around."

She walked back to the Tudor, Freddie's eyes following her there. He felt a boyish happiness for the surprise seaside rendezvous. Then his eyes glanced up at his chair all alone outside. He turned back around and dove into the Pacific for the first time. Watching the sunny sky in moving water, he felt purified, anew, like it was a christening.

That afternoon, without eating or drinking, Freddie couldn't resist falling into the chair again. He spent his time either napping or occasionally peeping inside Charlotte's living room, but didn't see anything he cared for. At one point the upstairs curtain moved, which made him excited for a possible new view, but he was fooled. Dark gray lenses covered his eyes as he fell back asleep, looking like a '50s gentleman—not dressed like one. He was interrupted by footsteps.

"I'm going to find you dead in that chair one of these days," Veronica said, approaching him from the driveway. Another unexpected visit.

"Please," he said, "bury me with it. No casket necessary."

"Jeez, Fred," she said, sitting on the chair's arm. "Don't talk like that."

She looked out to the water, something they seemed to do a lot. It was hard not to. Veronica's home had a nice beach view too, but it was up in the hills. She had the distant, tranquil view.

"You started it."

"You're getting color." A change of subject, Freddie picked up. "L.A. suits you."

"Don't know," he said. "Thinking about moving." Veronica made a sharp gawk. "I'm getting bored."

"It's not boredom, Fred. It's just routine. This is good. It's what you need. It's calm, not boring."

"Maybe. But you have to admit, routine can get boring."

"You do this with women you date too," she said. He sank deeper into himself. He didn't want to hear about his types, his flaws. "You think normal is boring, so you go for the difficult ones."

He ignored the analysis, pretending like it didn't hurt like a stab wound. "I think I need to get out."

"Looks like that's all you do these days. You need to find a new calling," she said. "Have an early midlife crisis and ride PCH with a sports bike or something."

A pause.

He said, "Free for a late lunch?"

"Already ate."

"Of course you did. I get it. Not everyone's retired."

"Something small to get your mind off stuff," she continued.

"You're in one of your moods, aren't you?"

"What moods?"

"This one's your, 'I'm Veronica. I like to tirelessly help people even when they don't want help' moods," he said, making one of his poor girl-voice impressions. She didn't like it; he could tell by her face. "What do you suggest I do, exactly?"

She watched the water as she thought about it. "You used to love bicycling, right? You traded New York City's cockroaches for Malibu's waves; enjoy. Or do yog—"

"Jesus, not yoga. You've turned full L.A. on me."

"Right, New Yorkers don't do yoga."

He appreciated the sarcasm. "Okay, I'll give my bike a shot." It seemed like a reasonable compromise, something to make her stop talking about him and his ways.

She got up and put a hand on his shoulder. She was fulfilled enough to leave him alone. Freddie grabbed her hand without thinking. He held onto her for a few moments; they were a few short seconds, but they lingered. He let go before he could feel embarrassed for it. "You're off?"

"Yeah, you were on my way."

He nodded. Her little visits were giving him mixed signals. He knew she was moving away soon; was she trying to avoid getting too close again before leaving?

She put her sunglasses back on from overhead. "Later, Fred."

Freddie kept looking at the water, listening to her click-clacking footsteps fade away as she reached her car.

It was a strange sensation he had. There was existence all around him—trees, water, a town up the street. He could imagine all the marine life, the water's very own economy. He became very conscious of the fact that he was alone on the patio again. Suddenly, the beach was empty. So was Freddie.

It was a cold night. The winds raged like a winter storm was coming. The trees were doing more than dancing; they were angry, ready for a fight.

A fight. Freddie hadn't been in one for some time.

He had the heater on, sooner than he thought for SoCal. He felt silly adjusting the thermostat; what was going on outside was nothing compared to the winters back east, but he dressed for it. He had one of those pullovers on with a zip-up turtleneck. When he was a teenager, he used to make fun of his dad for wearing them. Now he thought about taking out one of the old photo albums to compare their styles, but that required remembering where he unpacked them upstairs, and he was too comfortable lying on the couch.

The villa lights were dimmed, an attempt to alleviate the pulsing migraine that had him ready for a nap again. The sunset had become a dark night, and even though he thought he had closed all windows and doors, the sounds of the wind and water feuding infiltrated the first floor of the villa. And, somewhere, shutters rattled. He sat up from the couch to find the source, but the wind took care of it for him, knocking a door shut. Then he noticed the Tudor's outside light flickering again.

Someone was out there. Was it just another windy night messing with his head? With his migraine, he could see black spots flashing in front of him, making him want to wave them away like they were gnats. He closed his eyes hard so the circles went away, then lowered one layer of the shutters and continued to watch. He could see Charlotte and someone else. A male, he inferred based on the person's build.

He could hear them talking, yelling. Fighting. Vehemently. He thought he saw lightning flash, blinding his tired eyes some more, just as he also thought he saw the man push Charlotte. Both could've been missed with a blink.

Maybe she likes it rough.

But this wasn't like the other night. She wasn't leading this guy on; she wasn't liking it. Charlotte pushed the man back. He went for another shove.

Freddie dashed out of the side door and made his way down the hill more casually, as if he'd been on a stroll and was now returning to the grounds. He walked tall but wished he had pockets to hide his hands, not knowing what to do with them loose at his sides, and with no holster to rest them on. He did his best to appear cool.

When he was close enough for them to acknowledge his presence, he asked, "Everything okay here?"

Silence and distance between Charlotte and the stranger.

Freddie had seen these disputes dozens of times while he was a cop. He didn't expect this with Charlotte; she didn't fit the bill. Neither did Mystic Place.

Freddie looked interchangeably at the two, then said, "Charlotte?"

"Freddie, this is Nathan," she said. Freddie was expecting a last name, but Charlotte looked up at Nathan just then and said, "He's *leaving*."

"I'm not leaving," an angry Nathan said, waiting for an introduction as to who Freddie was.

Charlotte shook her head and walked closer to her door. Freddie wanted to tell her that home didn't make her safe, despite its façade that it could be. Home could be dangerous. It could make any gentle person yell at someone, hit someone, shoot someone. Charlotte wasn't there yet, but maybe she'd get there if Nathan continued being persistent.

"Nathan," Freddie said calmly, "it's dark, it's cold out here, you're standing on the lady's property. She's made it clear she wants to be alone."

"Who the fuck are you, then?"

"*Nathan*," Charlotte said in a reprimanding tone. "Don't be stupid." They all realized how childish it sounded. But she was fed up, tired, embarrassed, becoming short-tempered. Freddie felt like he was in high school again watching his two best friends make the shift to lovers and then break up.

"I'm a detective, Nathan." He realized the falsity of the statement before he saw the look on Charlotte's face, but he didn't find it the right time to correct himself. "I live right next door and was disturbed by the noise. I'm happy to drive you to somewhere you need to be. Can I do that for you?"

Nathan turned to Charlotte as if she would help him. Instead, she wore a look that told him he had no other options left. "No, I'm leaving," he said to Freddie. As he walked away slowly, he gave Charlotte another look Freddie didn't like one bit.

The two neighbors watched him disappear back onto the street, wind blowing against their bodies from all sides.

Freddie could feel his thick hair becoming coarse as he brushed it back. He wanted to follow Nathan, maybe get a license plate number to investigate like old times. But he didn't hear the sound of an engine or see any car lights.

"What the hell was that?"

"Come inside from the cold," Charlotte told him, her arms snug across her sweater. She led the way through her front door and closed it behind him. "Sorry you had to see that." In the kitchen, she leaned against the island's wooden countertop, putting her weight on her spread-out hands, and eventually let out a sigh.

"Was that something I should know about?" He stood somewhat awkwardly in her living space, not knowing what to do.

She smiled adjusting her posture and crossed her arms again. She was about to get defensive. *I'm no damsel,* Freddie could hear her think.

He put his hands up as if to surrender. "Not my business."

"No, thank you for stepping in. The whole thing was ridiculous. I thought I had it under control. I usually do." She shook her head again and looked at Freddie, who was confused, bewildered. He didn't know what he'd seen or who was at fault, if there was a person to blame. What if he'd just taken her side because she was the pretty neighbor?

No. He pushed her.

"What exactly did I walk in on?"

"He's just some guy I see from time to time." Freddie half nodded, not sure how to respond. She caught it. "I didn't mean for it to sound…"

"Not my business," he said again. "I just need to know if I need to call for backup."

Charlotte paced around her kitchen. When Freddie saw she wasn't going to say anything yet, he admired the exposed red brick wall behind her in the kitchen. Then his eyes went to the black metal chandelier above the island. He imagined it falling, the sharp, lowest edge puncturing someone. Puncture was a nice way to put it; it would strike someone standing around, blood splattering everywhere.

I miss murder.

Charlotte eventually sat on the couch. "There's violence around L.A. County all the time. Cops can't do much, even if a woman gets a restraining order. What are you going to do for me, Freddie, if I ask you to?"

"Favors can get called in."

"That's not fair, is it? To all those other people out there?"

"No, but it's one less issue, if I can help it."

She shook her head. "Nathan Roberts won't do that to me again."

Roberts. Nathan Roberts. He could figure the rest out.

She was so certain, almost like it was a threat. A promise. He left it alone, though he wondered for a few prolonged seconds if he should. They were just words. If Nathan ended up missing or found face down near the water, he'd know who to question first.

"I'll make some tea before you go."

That wouldn't take up much time before starting his own research. A minute on the electric kettle, ten minutes of conversation and tea drinking, and he'd be out of there to get to it. He'd top it all off with a drink and smoothly drift to sweet, sweet sleep.

He watched her move around in the living room he'd seen her in from his private view, then to the clean, blood-free kitchen. The only red in there was the brick, bright against her off-white cabinets. She reached across the island stovetop, held the kettle under the small sink and ran the water.

This was going to take longer than eleven minutes.

She put the kettle back on top of the stove and turned on a burner, which cracked a few times before it became a full flame. She shuffled through a porcelain jar next to the stove, taking out some tea bags, tucking away her falling hair to have a good look. Freddie just watched, relishing all of it, remembering that dream he had managed to cling onto, pleased by this new perspective. Her wavy hair was fully curly from the misty winds, looking shiny and almost red under the kitchen lights, blondish against her black turtleneck.

"Do you have a preference?" she said, holding up a few options.

His eyes went to the entry table on the other side of the kitchen wall where he'd watched her and Nathan—or whoever it was—ready to strip the other night, everything on the table perfectly back into place, then back to her prepping two mugs.

What if she planned tonight's encounter all to look the way it did? And Freddie, former star detective, was there to witness the whole thing. It couldn't be. Nathan pushed her. Freddie saved the day, the night. The cold, loud, unnerving night. He wouldn't be credible to attest to anything because he had felt tired, weak, ready to pass out. She couldn't know that.

Sound alert.

"Anything caffeinated," he said.

Shit.

That night, revelations flowed like currents—fast, destructive, and unstoppable—the storytellers a couple of incompetent sailors lost at sea. Fast, destructive, and unstoppable because it was unflattering yet inevitable for the two of them to open up about their pasts. Other conversations attempting to derail that particular one were eventually surreptitious roadmaps back to the same topic. All this despite the fact that Freddie put in a conscious effort to make it difficult to talk about himself. And as far as he could tell, Charlotte had no idea he was working so hard to keep the spotlight on her.

"How'd you end up deciding to give your money to troubled youths?" he asked, almost in awe, wanting to know how she'd managed to check off points on his list. The Perfect Woman List.

"Growing up," Charlotte said, "my mom and I didn't have the best relationship. She took care of me and did motherly things, but there was always something between us that was never settled." Freddie kept quiet though he knew exactly what she meant. "I was never good at school back then. I didn't take it seriously until too late. I was lucky to get into some good universities, but my essays are what got me there." She trailed off in thought for a moment, then smiled before she said, "It had to be. My grades were awful. I would've ended up in juvie if I didn't change some things."

"Juvie?" Of all the things she said, that was what stood out.

Veronica had warned him about his deceptive neighbor in the Tudor, but he had brushed it off, refusing to think it was anything other than play. But now, Charlotte was admitting to him, in some form, that some assumptions he'd come up with lately could very much be accurate, even if nothing could be labeled as breakthrough.

Charlotte gave him a shy smile like a little girl acting innocent while caught in a lie. They watched one another as Freddie tried to get more out of her by saying nothing at all. She said, "I used to get into fights at school. It started before I was in high school. But people would make fun of my mom, call her all sorts of names, the way kids do. I never liked it, so I'd fight back, using my hands instead of words."

"Juvie for some fights? Kids do that all the time. It's like a rite of passage. And good for you for sticking up for your family."

"I was sticking up for myself. They were making fun of part of my identity. They were wrong for what they did, but I was wrong for sticking up for my mother."

She was building an angry passion as she spoke. "You don't need to talk about it if you don't want to," he said.

She managed a timid smile. "You keep saying that, but I seem to tell you anyway." She readjusted herself on the couch. "I used to be quite the thief too, maybe what started the reckless behavior. The conscience kicked in and I stopped, but for a while I used to love the thrill. I didn't think I would be able to stop."

He recognized the thrill she was talking about. He wasn't able to stop seeking it, and he doubted she could either. Based on his experience, he was certain such a need couldn't vanish completely; it could only be tamed over time.

"And your mom?" he asked.

Charlotte's shoulders were high, tense, until she gave another smile and said, "How much time do you have?"

He pretended to check his watch. "A lot, actually."

"Retired life?"

"Again, you can stop at any time. You seem like a strong woman, though, and I'd hate to see Nathan come back to push you around just because it's something you're used to."

She thought about that and he wondered if he'd offended her. But he cared, and she had to have known because she was still speaking to him so openly. So openly that Freddie wondered if he was merely still *that* good at getting people to talk, if she had found everything to be so seamless with him, or if her story was a front to cover up something greater.

She shook her head. "Nathan…he's just someone," she said with a half shrug. "He can stay or leave like anyone else. But parents? You're stuck with them and they're a part of you, whether you like it or not."

Freddie's mind visited his parents, how he would've been a cop, a detective, whether he liked it or not. He would have been everywhere he had been, whether he liked it or not.

He felt helpless now, when in all that time he'd thought he had been free like wildfire.

"You still let her get to you." Freddie said.

She smiled wickedly as if he'd caught on. "My mom used to say my life wouldn't go anywhere. Sometimes I wish she were around to see me living here. She'd hate it, want to take it away from me, tell me I don't deserve it. But I'm here. That's why I donate to organizations that help youths making their way back into society. They should never feel stuck or put down." She had entered her past and was living there until she had enough. "What about yours?"

"My parents?"

She nodded. "Were you close?"

"Yes and no," he said. "Like any kid would be during teenage years. Then you grow up and roles change a little. My parents were polar opposites. They were good for each other, though. I lost them at two very different times in my life. Could've been worse for me, really." The sentence lingered in his head until he felt himself smiling.

"What's funny?"

"I was just thinking how I became a detective because of my dad and quit because of my mom."

"Parental pulls are a part of us more than we like to admit."

Freddie agreed, aware that he never really knew what he wanted out of life, and wasn't sure it mattered. He never cared for labels. Why did the labels matter so much to other people anyway? he always wondered. He hated the labels, the DNA tests for ancestry, the anthropology class he and Veronica were in. But now, talking about the past and present with Charlotte, the labels silently mattered, especially when it felt like years of therapy were being unleashed in one sitting. There was something about Charlotte forcing him to be honest with himself, something he hadn't been good at in the last few months. Seamless, he thought.

"It sounds cruel to say, I know," she said with an angelic smile that brought him back to where they were, and God, did he like it. "I truly believe I'm better off without mine."

That took a morbid turn.

"What made you come to that conclusion?" He didn't recall Charlotte mention anything about where her parents were, just that she liked the fact that they weren't around.

"My dad died years ago. He wasn't in the picture when it happened, which made it easier to cope with at the time. I distanced myself from my mom after I saw what an emotional wreck I was around her. Physical wreck sometimes too." She let out a sigh, moved her hair over her shoulder, and sat poised again. Freddie mentally recorded it all, how she could turn her grace and inner pain on and off. "I'll take you up on not talking about them," she said, and took a drink from her mug.

Dead or distant parents, a dead friend who was conveniently her source of money. Dead cats too.

She's going to get you too.

"Are you okay?" she asked. "I'm sorry if this is bringing back things of your own. You asked—"

"Fine, I just freeze up sometimes."

"Is that from the job?"

"It's a Freddie thing, not a detective thing," he said self-consciously, yet somewhat…seamlessly. Again. But he was careful not to ramble. "I haven't been sleeping well lately. I think freezing is my body's way of telling me it's time to call it a night."

She knows another one of your weaknesses now.

"Didn't mean to keep you," she said.

"No," he said, trying to assure her this wasn't a waste of his time, already assured himself of the same. "I'm glad to get to know you, but I guess the body doesn't lie."

She nodded and got up with him. When he reached the door, he turned around. He didn't expect her to be so close behind for him to flinch. "I'm sorry," she said. "I didn't mean to scare you. And thank you again. It could've been worse earlier."

"No trouble."

"I'll need to get you a plant that suits your place. A small thank-you. And welcome."

As much as he wanted to be, he wasn't sold on her stories yet.

"Or I could take you out," Freddie said, stunned by his unexpected boldness.

A hit, a date, whatever the night would lead to.

"Nothing crazy," he said, seeing she wasn't expecting the boldness either. "I still need to get to know the town."

"I'm sure we'll run into each other again to figure it out."

He opened the door, stepped out halfway, turned to her again. "Thanks for the tea."

"See you around." Her catchphrase.

Again, Freddie heard it as a potential warning. Yet, it was a statement he wanted her to uphold.

This isn't being free. You're trapping yourself. As a single man trying to enjoy bachelorhood, as a potential victim to whatever he was playing cat (or mouse) in.

Maybe wildfire was a trap, a prison rather than a blaze of freedom. It was destructive, wiping everything in its way, all of his hopes and endless possibilities, those alternatives he was thinking about earlier. Maybe he wasn't wildfire at all. Maybe she was.

Despite these musings, he shook his head on his way home and regretfully said to himself, "The body doesn't lie?"

5

Bicycle Race

The next morning, Freddie wobbled down the stairs to the kitchen like a zombie born fresh from the apocalypse. He opened the blinds above the sink, then rested against the counter with his head hung low and stared into the drain. The migraine thumped against his left eye, the type of migraine he'd get if he drank too much or too little. Based on the natural lighting in the house and position of the sun, he figured it was about nine o'clock. After a deep breath and good, long stretch, he set the coffee machine and opened the shutters to the backyard doors, the panels spitting dust into his face as he did. Just what he needed before that first cup of splendid sin—rum, coffee, whatever that morning required. This morning, it was just coffee. Freddie took his full mug outside and sat with his feet in the pool, leaving the back doors open to let in the fresh air.

You'll be caught dead if you bring glass by the pool, Freddie, he heard his mother say.

He let himself sink into the pool on the first step, his boxers-turned-swim-trunks and lower abdomen submerged. He picked up the mug beside him again. Every sip was enjoyed with a devilish grin, one he didn't realize he had until he did.

Later in the day, Freddie decided to skip the shower with a workout in mind for later, and went straight to his dresser to pick out a clean T-shirt and boxers. Feeling comfortable again, he picked up his laptop from the bed and logged in as he went down the stairs a revived man. He lay on the couch in the formal living room—just for a change of scenery—with the laptop on his stomach, feeling the lack of ethanol in his system. Only he wasn't imagining the smell of sweet liquor or even showing withdrawal symptoms—the shaky hands, the crabbiness, the inexplicable tension or jumpiness—all of which he could blame on caffeine withdrawals for those who showed concern. No, this uneasy feeling came from an event, a person, a disturbance right outside his beloved new private home. *Who the fuck are you?* Nathan had asked.

Who the fuck are YOU, Nathan?

Freddie clicked on the first link that appeared in his name search, a social media page. It wasn't too fun for Freddie since Nathan didn't seem to use social media all that much. Still, Freddie had a general idea about Nathan's habits with what little he could work with, like the fact that Nathan liked to ride his bicycle.

I like to ride my bicycle.

It was always surprising when he found a commonality with someone he already downright abhorred, like it couldn't be a possibility.

Nathan Roberts had photos, what appeared to be professionally taken, of him cycling at the gym, the captions going on about the equipment he was using. There were other photos of Nathan biking by the beach, probably in Venice and Santa Monica—the locale was different, touristy (though it was getting more crowded with tourists in Malibu). Once the sun set, the roadsides were crammed by parked cars filled with couples shaking things up, or teens smoking weed or drinking wine out of cans, the evidence always left behind on the ground from littering near the bins.

At first, Freddie thought his time and energy were going to waste. Nathan Roberts living in Malibu was the perfect man, a guy involved in preserving endangered plants and who liked riding his bike beachside. His social media pages were all public but vague—just a few pictures of beach views—nothing to single him out from anyone else in town. And nothing was new information. All in all, Nathan was a private guy.

I'm private, Freddie thought, again, hating that he and this person had something else in common. But there was such a thing as *too* private.

Freddie continued scrolling and eventually made it to the Images section, desperate to find something more on Nathan Roberts, the aggressive man, the man with a dark side who liked to skulk on dark, windy nights.

Freddie scrolled and scrolled until his finger felt a cramp. Then, finally, he found something new to work with. Massaging the cramp out, he read:

Nurse Detained for Administering Lethal Drugs

Nathan's license had been revoked and he would be sent to prison if he were to ever be caught anywhere near a hospital, doctor's office, or patients and drugs again after his year-long sentence. Freddie had never been happier reading such bad news, to know someone had lost the opportunity to live a normal life. But what did Nathan Roberts want with Charlotte? Money, control? Freddie thought, *Get in line, pal.* Something had to make him different to go to extreme measures.

Extreme measures.

This wasn't extreme, was it, reading up on Nathan?

The occasional web search isn't anything fanatic.

It would be worse to be so obsessive on the job, wouldn't it? To go over the line obsessively. This, sitting in the comfort of his own home with a spectacular view, alone with no one to bother him, was the right time and place to be an interested—no—concerned man.

He continued browsing the different webpages, all open in different windows covering his bright screen, reflecting off his face until his vision started to go blurry.

Next on the search was an address, which Freddie immediately copy-pasted into his phone's map. A fifteen-minute drive from Mystic Place. With Freddie's speed and agility (to the best of his biased, denial-driven knowledge) the trip was probably just as long of a bike ride. Nathan lived in the hills, halfway to Veronica's, and Freddie hadn't exercised since his last case was in trial months ago.

He kept the address logged into his phone and headed toward his car, his bike mounted on top. As he brought it down, he couldn't stop eyeing the filth on his car from birds and dried mist on dirt. He struggled at first with the tangled hose, then rinsed off the car. The bike too while he was at it.

The hot day settled on his head and a drop of sweat ran down his neck while the sun dried the car and bike for him. He was glad he hadn't taken that morning shower. Once he'd satisfied his compulsions to clean, he locked the front door and decided to make his comeback at bicycling, and he knew where to go.

It took Freddie just over half an hour to get to Nathan's house, a two-story modern, after being in a bicycle race with himself. He planted his feet on the ground, still on his bike, and checked his phone for the time. He was disappointed by his speed. That, and at forgetting to bring his good camera along for the ride. Not to capture the pretty views, but to capture a view nonetheless. The kind private eyes get.

He yawned like a lazy cat while he waited for something interesting to happen. Nothing did for a while. He had his phone in hand waiting for the picture moment. Instead, he opened a wellness app to record his exercise, diet, and mood. This, of course, was something he would never admit to most people. If he had a younger sister, this would be the type of thing he'd give her hell about. At least he could report something useful to Veronica if she asked. Trying to follow through, he placed his thumb over the Mood icon, but he angrily refused to tap the screen. He exited the app and switched to his camera. All he had to work with was his phone, which was due for an upgrade. The few pictures of Nathan's house he attempted to capture ended up in the Trash folder due to poor pixilation. If he couldn't take a decent picture on the fly, there went his potential for doing PI work if retired life didn't work out. He stretched while remaining seated on the bike, feeling good about his back cracking but disturbed by its sound.

No more slouching in the chair.

He realigned his spine, then sat there some more with better posture.

This was boring; his mood hadn't changed. He restored the deleted photos and yawned another time. His frontal lobe thumped, near his eye, before he saw his phone go black. The trees brushed swiftly to the gentle breeze. They were turning black. Everything around him slowly closed into darkness until he could no longer hear his thoughts.

He woke up on the ground, the bike flat below his feet. What was touching him, poking at him. An animal? No. It felt like a couple of cold fingers pressing against his neck. Shit. Had he died, and had paramedics brought him back to life? As he thought this, he grabbed whatever was invading his personal space. Reflex. He squeezed, hard, ready to put up a fight before he knew if he needed to. Life became colorful again and he clutched on harder, trying to pull himself up this time.

"You're okay, you're okay," he heard a voice say. A man's. *Shit,* he didn't like where this was going. *I'd rather be passed out.* "You're holding on really hard. I need you to let go. Let go." The man tried to loosen Freddie's grip.

Freddie blinked rapidly until he could see straight. He'd gotten the routine down from waking up after having had too many drinks.

Yup. Nathan. If only Freddie knew how long he had been on the ground, and with Nathan kneeling over him. Where had Nathan been? Freddie finally let him go as he came back from a place of confusion.

"I was just checking your pulse," Nathan said, rubbing his throbbing hand. Freddie could see it changing color—*boom, boom, boom.* "You're okay," he insisted.

Freddie sat up, his hand moving to the back of his head where it also throbbed. *Jesus, if it's not the front, it's the back.* But when he looked down at his hand, he was thrown off by the color. He blinked hard some more then realized just how hard he'd fallen.

"The good things in life are fragile," Nathan said, his hand with a latex glove. It was odd to see, considering they were alone on the side of the road, wilderness below the hillside. One push from where he was could cause someone to plunge to their death.

Did Nathan just carry gloves around? Did a car repair-person carry jump starters? So, he was just a prepared nurse. Normal. *Except Nathan is a nurse who's done time.*

Nathan gave Freddie a gauze and took off the glove. "Just keep that on for a few minutes. You won't be needing stitches." It was all so accommodating, so routine that for a brief moment Freddie didn't feel like he failed something as simple as a stakeout. This was rightfully apparent when he noticed Nathan starting to realize he'd seen the face on this wounded head before. Freddie stood up, still holding the gauze to the back of his head. "Don't get up so fast, you'll fall right back down," Nathan said, moving hastily as Freddie did.

"I'm fine," Freddie said firmly, something he had been saying too much and noticed how he didn't mean it each time. He picked up his bike, examining it, mostly to avoid eye contact with the guy he had attempted to secretly watch. "Sorry for the trouble, and, uh—" He really didn't know what to say next. Not because he was speechless and worried; because his brain was working hard to reproduce the English language. He eventually said, "Thanks for the help."

"Low blood sugar?"

"No, I'm fine." Again.

"You live around here?" Nathan asked skeptically.

He knows I don't.

If he could get away...

Freddie felt his pockets, noticed his wallet was still there, so Nathan didn't ID him, unless he did check for ID while Freddie was unconscious. *Crap, where's the ph—*

Nathan handed Freddie's phone back to him. "No cracks. You're lucky."

Freddie grabbed it as coolly as he could without throwing what would've been an unsteady punch. He pushed his bike along, ready to get home to have a beer on that chair.

"Do you?" Nathan asked.

"What?"

"Do you live around here?"

"This is my exercise route." Freddie couldn't tell a proper lie while losing blood or thinking about the photos of Nathan's house in his phone.

Nathan took a step closer. Freddie stood still. If he couldn't lie, he could at least act like he wasn't intimidated.

"You're the guy from Charlotte's house," Nathan said. "Her neighbor from yesterday."

Freddie sat on the bike, ready to peddle away (even though it was a downhill ride). "Thanks for lifting me up," he said and rolled a few feet forward.

"Yeah," Nathan said. "I saw those pictures on your phone."

"I don't know what you're ta—"

"I deleted them, then deleted your deleted stuff," Nathan said.

That's one way to erase an ex completely.

"New hobby out here in L.A., you know, with the whole movie scene. Just some freelance scouting," Freddie said. A shot was a shot.

"Charlotte know you're a stalker? Maybe I should visit her more often, tell her all about you."

That got a chuckle from Freddie. "Tell her what? That you helped her neighbor from bleeding into another fainting episode? I can see how that makes you a hero, Nathan."

"You do remember me, then?"

Fuck. Cockiness getting in the way again.

Freddie dropped the bike. It wasn't so much that Nathan was threatening him, or Charlotte, but it was a contributing factor. It was really the fact that Nathan gave off a bad...aura, in lack of a better word, the moment Freddie had laid eyes on him. He could go back to playing God's apprentice with all the right pretenses, and he would still create a bad vibe.

"Did you forget that I'm a detective, Nathan? Let's also relive yesterday and establish the fact that I was there, I saw you with Charlotte, and it didn't look pleasant. Or healthy, for that matter. A nurse would care for someone's health, right? Or do I need to call the board and have them remind you what good practice is?"

Nathan stared into Freddie's eyes like he enjoyed hunting season. No wonder he lived in the hills. Then he took a step back, giving Freddie faith in his cockiness again.

"Stick to Mystic Place," Nathan said, then went back inside despite Freddie waiting for the Or Else part.

All that remained were the distant sounds of seagulls flying over the water below the canyon, and some Black Phoebes chirping their short, elegant sounds amid Bewick's wrens sounding like car alarms. This was very different from the sandpipers pecking away at the wet sand. There was something eerie about the sounds that slinked through the valley. Freddie continued thinking about what an Or Else speech would've entailed.

So, he tracked Nathan Roberts for a week.

Each day, Freddie was disappointed yet relieved he hadn't witnessed anything unusual. Nathan hadn't even visited Charlotte to tell her about the little encounter. Freddie felt his lowest then. Had he been wrong to check Nathan out? Because, if he had been wrong, then he really was just a creeper.

During his last stakeout, he pretended to be biking (though he did bike there) and tried to stay hidden behind trash bins or trees, waiting for Nathan to zoom out of his driveway. Freddie stationed himself on the bike securely, his feet on the ground again after Nathan was well down the hill. He waited, figuring he might as well enjoy the ocean view from a new perspective. He thought about seabirds, only because they were flying around his head—literally, not because he was seeing a mirage of floating stars or birds. He continued a stakeout while Nathan left and returned home. He had come back with groceries.

Okay, he showed love for the environment and was athletic. So what? Again, hatred ran through Freddie knowing this was too good to be true. There were people out there who did horrible, violent things because they claimed it was for love. Love was a real feeling, and violence was a real act. The fact that a person could love didn't make them good.

Freddie needed to get out of there before someone noticed a man on a bicycle lazing in front of the house for—he checked his phone—1.5 hours. He was cognizant of the passed time now that he could feel trapped heat beneath the flesh of his nose.

He'd returned home after every stakeout and rewarded his efforts with a beer—a reward for snooping and cycling. *Another chapter title.* Then he would drop onto the beach chair, proud he'd gotten some exercise. Thank goodness, the beer was safe. He'd gotten the hang of falling back without causing any spillage.

Once in a while, he'd touch the back of his head to check for sporadic bleeding. Nothing there either.

He rubbed some aloe on his nose hoping the burn would become a tan by morning. For now, things were clean.

6

Dark Necessities

Thinking about how many open cases there had to be in L.A. County and New York City's boroughs combined had Freddie admitting to himself that he missed work. He didn't want to, but he was facing it in his everyday life, whether he was creating scenarios about his neighbor or watching her from a distance, or waiting for life to waste away or pick up again. And he often did the thinking in the beach chair.

Leaving detective life made him miss detective work, just like making detective had made him miss being a cop. Most detectives hated their days as cops driving around in a patrol car—midnight drug busts at iffy street corners and profiling people for the casual pat-down, all things he didn't think he'd miss until he was behind a desk. And now. He missed the action.

If only there was someone on the force he could trust to help him have that action. He needed McKinney and decided to give him a call. New York was three hours ahead, already experiencing its midday rush, and he'd called before realizing it.

"McKinney here."

"Frank?" Freddie's tone was that of someone about to deliver bad news. "It's Freddie."

"Freddie! No one in L.A.'s gotten to you yet, huh? Good to hear your voice, kid."

Kid. He'd always be kid. Always older by a year, could be married, have kids, grandkids; but if McKinney was around, then he'd still be kid.

"It's good to hear you too."

"Wait. Let's get this out of the way," McKinney said. Freddie dropped deep into a scare as he followed his old mentor's orders. "How's the weather?"

"Jesus, Frank. I thought someone died."

"Thought that's why you left, kid. What can I do for you?"

"I need a bit of a favor, Frank."

"Sure, kid, if I can do it across the country. I don't do hits anymore," he said before heavy laughter. "I'm just messing with you. Tell me."

"Know anyone out here? Anyone who I could talk to about...things? Some crime things."

"Christ, kid. Bored already?"

"Getting there," he said, shuffling his foot against the patio tile.

"Fred, I can give you information for a support group you can go to, but that's about it. Think that's all that'll be good for you. Taking any real time for bereavement, or, you know, plain pleasure?"

"I'm not joining the force out here, Frank." He sounded like a toddler trying to convince his mother to buy candy at the checkout line. Freddie always used to. If she refused, he'd bring his dad into the conversation to say he would let Freddie have his way. Even then, the answer was no. He had wondered if she would deprive him of anything he wanted just to make him feel as worthless as a small pack of candy on the shelf.

"Not this again."

"What was that, Fred?"

He thought it; did he say it? Talking to himself at home, passing out in front of a stranger's home, loss of memory and cognitive skills. Things were great.

Freddie paced in meaningless circles, rubbing his eyes to see clearly again. "Nothing," he said, still rubbing, but he knew McKinney could detect a lie, among other things. "I've been seeing my mother."

Freddie didn't like the silence before McKinney said, "Uh, Fred. That number I can give you…"

"I don't mean seeing, like I'm seeing dead people. No imaginary friends either."

"Just pays a little visit, huh? Any hallucinations?"

"It's fine, really. I'm not starting up a mommy-and-me motel or anything. I'm grieving, remember? All I need is a distraction," Freddie said. "Someone close to the crime beat around here. Someone to—" *Someone to feel like you're around.*

"Okay, okay." McKinney's tone sounded like what Freddie hoped his mother would sound like at the end of the checkout aisle. "Just quit using my name like that. *My* mother's been in the ground for over a decade, kid, so quit with the 'Frank' business."

I'm like my mother after all. He made a conscious effort to stop repeating McKinney's name.

"Listen closely," McKinney said. "I'm only going to say this once and fast and hope that you miss it." Freddie searched for the notepad he'd found along with his mother's pen until he felt it against his fingertips in the back of the drawer. "His name's Daniel Wesley, usually goes by Wes. Let him know I gave you his info. He's a good guy. Tell him I say hello. And sorry."

Freddie chuckled, something in the pit of his stomach giving him the childish thrill.

"Thank you, Frank. I'll be on my best behavior, promise."

"Yeah, you will. And that's McKinney to you, kid. Take care of yourself."

Click. It was then when Freddie realized he'd called the home line.

Freddie now had something else to do. But he waited. He sat in the chair again, feeling relieved and content from hearing McKinney's voice for the first time since he was off the job.

He did a web search on his laptop, feeling better that he was searching for a man of the law rather than a Nathan Roberts type. He did this lounging on the beach chair, listening to the water, even catching glimpses of dolphins making their domes when he'd look up, while the study upstairs collected dust. He imagined opening the door to the study years from now if he decided to stay on Mystic Place. The door would open with a sharp creak, cobwebs in all corners of the ceiling, windowpanes, and empty shelves. The outdoors felt fitting, though the lighting wasn't all that great for viewing the screen, but he thought it would force him to put technology away for a bit, let him stop himself from going out to find crime. Okay, not crime; a detective, he told himself cheatingly. A very particular detective.

Daniel Wesley. Dan Wesley. Detective Wesley. Freddie waited impatiently with each ring until a receptionist answered. That was when he realized he had no plan ready other than asking to speak to the detective.

"Is this an emergency, sir?"

"No emergency. I'm a friend of Detective Wesley's. Of Wes's," he said, hoping the nickname would catch someone's attention.

"Please hold, sir." A long period of silence. Then she returned. "May I have your name?"

"Freddie McAllister."

"Fre-der-ick," she said, likely writing the name down on a sticky note to hand off to Dan Wesley or anyone with more authority walking around.

"It's just Freddie, actually," he said, unsure about why he bothered. "Is he in?"

He could hear commotion in the background, a man speaking and possibly the phone being passed to someone else. Dan Wesley, he assumed. Sure enough…

"Yeah, you've got Detective Wesley."

"Detective. This is Fred McAllister. I'm Frank McKinney's friend."

There was a sudden boost in the detective's voice, like a struggling engine finally ran smoothly. "How is the man?"

"Better than you and me, I'm sure."

"Great, great. Grandkids must be gettin' big."

"Probably. We're not getting any younger."

"Ha! Hope not, or some of my old cases would still be open." That would be a nightmare come true. "What can I do for you, son?"

He had graduated from kid to son.

"I'm living in L.A. now. I'm out of the job and Frank said you're the next best thing to having him around." He hoped Dan Wesley could hear the joy in his voice, though he was trying to tame it.

"You've got the summertime blues. Homesickness or what have ya."

"McKinney's spoken very highly of you over the years. Thought it would be an honor to get you face-to-face."

"I can't say no to my very own fan club, can I? Come by our offices…Freddie, was it?"

"It is."

"Well, come by, son. We'd love to have some fresh blood down here."

"Thank you, will do. We'll talk soon," Freddie said and hung up like he just got a new case.

Freddie had told McKinney years back, during small talk at a crime scene, that cops got more action on their beats than detectives did behind their desks. Freddie had caught him by the crime scene tape surrounding the property, his first time at a homicide scene as a cop. All he could do was serve as the bouncer for all the nosy rubberneckers and reporters.

McKinney was slipping on a pair of latex gloves when he'd said, *If you think detectives don't get more action, you're living in a good town. A safe one. Trust me, kid, action comes. And with detectives, it's more painful because it comes in high volumes and at a slower rate.*

It was a shame they were never partners. Freddie could've achieved so much more if they were, but he had already felt the years of the job. He was roughed-up as it was. But being roughed-up meant progress. And now, he was roughed-up more than ever, and he had a detective to meet.

Over the years, Freddie had come to realize that he loved the prospect of murder cases—the phone ringing, where the story would lead—but he never liked the mess, the loss. Still, he liked to feed the chaos in his life, because what would he be without it? So it was a homicide detective's wet dream walking into the department.

There were cubicles everywhere, phones ringing. The coffee was brewing, the windows bright despite the grime casting shadows. It was roughly happy for what it was. The opposite of what it was like in Brooklyn. Freddie and the squad had been in the basement. No windows, no natural lighting. Abundant lamps created a glare on any boards plastered with newspaper clippings, glossy photos, and police documents. Best homicide squad there was and those were the conditions they worked in. They gave themselves an extra pat on the back for it.

Dan Wesley skipped a formal introduction with, "McKinney's boy! Follow me." Freddie obliged, thinking about how his name was now in a new police database the minute he handed over his ID to check in.

"Here we are." Dan Wesley sat at his desk, then leaned back in his rolling chair and rested his intertwined hands over his belly that was pushing against the buttons of his shirt.

Freddie continued making mental notes on Homicide. It was similar to a corporate environment, for anyone who walked in and didn't know where they were. All of the old-timers had desks in the back away from cubicles in an open space.

He suddenly felt like he was interning for a political campaign like he had done the year before his father passed. He didn't want to, having only hot summers at Coney Island on his mind, but his mother convinced her well-connected friends it would be useful for everyone involved. He resented his mother for it, feeling like his childhood was nonexistent. He could have gone to work with his father to hear about paperwork or new computer software; or he could tag along with friends to do what typical kids found fun.

Carousel music was playing under Homicide's florescent lights. Freddie was taken back to the crime scene his father had been called to on a particular afternoon near the Brooklyn Bridge. Freddie was in a car to Manhattan with his mother. A day with mom. Freddie had dreaded it, thinking about ways he could conveniently get lost after stepping off the carousel. But he'd stuck around to stop her while she was behind the wheel, yelling, *There's dad!* How proud he had been to watch him work, completely oblivious to the fact that there was a dead body surrounded by yellow tape and several other cops securing the area, forensics all over the space like ants feasting on honey. When Freddie saw the body, realizing the full scope of it all, it took his breath away. All of it. Not in a sad, shocked kind of way. He had felt enthused, impassioned. *This is what I want to do.*

"So," Dan Wesley said, "what's on your agenda?"

"The agenda." Freddie hadn't thought that far ahead.

"Want a tour of Hollywood, or do you just like florescent lighting and the smell of sweat, fear, and shit coffee?"

Freddie's eyes gravitated toward the drawing board on wheels standing between Dan Wesley and another detective's desks. He could see the faces of victims displayed on there, all four of them side by side. Freddie nodded at the board and said, "Should it be out like this?"

Dan Wesley glanced at the board casually. "Private guests only allowed back here. You're getting the VIP treatment."

"Don't I feel special."

"You may not know this, but I got a call from McKinney not long after I hung up with you."

Freddie was surprised by his own surprise. *Of course he did.*

"Said you'd be doin' exactly what you're doin'." He kicked the board. It moved only a couple inches before coming to a full stop. What made McKinney a loyal friend to this guy? He looked at the board again, then back at Freddie. "So, that agenda…"

How was Freddie going to put this?

"Ever work in Narcotics?"

There was a conversation starter.

"Fuck, no. One of my former partners did undercover for them when I was first starting out. Evidence went missing and he lost his job. And life. Stayed the hell away from that and still mourn the loss of a partner, even if he's still alive."

Freddie took his time to think about his next move, remembering there was something he needed from the detective. This was their first meeting. He needed to keep his options open. It was like interviewing a suspect for the first time; he'd need to establish some friendly layer before getting deeper into anything.

"But you remember your first case you closed, Detective?"

He nodded, recollecting. "That why you're here? For us to share about our first times?" Dan Wesley got more comfortable in his chair, crossing his leg over the other, hands pulling in his knee as much as he could without his shirt buttons busting. He paid attention to Freddie like he was forced to interview a nutcase.

"You felt good about it, didn't you? Like a high?"

"You can call it a kind of high," he said, still recollecting.

Freddie took a deep breath, let it out before he spoke. "My first case involved two druggies. One of them had overdosed. The other guy was arrested on the scene with murder charges and possession. I saw him shoot up before we cuffed and searched him. I'll never forget his face the moment he stuck that needle in his arm. I knew the feeling and I've never done heroin."

"We all have our heroin." Dan Wesley was focused, wondering where the story was going. He was entertained, that was for certain.

"I'm looking for that kind of high."

"Son," Dan Wesley sat up and leaned forward. "Didn't you just quit and move away from the detective life? What in God's name are you doin' in here? You a masochist?"

The questions were flooding, or they only seemed that way because Freddie didn't feel like explaining himself.

"I did quit. I'd just like to offer any professional services I can without being reinstated."

"You want me to feed you info under the table."

"When you put it like that, you make me sound like a bad guy."

"Do I need to have another conversation with McKinney?"

"No," he said, perhaps too quickly. "I just need something familiar out here, that's all this is. And maybe I can help. I'd be staying out of trouble if I was able to help rather than sitting at home wondering about all this on my own."

"What are you interested in, Fred?"

Freddie pointed at the board. "That, right there, has been bothering me since I read about it."

"Oh?" The detective didn't turn around; he knew what Freddie was referring to. "It's one of those that'll probably move slowly. You're telling me you want info? We're afraid of losing funding and calling it a cold case. How's that for info?"

Then Dan Wesley looked around the large room, like he was trying to hide something. He failed at being stealthy, but no one else was around to notice. "Not here." He looked around some more then leaned in. "Show me that fancy house McKinney was talkin' about. You drive. I'll get one of those car services back." He tapped on his smartphone. "Unbelievable what you kids come up with."

Dan Wesley led Freddie to the elevator, waving at colleagues as they walked by. He gave them a simple "Hi, how are ya?" or little boosts of encouragement to keep on with their cases. They rode the elevator down to the main floor and went out under the sun. Freddie started to sweat as they walked to his car. He was already nervous as it was, and now impatient, wondering what it was Detective Wesley had to say that it had to be done at the villa—a place where he wanted to start over, a place he promised he wouldn't bring any more work to.

Another promise broken.

Freddie had never hosted anything before; not even a party during his college years. The closest he'd ever gotten was by serving his Uncle Harry a beer at his dad's wake. Freddie was thirteen and had never tried alcohol before. After he gave his uncle a can, Freddie went back to the refrigerator to sneak one for himself. He cracked the can open alone in his bedroom and slurped his first bit. He didn't expect the carbonation to burn his throat; soda didn't do that to him. Maybe he hated the taste. He feared he'd hate it forever, the golden, manly drink.

Serves me right, he'd thought.

If his father had caught him, he would've taken the can away. An intervention would follow, joined by another precinct detective to talk about the serious consequences of underage drinking. They would've made him sit in a cell for an hour to traumatize him into never doing it again.

Now, helping Detective Dan Wesley to that golden, manly drink at Mystic Place, Freddie took a bottle out of the fridge—just one; he refused to add on to the recycling bin that was already full of past nights' cans and bottles. Freddie popped it open and handed it to the detective sitting on the edge of the couch, sending himself back to that sorrowful day.

"So," Freddie said, "Dan or Wes. Have a preference?"

"Don't care what you call me, son, as long as it ain't foul."

Freddie got comfy in the armchair diagonal from the couch, facing the window to his neighbor's house. "I'm used to calling my older colleagues by their last names."

"Huh. Well, Wes'll do just fine." He took back a gulp. The sound of the liquid hitting the bottom of the bottle again made Freddie squirm in his seat, like he'd just left Uncle Harry and sat on his bed, just the can and him. Wes was oblivious to this, of course, admiring the living room, kitchen, and the view beyond it. He said, "Nice place you've got here."

Freddie nodded in agreement, wanting to move past the small talk. "I take it we're not here to give you the tour."

"No, we're not." Wes took a coaster from a stack and placed it under the bottle. "There are certain things I can't talk about back there with a guy that's not involved or part of the squad."

"You have my full discretion," Freddie said, then waited for the detective to continue.

"The big case on your mind?"

"Can't be all that big if you think it might end up a cold case. But all over the papers? Something's bound to pick up."

"People don't read, son, that's the problem. No one reads, no one comes forward. Not any closer to closing."

"Still talking to the victims' families?"

Wes nodded as he reached for the bottle, then made himself comfortable again. It made Freddie wonder if he was trying to get in an ab workout reaching for the beer, creating reps. That was what Freddie would do, now that he had gained a few pounds.

Freddie leaned in closer, rubbing his hands together impatiently, like he wanted to say, Give me the good stuff. He asked, "Any patterns, M.O.,...?"

"I've got a man in his thirties who died of sudden cardiac death. Then, three men in their thirties go missing. They make good money with different professions, no commitments—no one to notice anything wrong right away, no one to go looking until it's too late for us. And no bodies have been found. And the only connection we've identified so far is that they know each other."

Freddie was stunned. "No bodies? Why are you on the case if you can't rule out missing persons?"

Wes made a face as if a two-year-old beat him at a game of chess. "This ain't no boys' trip gone bad," he said. "We've had this open for almost three weeks now with pay cuts and budget issues. This ain't no small town. Geographically, at least. I think you'll find that gossip proves otherwise. Anyway, I'd say it's past the mark of missing persons."

Freddie nodded and said, "But no evidence to rule homicide."

"But a pattern."

"And these guys know each other?"

Knew each other?

"Indeed. Different jobs, different backgrounds, no one's a connection except each other, at least not anyone we could label a person of interest."

"Meaning?"

"Now that we think the death of Hudson Ross might be connected to these missing men, we interviewed some people, but no one is a person of interest. So back to square one with these men being the only connections between each other. I can only think that someone's been watching them, targeting them. The only good news about the case is that no one else has been added to the list. If it is in fact murder, the killer has gone dormant for the time being."

They both let the facts speak for themselves for a few short moments.

"It usually is someone they know. Something will turn up. It always does. Either way, sounds like you might have a serial killer."

Just saying it sent all his blood rushing.

"Bingo," Wes said. He reached for the beer again, this time with a face like he wasn't enjoying the drink. "Say, Fred? You're a man in your thirties, aren't ya?"

Freddie, hunched over, still rubbing his hands like he was ready for a good meal, raised a brow to say, So?

"And you've had a successful career, wouldn't you say?"

"I have, I suppose, yeah. Nothing fancy like these guys, though. What are they? Doctors, lawyers?"

"Hudson Ross was a real estate agent for the area. I mean *this* area. These four men are from about a fifteen-mile radius from where we are right now. From your not-so-humble home. I'm concerned this number will add up to five. You watch out for yourself, Freddie."

"You sound like you're on the right track to catch your man," Freddie said to offer some solace.

Or woman. A light bulb illuminated in Freddie's head. *Real estate. Does Veronica know more about this than she's led on?* She seemed to have had purposefully avoided discussing it when he'd brought it up. He didn't mention the hunch to Wes. Veronica's name didn't belong on his list. She didn't like talking about anything personal or sensitive. She and Freddie had this in common. More information from the detective would give him a better conversation with Veronica about it later, and she wouldn't like having a detective on her doorstep.

Freddie was ready to speak, but both he and Wes turned toward a loud bang of a door, Freddie lifted out of his seat to make sure Nathan or anyone else wasn't coming around for more of whatever he'd interrupted the other night.

They spotted Charlotte walking toward a man near the center of Freddie's backyard view. Freddie recognized Earl, and Charlotte made her way to him with a smile. When Wes faced Freddie again: "I do like your view."

Freddie, beside his friend now, lowered a shutter strip and looked out. She was probably helping Earl with something or just stopping by for a friendly chat. He'd remembered Earl mentioning Charlotte helping him around with things that needed lifting—putting out the trash or whatever his frail arms couldn't handle much of anymore.

"Pretty and doesn't discriminate."

"Easy, Wes."

He stepped away from the translucent door. "I see why you like the place so much."

"No work. Leaves my to-do list limited."

"To-do, you say?"

"All right, Wes. Don't make me report you to McKinney."

Wes put his hands up. "I'll leave you to it, son." He picked up the bottle from the table and chugged it all away and handed it back to Freddie hollow. Freddie was concerned. Wes chuckled and said, "I'm not drivin' and I didn't drink bourbon."

Freddie walked him to the front door, realizing there was absolutely no purpose to the visit. Maybe he was a drifter like Freddie who needed an excuse to find company or a drink. Freddie's father had said that every detective had some type of addiction. Maybe drinking and awkward social gatherings were Wes's.

As he watched the detective use his cell phone to hitch a ride, he thought, if this were his case, it would've been ready for trial.

They waited on the street for an unknown driver to arrive. Freddie said, "Anything I can help with, Wes, say the word."

"You're not a detective anymore. You watch out for yourself, you hear? If you do see anything suspicious, you have my number."

Freddie nodded, pretending to agree, still not satisfied. He had his hands on his hips standing tall and feeling the cool breeze on the warm, sunny day, cars on PCH zooming by as usual, and the palm trees accentuating the fact that Freddie was a West Coast man now. He stood behind in his same position and chuckled with awe over Detective Wesley hitching a ride with a stranger to get back to Homicide.

Wes turned around and said, "Keep a low profile. We don't need you to be next."

She's going to get you too.

"Me? I'm just a nobody who knows how to use a database, cuffs, and a gun."

"You've got a good head on your shoulders, but you and I both know that the job we have—I have—can ruin you, put you down in a dark pit where there ain't no light up top."

The morbidity humored Freddie. He always laughed at the wrong instances. "What are your interests in the case right now?" Freddie asked, realizing his interviewing skills could use some work. His questions were way out of order.

Wes lowered his phone and got closer to Freddie. He was going to say something serious, private again, even though there was no one around except for the bicyclists peddling away down the street.

"My instinct tells me it's a woman doing this heinous shit."

"A woman," he said, both pleasantly and horribly altered by suspicion. "*Potential* heinous shit. Labeling sex calls for narrowing down a search. Don't want to miss anything without real reason to believe that."

"No," Wes concurred. "But I don't have a single motive for a man, and definitely no man who's a common link."

"Most homicides are done by men. It's just stats."

"But not all."

He had Freddie there. But Freddie disagreed with his tactics and deductive reasoning. Then again, Wes was the detective.

A car came rolling by and stopped at Wes's feet. He gave the driver a hand salute and walked around to open the passenger door. The driver was in for a treat, Freddie thought as the car made a three-point turn.

Wes had his window down. Of course he had to have the last word. "See you around, son." Then the car rolled away.

It all felt like the ending to a Western movie, only the sheriff was a detective and he was riding in a car, not on a horse. Regardless, Mystic Place suddenly looked unadorned, all abandoned but the dark necessities crawling back to Freddie.

A woman. She's going to get you too.

7

California Dreaming

Veronica was coming over. This time, she was invited. Freddie waited in his usual spot outside in the shade, sunglasses on, body resting comfortably. It was mid-week and even the distant, public beach had been quiet all day. Freddie had changed into his trunks and enjoyed a swim in the ocean, then decided he had enough of feeling seaweed wrapped around his ankles like some eel or other slimy sea creature was draping his skin.

Once Freddie came back from the beach, he lay back, sinking into the seat as much as he could until he fell asleep in his cadaverous position. Not even Veronica's footsteps getting closer brought him back. She gently pushed his shoulder.

"Jesus!" He jumped out of his seat. "Don't do that again."

She looked around the porch. "Got another one of these?" she asked, resting her hand on the back of his chair. "Maybe one that's better."

He sat up. "There's a folded chair in the pantry."

"You've organized." She was being sarcastic, of course. A beach chair didn't belong in the kitchen pantry with cans of broth and sauce and boxes of macaroni. "You used to be worse than me about stuff like that. What happened?"

"Exactly. Didn't want it out, and it was either the garage or pantry. Pantry was closer, so there you have it." He didn't get up.

"Are you really going to make me go get it? In this polyester shirt, pencil skirt, and heels?"

"Polyester? I thought you could afford better."

"Tell it to every designer. Or you can take me to Rodeo Drive for a shopping spree."

Freddie lowered his sunglasses down his nose and showed Veronica his eyes. "You women say you want equality. I guess you all pick and choose as you please."

"If you learn the difference between common courtesy and sexism, maybe you wouldn't be sitting out here alone."

Freddie rolled his eyes up and down against her existence. He pushed his glasses up his nose and got up. He went inside from the door that led into his most-used living room, shut the door behind him, and locked it.

"Come on, Fred," she said, putting her hair up to fan the back of her neck. Freddie didn't budge. "I can leave."

He didn't want that. He'd called her over after all. He needed her and she knew it. She knew how to push his buttons just as well as he knew how to push hers.

He unlocked the door and slowly opened it. "No need to get all worked up," he said uncomplainingly.

He joined Veronica outside with the chair and unfolded it open beside his, careful not to obstruct his beach view. Sitting again, he lifted his shades and looked out to the ocean. Veronica could see his bloodshot vessels from the corner of his eye, his dark, long eyelashes showing a twitch every now and then.

"Are you stoned?"

He ignored her.

"Are you?"

"No."

"Drunk or hung-over?"

"No."

He wanted to tell her about his encounter with Nathan in the hills. But she'd ignore the details that mattered to him and jump straight to punishing him for doing some mild stalking. And why make her so angry while she was being all sweet, catching a loose eyelash at the corner of his eye onto her fingertip.

"Make a wish," she said.

He furrowed a brow at the childishness of the command. He blew against her finger anyway until the eyelash was dust in the wind. He said, "I've been crashing when I want to be awake, and I never know for how long I've been out unless I see the change in sky. If I fall asleep while we're talking, I'm sorry." At least the sincerity was there. He hoped she would notice it and be gentle.

"You don't sound like someone who's enjoying retired life."

He liked that she called it that.

He stopped rubbing his eyes and checked the inside of his hands, afraid that he'd see all his eyelashes clinging to his skin like in a nightmare. "Weird sleeping habits from the job, I guess."

"Maybe you should quit the drinking and go back to counseling." He kept quiet. He wanted to respond, just to shut her up, but an idea never came. "Or give your guy Mickey a call and talk things out."

"McKinney. I've talked to him already. Thanks, but I think I've got a handle on it."

His code for Shut up.

Silence lingered between them for some time, but he didn't find it awkward. He appreciated silence once in a while, even if life had become too quiet as of late.

Veronica cleaned her sunglasses on the edge of her sleeve. "Why have I been called here on this fine, sunny day?" She put her sunglasses back on.

Freddie removed his, almost like it intended he meant business. "Why didn't you tell me someone you knew was in the news related to an open missing persons case?"

He could see her eyes sharpen behind her lenses, like a suspect caught off guard. She wasn't expecting this conversation during a visit. "With your condition—" He looked at her then. "You know what I mean. You shouldn't have to hear about it. Or want to."

"You okay?"

"It's been hard talking about it with people in the trade, but I'm fine. He and I weren't all that close. It's horrible, though. It could happen to anyone at any time."

Freddie nodded. "How's everyone else handling it? Anyone grieving a little too much or too little?"

She let out a sigh and went back to ironing her skirt with her hand. "No, Fred."

"What exactly do you know about the girl next door?"

Veronica pressed her lips with a head tilt and eventually said, "You seem to have cozied up to her. Wouldn't you know more than I do?" A sly smile stretched her lips, bright in the natural light.

Summer suits you.

Summer suited every woman, he thought, and not just because it meant they'd be half-naked in the heat, particularly on the beach. He liked how summer was the time of year when women he'd been with had a certain, almost careless, type of confidence. The heat could disagree with hairstyles and makeup, and, after a certain point, women would stop caring what they looked like. Summers in New York City were like that with Veronica. He remembered summers off from school and meeting her at Central Park. She'd be in shorts, a T-shirt or tank top, and sneakers. She'd show up with her hair down, but would later tie it up in a messy bun, some hair falling loose. No makeup, no jewelry. Just stripped. She'd still look good. The lack of stress or care, the simplicity women had that time of year attracted Freddie. There was nothing to hide, nothing left to do but just be.

"You know what detectives think about a question being matched by another question."

She gave one of her half shrugs. "I know what you know, probably: poor rich girl living her dream life out of thin air in an expensive neighborhood."

"'Poor rich girl'? You're either victimizing her or showing a hint of envy. Which one it is, I can't quite tell."

"Neither. Just telling you what I know."

"Did you sell her the house?"

She shook her head. "A colleague of mine dealt with the house after the resident's passing. Do we need to call him here, Detective?"

His shiny eyes showed he found the idea brilliant.

Veronica shook her head again. "I can't call in favors just because you feel like playing detective for the day."

"Did you sell the house to the previous owner?"

"No, she'd been there for years. I remember being in shock—just the 'Oh my gosh, how sad' kind of shock—when I learned she passed away after she'd lived there for all those years. Never knew her. At least she died by the water. She had to have been happy. Her grandson used to live here in your house. He moved after she died. I felt bad for him."

"Bad how?"

"How would you feel if your mom and dad left you nothing? This guy cared for his grandmother for years and she died leaving everything to some girl rather than family."

"Cause of death?"

"Natural, I think. Old age. Oh, and you'll love this. Ms. Hottie next door used to *date* dead woman's grandson. Southern California is incestual, I know."

"Charlotte dated the guy who used to live here?"

"Mm-hmm. It should make for an interesting conversation the next time you two meet."

After thinking in silence, Freddie said, "My guy McKinney gave me the name for a detective out here. I paid him a visit this morning. We got to talking about missing people, around this neighborhood."

"Okay…"

"I'm keeping an eye on Charlotte."

She scoffed. "I'm sure you are."

"A different kind of eye, Ron."

Ron? It had slipped Freddie's mind he'd ever called her that. Veronica hadn't heard that since undergrad. By the time she started grad school, she went by Veronica and every man savored the sound of it. She hated using her full name at first, but once it stuck, anything but sounded bleak. Still, she didn't seem to notice Freddie use the nickname. Maybe it was perfectly natural to both of them for the name to roll off his tongue.

Veronica gave Freddie some judgment. "Oh, *seriously?* I think she's deadly for selling this house—which seems to be a broken curse. I don't think she's actually out there making men disappear."

"Mind giving me the name of the realtor you mentioned? The one that's alive."

"I don't want to do that, Fred."

"His name and we don't need to talk about this again."

She wanted to believe him. And she did. "Tom Coaster."

The name rang a bell. Freddie remembered that Tom and Veronica had been a couple. He hated seeing online photos of their time together, and it had been one of his happiest days since he had gotten engaged to learn the two of them had split.

"You can see how the name was set to give him a great career out here. He was a smooth talker. That helps on the job."

And bedroom, apparently.

They stared out to the water, the same stupid way they had many times before. *California dreaming,* he thought, sitting in his old chair next to an old friend, facing the ocean, and making casual talk like old times.

The moment was interrupted by a noise from down the sandy trail. It was Charlotte's door slamming shut behind her as she walked toward the beach. She was in swimwear and had a towel in hand. Freddie and Veronica silently watched her at the edge of the foamy water. The waves crashed loudly, far enough so that their murmurs could go unheard.

"This is getting too 1950s-suspense-movie for me, Fred."

Nothing was like old times, like when they were still living in Manhattan for school. Freddie used to walk Veronica back to her apartment after he spent his night in the library and Veronica had gotten out of a late-night class. Freddie had made up his mind about the police academy after graduation. Veronica decided to go for another degree. They were walking to her off-campus apartment, iced-coffees on the go during a humid night.

That's great, she had said. *Good for you.*

It feels good.

You'll be around for your mom and do what you want to do. Best of both worlds.

97

Sure, Freddie had said, less than enthused.

Okay, she said to lighten the dimmed mood. *If you weren't aiming for the academy, what would you be doing?*

You mean, the 'I need a job, so I'll do anything' kind of job, or something more permanent?

Permanent, I guess. The dream job. What would you see yourself doing and really liking?

Freddie had thought about it before, so he answered honestly when he said, *I always wanted my old man's job.*

What if the academy doesn't work out—

It's going to work out.

—and you land a great career. What're you doing then?

Uh…journalist, maybe?

You look really serious, she said with a smile in her voice.

I don't know. It's the closest thing, isn't it?

An investigative reporter! I can see it.

Takeout coffee cups everywhere, papers stained with coffee rings, stacks of paperwork and notes all over the place, no sleep unless I've been passed out at the bar. Same shit as detective work.

Is that how you saw your dad? she asked seriously, as they walked side-by-side.

No, but that's what's coming to me in this dream world of yours.

She saw he wasn't being so serious.

He said, *You?*

Lawyer.

Now that I can see.

She gave Freddie's shoulder a light punch. He didn't flinch back then. *The fuck's that supposed to mean?*

Well, you do love to argue. You just go on and on. He stopped her. *And on.*

Shit. Maybe I need to apply to law school instead of going for my business degree.

Freddie pulled back on her wrist until she came to a halt and turned around to face him. *We're in this conversation because you started it. I think you'll do grand whatever you decide to do.*

Grand?

Freddie nodded with his big doe-eyes.

Okay, but grand in the Irish way or American way? Because they mean different things. Grand the Irish way just means okay or fine, she said. *Grand in American English means fantastic and big.*

American. Definitely, he said.

Eventually she said, *Yeah, I know I will be. See you later,* and walked up the stairs to her building.

Freddie had smiled and stood there a couple minutes until he realized his cheeks started to hurt. He had worn that smile all the way to his lousy studio.

It's not a meeting, it's a date. And a date is not an interview, Freddie repeated to himself, doing one of those cheesy but necessary pep talks in the steamy shower mirror before going to bed. This was something he hadn't done in some time, but it seemed inevitable when contemplating his actions: trying to get a girl, before a job interview, or moving to another coast.

Living right next door to Charlotte made things more advantageous. He could look down at her house and see if she was home, knowing when to stop by or call, or if she had any other male company. Or female company, for that matter. Freddie hadn't seen any friends visit. He couldn't judge; it was very possible for Charlotte to see Freddie on his patio with Veronica on their few occasions since he had moved in. What would her thoughts be about them?

He was stalling. *You need to do it sometime, before either one of you loses interest.*

The only faulty aspect with this thought was that Freddie would never lose interest now that he had something to consume his other thoughts.

He had gotten Charlotte's number from Earl. He felt odd doing it, but asked himself, *What if there's an emergency?* He got Earl's too, so he wouldn't feel like a creep for having hers. While he was at it, Freddie had also asked Earl if he'd seen anything suspicious recently.

"Around here? Oh, no," Earl had said frailly. Freddie could barely hear him as they stood close to the waves. Too bad Earl kept talking. "No," he said, "I haven't seen anything strange. Not since the seventies."

"Figures," Freddie said under his breath.

"What?"

He's good at hearing for someone who acts senile.

"Good figure you have, Earl," Freddie said, patting his abdomen. "I could use a few pointers." That got Earl to give a great smile. Freddie decided it would be best to leave Earl happy. And before he'd open his trap again.

Freddie paced in the living room before building up the courage to pick up the phone—the home line, plugged into a phone jack, with a chord attached to the dial, entangled like a double infinity sign that made walking away from the table difficult. He took out his cell phone to see the number nice and bright. He could've used his cell phone, but he hadn't used it much since leaving work. He liked being detached from it, but also wished that someone from the precinct would call (not his ex).

You really could pick a better spot, he thought, very aware that he was standing in plain sight in front of the glass door.

He dimmed the lights and went back to the phone. That was no good. He slammed his foot on the table by the couch where his phone and notepad were. "Shit," he whispered, then felt like a fool for it, all alone in his house. In the silence again, he reached for the phone, but his gaze suddenly lifted away from the table as he heard a large thump and crash from next door. Not Earl. It was coming from the Tudor. The only sound missing was that of a distressed cat. He leaned closer to the glass door to see if he could see anything out of the ordinary in the black night.

Nothing.

He dialed her number, then the rings went quiet with a mannerly, "Hello?"

Did I wake her up?

Ten o'clock.

Then he heard a ruffling sound that took him back to when he'd seen his then-fiancé in her wedding dress. *Bad luck!* she'd said, pushing him out of the dressing room. She and her girlfriends had gone shopping, and Freddie knew where they'd be and happened to be around. He was never superstitious—his job couldn't let him be, not with facts, truths, and evidence that challenged coincidence.

"Hello?" Charlotte's voice brought him back.

"Sorry to wake you," he said.

"Freddie," she said, her voice slightly higher, a sign of recognition. "I wasn't sleeping. Is everything okay?"

Did they both always assume the worst?

A concerned Veronica suddenly entered his brain. *You've lost your touch lately, don't you think? You used to be able to keep a good cover, a bluff. Now you'll blow it.*

Freddie was certain he'd heard the sound of sheets ruffling. He imagined her in bed, trying not to think about her there with someone else. Maybe she was in another kind of action. A messier one. A bloody one, wrapping a body in sheets. She sounded out of breath. Either action could induce that.

She sounded focused and slightly irate.

"I heard an upsetting noise and thought I'd call to see if everything's all right."

"Everything's fine. You don't have to call or come by any time you hear something. I just dropped some books in the home office."

Bullshit. What he'd heard was too much of a bang for a stack of books falling down. Her somewhat defensive response was a red flag to his detective senses. He'd heard suspects in the interrogation room use squabble like that all the time, and most were found guilty at the end. *No, I wouldn't know if she died in her apartment last night; I wasn't there, was I?* or *No need to get all angry, Detective. Jesus, I was just being sarcastic,* or something along the lines of those adaptations.

Don't piss her off.

He tried to let it go.

Say something before she hangs up thinking you're gone.

"While I have you on the phone…I've been thinking about that d—" *Don't use that word; it'll scare her off after what happened the other night.* "Outing." *That'll determine if she's with someone. Someone alive.*

"What did you have in mind?"

Could she really expect an honest answer from any man about what *exactly* he had in mind?

"Something simple. Nothing to get you worked up about."

"Worked up? You think I have a bad temper."

"No," he said. Yes, he'd lost the touch. "I don't know you well enough to think that, but I'd like to. Get to know you, that is. I just meant something simple, nothing out of the way. A casual dinner someplace around here. I can leave it up to you if it's not too much."

She was the one pausing now, and it made Freddie's heart drop. If she said no, her answer later down the line would likely be the same. He wouldn't be able to get her alone for too long again to get more out. Not without another professional with a badge present; even that professional would need sufficient reason without getting the roundabout.

"Anywhere's fine by me."

That was a yes.

"There's this place called the Blue Lagoon," Freddie said. "I've seen it driving around before, lots of people, good atmosphere. Heard of it?"

"Can't say I have. When are you free?"

He heard the ruffling again.

"I'm suddenly very free," he said, then clarified to keep from sounding too available. "...without a job."

"Right," she said. "Day after tomorrow okay?"

"Works great."

Freddie wanted to leave it at that. But from the job, he had it embedded in him to never be the first to hang up so that he wouldn't miss any information. All information was important, even if he didn't know it yet.

But the silence between them lingered again. It prompted Charlotte to say, "Freddie?"

"Still here." He felt like he was in high school again talking to his first love late night on the phone.

"What should I wear?"

"Wear?" His mind went back to the lace blouse she'd worn the first time he'd laid eyes on her.

"Just trying to get an idea of the place. Do I wear my sweater or trade it in for a dress?"

"Either." He couldn't think of anything more to say.

"I'll see you soon."

"See you soon."

She hung up first and Freddie realized he hadn't finalized the details, really. Would he pick her up or meet her there? It wouldn't be difficult to figure it out. They were right there, partly sharing some square footage of sand. He hadn't asked a woman out in a while; maybe he had grown incapable of it. It made him wonder what else he had become incapable of doing.

He walked into L.A. Homicide sporting a visitor's badge clipped to his button-down pocket and carried a cardboard tray with two cups of coffee from a non-chain but trendy (a superior word for overpriced) shop from a couple blocks down. Because he needed a second cup; because the alcohol had amounted to zero cups that morning, and he had things on his mind that required an extent of placidity to relay them.

He was escorted to Wes's desk by an officer, where the detective was reading his way through a small stack of newspaper clippings that one of the guppies had cut out for him. He pushed them aside to the corner of his desk when he saw them approaching. "What brings you in today, son?" He motioned for the officer to leave them alone.

Freddie listened to the officer's steps fading away. When they became nonexistent, he handed the detective a cup. The gesture of friendship, the friendship he needed to earn favors.

"With coffee!" Wes said. "Welcome any time." He took a sip. Not even a full gulp through and nodding his head to the counter by the water cooler, he said, "Good call not drinking the piss over there."

Hopefully the coffee Freddie brought didn't taste like the piss two men in suits were drinking.

"I'm wondering if you can do me a little favor," Freddie said.

Wes shot him a skeptical look. "I ain't gonna answer until I hear it."

"I need you to run a name."

"Why?"

"I have a feeling and I'd like to be sure of it."

He pulled out one of many uniformed pens from a cup on the corner of his desk and licked the tip, then put it to a yellow pad of sticky notes. "What's the name?"

Fuck. He'd forgotten her last name and he felt too dirty to cyberstalk her.

"This is really preliminary, Wes. I've got a first name and an address, and I'm curious to see what you find."

"The name," he said again.

"Charlotte."

"Address?"

"Six-six-six Mystic Place."

Fitting, he realized.

"Mystic Place," Wes said. "That's where you are, ain't it?" Freddie was silent, letting Wes do all the inferring on his own. "Is it that pretty girl? It's always the pretty ones. What's your game here, son?"

"No game. Can't help it if information falls onto my lap naturally."

"The hell you ever quit for? Most investigators beg for information to fall onto their laps."

"I didn't want it to," Freddie said, almost sensitively. "Just think it's something to look into. That and a few other things. People."

"Anyone else?"

"The guy who used to live in my house. He and Charlotte had a fling for a while. I want to confirm and see what he has to say about all of it."

Freddie felt crummy as he continued giving Wes the list, like he'd betrayed Veronica by doubting her memory or intelligence, or he felt plain stupid for checking in on his neighbor under the table. *Just doing the job,* Freddie thought, but felt crummy about that too. *You have no job.*

"Are you expecting anything to come up?"

Another look from Freddie. "Meaning?"

"Well, son, to be honest with you, I just want to figure out if you're paranoid and wasting my time. I ain't no PI. There better be somethin' in it for me."

"One way for you to find out," Freddie said.

After a moment of deliberation: "Yeah, fine." Then Wes pointed a finger. "One thing, though." Freddie waited for it. "Don't tell me how to do my job."

"You got it."

"No, *you* got it. Got it?" Wes leaned back in his chair and motioned for Freddie to take a seat in the chair across his desk. When Freddie finally sat, the detective said, "This is all background, right?"

"Background, as in, off the record?"

"Background, as in, just for peace of mind."

Freddie looked ruefully into his eyes, tried to find something else to set his eyes on but failed.

"People have baggage," Wes said. "Something had to bring you to this, and you haven't given me any of that information that fell onto your lap."

In that split second that followed, Freddie deeply debated, *To tell or not to tell?*

"She's got a rocky history. One of violence." He decided on the summary version. "Something's off, I can feel it in my gut." He gave a wise-guy shrug. "I haven't been wrong, and I love to be right."

Wes sat on the edge of his rolling chair and leaned against the desk to speak more privately with Freddie, not that it mattered; it was busy and loud in the office space anyway.

"Well, I suppose it's better than thinking with some other body part of yours."

Freddie leaned back with his arms crossed waiting for Wes's next piece of whatever.

He eventually said, "I'll give it all a run and see what I can find, but this ain't my priority, you hear?"

Freddie acknowledged this.

Wes put on one of those hats sheriffs wore in films. Was he trying to pull off a 1940s archeologist look? There were those images of the detective in a Western movie again. He said, "I'm workin' with Missing Persons, but I've got a killer to catch."

Freddie strolled through his house that evening. He was waiting patiently, at first, for a call from Wes. The anticipation would have killed him if he didn't choose to occupy his time by exploring the study upstairs. He felt a certain exuberance looking inside, something he hadn't felt since he first shot a gun.

The study had a stunning view and made him feel important. If only he had a use for it. Sure, he'd had a desk job (sort of), but he had no business in that empty room. Just for kicks, Freddie sat in the leather chair he managed to keep salvaged from his old studio. He pulled out a Cuban cigar from a box one of the detectives had given him for his birthday. Freddie didn't smoke, but he thought if he was ever going to start, it might as well be with a good-quality Cuban and sitting in that leather chair. He sat with the unlit cigar in his mouth and began to play.

"I want a grand party, Houston."

Houston? He didn't know why either.

Then with an English accent: "What a jolly good idea, sir."

He put the cigar away in the box on one of the book-shelves and wanted to fill the other shelves. If only he'd read something. Freddie hadn't owned a book since college. Even then, he'd rented from the library, borrowed from a superior, or simply didn't give a damn to bother getting his hands on one. He didn't have time for books, but he was always reading something: paperwork, files, evidence boxes, databases—but not substantial books he was interested in.

He still had the compulsion to fill the shelves. But with what?

Downstairs in the living room, he retrieved Charlotte's book, feeling bad he hadn't even read the dedication page. He got over it quickly, though, and went back upstairs to the study with the book in hand. He finally picked the cen-ter shelf and placed the book to the far left so that it leaned vertically against the divider. When Freddie backed away to appreciate the improved decor, the book had already fallen flat on the shelf. He left it that way then stepped out onto the balcony.

In awe of the view, he leaned against the rail and looked beyond the backyard to the bay. He wanted to take a pic-ture, but then thought, *What for?* He had no one to send it to, and any time he wanted that picture, he only had to step outside. He'd have the view for as long as he lived there—assuming no climate change would ruin those chances in the next few days. And his friends were always going on about how the Big One was coming.

Freddie slid his hand down his denim pocket anyway. But about halfway through the reach: *Shit.* He had left his phone downstairs, unable to take advantage of the photo op, unable to hear a call from Wes. He walked away from the short-lived moment and returned to the coffee table downstairs, where his phone laid. He picked it up, the screen glowing, letting him know that the detective had called twice already but hadn't left any messages. Freddie tapped on the lit notification to call Wes back and listened to the rings anxiously.

"Freddie, you all right?" This barely audible, as the detective sounded like he was in a moving car.

"Fine. How are you, Wes?"

"Can't hear you all that well, son."

"You driving?"

"Sure am. Headed to Mystic Place with some information for ya."

Freddie didn't like that. "Not here again, Wes."

"Ah. Don't want to mix business with pleasure."

Freddie hadn't told Wes about the progress he'd made with Charlotte. Little progress, but it was enough. What could the detective have, and so quickly? With the right order of command, he could have phone records. It had to be that.

"I don't need anyone seeing a detective around here," Freddie said firmly.

Is he actually a crazy fucker who'll mess all this up? It seemed odd considering he was McKinney's recommendation.

"All righty, where do you want me to go?"

"Heard of The Reef?" It was a bar Freddie recalled, having driven past it once and decided that would be his go-to place for drinking when he didn't feel like restocking his private stash. And the good thing about bars: They were open until 2 a.m. unlike grocery stores. "It's not far from Mystic Place. Meet you there."

"Give me an hour," Wes said.

Freddie hung up and remembered his other concern.

I have a date tomorrow.

Freddie considered taking a twenty-minute walk—no more than a three-to-five-minute drive—down PCH to meet Wes at The Reef. He was used to staying in shape. He'd made it a habit to run on the treadmill daily at his studio back in New York, and to lift weights at the twenty-four-hour gym. He'd gotten lazy since the move. *Part of retirement,* something he told himself to feel better in times of self-pity.

Freddie started his walk once he received a text from Wes with an estimated time of arrival. He looked like a hitchhiker from out of town, or from the wrong decade. He hadn't had a good shave and his thick locks had grown longer. The night before, Freddie could tie a little man bun that eventually fell loose. His new hairdo wasn't the only change he'd accepted; he was getting out of shape. Stalking didn't exactly mean bicycling regularly, and he felt tired on normal walks.

Any breeze the tides forced into the valley felt like a blessing as he walked to The Reef. When Freddie made it there, he was surprised to find Wes already sitting at the bar, a couple of shot glasses emptied in front of him. Freddie checked his watch. He was fifteen minutes late and perspiring.

"Hey there, Fred!" Wes shouted across the room, prompting Freddie to slip his phone back into his pocket and walk over.

"Sorry to keep you waiting."

"Swim here?" Wes asked, eyeing Freddie from head to toe. Freddie took the seat next to him, a swoosh of leather when he did. He put his sunglasses overhead and Wes motioned for service. "Tell the bartender what you'd like."

"I'm a mixologist," the bartender said to Wes with a stale attitude.

Neither of them on the other side of the counter expected it. The guy was probably over fifty and didn't pass as the hip-shit type.

After Wes and Freddie stared hard with surprised expressions, Freddie said, "Rum on the rocks."

"Attaboy," said Wes.

"Mixologist, that man. Who would've thought he was an ace at the science of mixing."

It didn't go unheard. "It's more of an art than a science," said the man behind the counter.

Freddie didn't know a thing about crafting drinks. He knew how to drink. And that the bit of information from Mr. Mixologist was wrong. He knew that much, and it didn't help the man's case.

"So," Freddie said to Wes. "What've you got?"

"Want your drink first?"

"Will I need it?"

"We all need a drink."

"I'll drink to that," Freddie said, but Mr. Mixologist was taking his sweet time. "Just tell it to me."

Wes had a grin on his face like he was ready for the big reveal. He leaned over and pulled out a manila folder from his leather attaché case, something Freddie didn't expect him to own.

Conspicuous for at a bar.

"You know," Wes said, "there are these things called public records. They have home history and phone numbers. You should give the internet a try, or I'll start charging you for private work."

"I'm trying to stay away from doing the investigating. Besides, your drinks are on me."

"In that case, where do I start?" Wes flopped the folder onto the countertop.

"Basics. Anything suspicious about her?"

"Sure is."

Mr. Mixologist placed Freddie's drink in front of him on a thin cardboard coaster, displeased that the two friends weren't leaving any time soon.

Wes caught it. "Don't give me that," he shouted. "We're paying customers and don't get me started on how you serve underage ladies on Tequila Tuesdays."

Mr. Mixologist's face went blank and he walked away slowly with a hand inside a glass, wiping it with an old cloth.

Freddie waited patiently.

"Phone records aren't long," Wes went on. "You were the only number on there the last few days, which is why it stood out. All others were for business. But business must not be good if those were the only calls she was gettin'."

"She's a florist. Most orders are made online these days." And Freddie knew, in love more times than he could count on two hands, and with even more counts of screw-ups.

Next.

"Charlotte Walker was married, Walker being her family name."

Freddie turned his head. "I don't want to know the guy's name, unless you think it's important."

"Afraid you'll social stalk him?" This was somehow funny coming from Wes, who continued flipping through his stack. "Divorced two years now. No kids."

"Reason for divorce?"

Wes was unusually silent for a moment before he said, "Her number ain't new to the police."

Is that who Nathan is?

"Where's the guy now?"

"Don't know. He could have a whole new life in another state or be dead at the bottom the ocean as shark food.

It's not unusual for abusers to take on a new identity. Abuse victims too. Your lady is brave for keeping hers."

Freddie knocked back his rum on the rocks, the rocks almost falling out of the glass, some rum still trapped underneath. He said, "She had a violent past before him."

"You can say that again. So violent and so *young*, she landed herself in juvie."

Freddie woke up then, stopped circling the glass in the air above the counter. "She *almost* went to juvie, you mean. Could have."

Wes shook his head. "She was *in* juvie, as in committed."

Freddie leaned back, balancing himself after remembering a little too late that the chair didn't have a backrest. "How long?"

"Two years. Seems to be her number. Fifteen to seventeen. Lucky to have been behind bars and out before eighteen."

"Jesus," Freddie said under his breath. She sounded like a girl lost. Just lost. "That's a good part of growing up, gone."

"Yeah," Wes said, reading his paperwork. "She's done real bad for herself."

Freddie got the hint. "Still," he said, feeling sorry for Charlotte. "That time of your life, nothing can buy or bring it back."

"I'd say she's recouped. Got married at age twenty-six. Married a little over two years to the fella, then divorced. There you go," Wes said and smacked the pile of papers on top of the bar.

Freddie twirled his glass some more. He zoned out, beginning to pay close attention to the sound of the ice cubes knocking against each other in the glass. *Clink, clink.*

Eventually he said, "Was she in that house already when she was married?"

Wes continued flipping through his manila folder, confidently, not needing to study it hard to find Freddie his answer, and Freddie picked up on this. "She moved in after her divorce was finalized. The property was in her name by inheritance, a woman named Kelly Finley."

"What's her grandson's name?"

Wes slid the folder away. "You've done your own investigatin', I see. Don't tell me you asked her all this yourself and I'm wastin' my time." Wes said this perhaps a bit too loudly, causing Mr. Mixologist and a group nearby to stop and stare.

Freddie was somewhat embarrassed by Wes, like he was a visiting uncle dragging him around town to force kinship. "I didn't ask her anything. I don't want to until I've got the facts from someone I trust. That's you, Wes."

"Ted Finley lived in your house," Wes said slowly, watching Freddie and his arrogance. "But you knew that," he said, turning himself in his seat so that he was fully facing the bar again.

"We know where he is now?"

"Didn't think to check on his whereabouts. But he's not the ex-husband, if that's what you're thinkin'."

They hung around the bar in mutual silence, the music morphing into the sounds of a slightly larger crowd now.

Freddie eventually said, "She lied to me."

"Who?"

"Charlotte. About being in juvie. She said her habits *could* have landed her there."

"I may be an investigator, but we're all entitled to our privacy. Your neighbor, Earl, had nothin' but nice things to say about her and Mr. Finley. Nothin' seemed off. Perfect couple, how Earl put it."

"You talked to Earl? What was that bit," Freddie said, looking at the ceiling, pretending the answer was there, "about being entitled to privacy? Besides, that's how 'perfect' couples always look, right?" He played with his glass, coming around to the idea that he wasn't going to finish its contents as long as he was talking to Wes.

"Least it increases your chances, wouldn't you say?" Wes said eventually. "Just figure everything out before the two-year mark." He slapped Freddie's shoulder with the folder as he got up from the chair.

"That's it?"

The detective stopped packing. "Just 'cause you spoiled my meeting agenda with your own digging doesn't mean I didn't find anything good."

"What do you do now with all of this?"

"Nothing I can do," Wes said, "but keep this file in case it ever needs to be anything more."

Freddie looked down at his half-diluted drink disappointedly.

"What," Wes said, "you didn't think I was gonna let you keep this, did ya?" He shuffled the papers into the folder and put it away in his bag. "*My* information."

Detective Wesley, full of liquor shots and acting like a preschooler, saying *my* this and *my* that.

"Anyway, you don't want her finding this in your possession down the road." Freddie appreciated Wes's faith in his charisma with the ladies. "As far as we're concerned, it's nothin'." Wes stood up and secured the bag's strap across his chest. "Know what you can do? Have fun. Quit thinkin' about detectives and investigations or murders. Go on a date. I'll warn you about L.A. ladies being a bit superficial just as the men are."

"Thanks for that. Reminds me, I've got a date with Charlotte soon."

"Attaboy," Wes said shoving Freddie's shoulder. "Sounds like you two will have plenty to talk about. Where at?"

"Place called Blue Lagoon. Heard of it?"

"Yeah, I know the place. I'll meet y'all there."

Freddie nodded at first, still fixed on his drink. Then it registered. "Why?"

"Take the edge off you two."

"Didn't know we needed your help with that."

"It'll be fun."

"For you and who? How am I supposed to explain that?"

"Well, you can tell her I'm joining, if you feel bad. But know she'll change her mind. You say nothin' and I show up, what she gonna do then? Watch her sweat a little. See how she reacts. Then you'll know if she's one to keep around."

For a brief moment, Freddie wondered what Wes's dates had been like back in the day or even presently. Then he wondered why he ever chose to call Wes in the first place. He was an interesting man, to say the least, no matter how good he was at his job.

But with tomorrow being Freddie's first first date in a few years, he wasn't just nervous, and a drink wasn't going to help take care of that. He needed a gun. And a target.

8

Hypnotized

Freddie woke up the next afternoon on the couch with a sore back, certain that he smelled like yesterday: the smell of drink, sweat, and guilt. After showering for longer than usual, he rubbed the mirror with a fist, towel draped around his waist. Once he could see himself clearly, he thought about having a nice shave—he'd gotten one of those mail-order kits—but he decided he liked the new scruffy look. It matched his longer hairdo, reaching to the sides of his face now all wet. He felt okay about it, maybe even confident. He wore a white T-shirt and slipped on boxer shorts, feeling more like his teenage self than an underwear model, and looked for his laptop he swore should've been on the bed. Where the hell did it go?

It can't go anywhere, he thought.

He eventually found it on the kitchen counter. Once he logged in, he did a search for Blue Lagoon to read reviewer comments and scroll through photos. This was his routine, his prep for anything he could apply it to. He felt better about telling Charlotte to wear whatever, seeing the attire ranged from just about anything, depending on the people and their occasions. And he knew to always tell a woman she looked good.

Upstairs, the walk-in closet looked like a store having a going-out-of-business sale. It was empty with several shelves vacant and plenty of hanger space. The shoe rack, however, was nicely stocked with his colorful sneakers and two pairs of dress shoes. Freddie pulled out a navy button-down with a pair of jeans and his brown dress shoes.

In the master bathroom, he ran some hair product he'd had forever through his hair now that it needed more maintenance. This was too much effort for him, and he wondered how women got ready every day.

Back downstairs, he picked up the landline and called the Tudor.

The phone rang and rang, eventually going to voicemail, but right after the beep, Freddie heard the hello.

"Charlotte? It's Freddie."

"Hi."

"Hi."

Another word would be good.

"Meet you out front when you're ready? No rush."

Now that Wes was tagging along, Freddie somewhat hoped he'd hear her say she'd changed her mind, that she couldn't make it but would really like to reschedule for another day.

"I'm ready. Meet you at yours in five."

She invited herself over.

Freddie was perfectly calm until he heard the doorbell. It was fair, he supposed. He'd been over to her place unwelcomed and without any plans. This was nothing in comparison.

He scanned the first floor as he walked to the door, making sure the notepad with his scribbles wasn't anywhere in sight, and to make sure there wasn't any dirty laundry from midnight swims...or any other dirty laundry, figuratively speaking. But he'd only left clothes outside overnight once and he was usually right on point when it came to organization, just not to Veronica's standards. His cleanliness all around was never an issue in any of his relationships.

The second floor was clean too, bedroom included, but imagining Charlotte in that room was wishful thinking.

She wore an ivory lace dress that made Freddie want to crawl out of his skin and over to her knees.

"You look nice," she beat him to it.

He fixed his collar. "It's not too L.A.?"

"You're in the right place."

Freddie opened the door wider for her to walk past. "Want to come in, see what the new guy's done with the place?"

She tacitly accepted the offer. Freddie closed the door behind her without locking it, put his hands in his pockets, and watched her explore the main hall and further, to his view from near the kitchen.

"Who couldn't love this?" she asked, her eyes fixed outside. Then she looked over to her home.

"I like the view from upstairs best," he said, trying to get her to turn away from the Tudor, though, really, she was the one to rightfully look at it as much as she pleased. She moved to the kitchen and checked out the beach from there. "Enjoying a new view?" he said.

"I've been here before."

Freddie knew that, of course, but he was surprised by her easy admittance. "Almost move in here instead?"

She seemed relaxed; Freddie silently gave her props for that, but he could hear her filter kick in. "The lady who left me my house...her grandson used to live here. He'd keep an eye out on her while she still owned my place."

"And that made you come here?" There was never a good time to do the first date grilling, he assured himself.

"He and I went out for a while. It was pretty serious. That's how I got to know his grandmother." She somehow angelically affirmed this was the end of the conversation without saying so.

"How long did you know her before the house was yours?"

"About a year," Charlotte said, getting cautious with her words. "She helped me through some things." She looked around the villa again. "It's less like a man cave now."

That made Freddie smile. It meant he'd actually done something adult and right since being on his own.

He watched her in his home as she stood before the backyard, the doors open and letting in the evening breeze. He liked it. He liked it all.

She continued the tour in the living room. "You don't have much, do you? It's like you were robbed."

"I try not to be materialistic."

"Not even coffee table books."

"People don't really read those."

"Or mine."

"Yours is upstairs," he said, "in the study." Their eyes met and even the second of silence was overwhelming for him. "Should we go?"

Can't keep Wes waiting.

"We should," she said.

Freddie felt his pockets, and their emptiness. "Just going to grab the essentials. Meet you by the front door." He went to the table by the couch, closer to the back doors, and pulled out his wallet and phone from the drawer, then made sure the doors were closed and locked. Next, he texted Wes to let him know they were heading over. Then he double checked that the frequently used doors on the main floor were locked and met Charlotte out front.

"Should we walk?" she asked.

Freddie stumbled for the answer as he helped her put on her light jacket. "Can we?" he asked, his thoughts on his walk from the night before.

"It's not far from here and the weather's nice. It won't ruin our efforts."

He liked that she didn't care. But soon their sense of ease would be lost at the sight of Dan Wesley, detective. And date crasher.

Their walk to the restaurant was pleasant, enough for Freddie to temporarily forget about the guest appearance awaiting. How would it all play out? How was he going to explain to her that he'd conveniently forgotten to mention a friend (?) was joining them?

As they walked in, Freddie was on the alert for the detective. After blindly searching the crowd, his eyes met Wes's. He was already seated at a square table that overlooked the perfect view.

"Shit," he let out in a little more than a whisper.

"What is it?"

Very few times had Freddie lost confidence to wish he could disappear into nothingness. He couldn't even complete this thought because...

"Freddie boy!" Wes stood up, aggressively pushing back his seat in the walkway, nearly knocking over a waiter in his clean uniform holding a bottle of red.

"Shit," Freddie said again.

Wes waved for them to come over.

Freddie glanced at Charlotte, but she was smiling, amused but baffled.

Freddie led the way, gently pushing Charlotte along by her shoulder blade. When they reached the table, he said, "This is Dan Wesley. He's...a friend of a friend."

Charlotte took Wes's extended hand.

"You've got a strong hand there," he said.

Charlotte smiled steadily. Freddie didn't want to know what she was really thinking, and he surmised that his cheeks had turned scarlet since they stepped foot onto the patio. He could feel his ears burning up.

"*Detective* Dan Wesley. Homicide."

"Oh," she said, then turned to Freddie while they picked their seats at the square table. "You have friends on the force out here."

Did she have reason to be apprehensive around law enforcement? Though, these days, many people did. "Detective Wesley is a new development," Freddie said.

They sat in a triangle, Charlotte and Wes across from one another, Freddie at the head of the table.

"Fred tells me you live next door to him on Mystic Place."

Freddie had the bottom half of his face in his hand, elbow on the table. His mother would smack his arm away if she were around. He shook his head at Wes.

"Well, I was there first, so Fred now lives next door to me," she said looking at Freddie, almost lovingly, like they'd been together for a while and this was meeting the folks.

The warmth from the heater radiated down on them, maybe comfortable for all but Freddie, who felt like he was in the hot seat. He took his jacket off and hung it on the back of his chair. He ran his hand through his hair as a nervous tic. He picked up on this, hoping no one else did.

"Hard to own a house like that at such a young age, ain't it?"

"Not when you have the money for people to take care of it for you," she said. Freddie hadn't known her very long, but he knew she was joking. Also, he hadn't seen any house staff going in and out of the Tudor.

"Ah, she's a sharp one, Fred." And to Charlotte: "It's no wonder you're not intimidated sitting here with two homicide cops. Well, former homicide cop in Freddie's case."

"You worked Homicide?" she asked Freddie.

He nervously adjusted his collar. "Did I not mention that?"

"You just said detective. I suppose it's my fault for never asking."

"Homicide," he confirmed. "Narcotics for a short time before that."

She watched him intently. He knew what she was thinking: He was an addict of sorts.

Takes one to know one.

But the intentness of her stare also told Freddie that she saw something, that she immediately understood there was some type of pain that ensued pity, pity he didn't want.

"Speaking of sharp and homicide," Wes went on, "those papers about the murders keep piling up. Don't think I've ever read so many goddamn papers in my life. Usually clean up spilled coffee with 'em. That's about all they're good for. Maybe when I'm incognito in the car. Newspapers will never go out of business. Someone always finds use for them, even if it means using them as dog mats."

"Or wrapping flowers," Charlotte said.

Was this her changing the subject? It was about time, Freddie thought. For now.

"That's right, Wes," Freddie said. "Charlotte is a business owner." Just then, he caught Wes checking Charlotte out as she adjusted the napkin on her lap. Freddie cocked an eyebrow, embarrassed for him and very curious as to what he was doing in very plain sight. Wes caught Freddie's stare and sat up straight again.

"I'm sorry, darlin'," he said to her. "It's just, we haven't ordered wine yet and you've got something red on the edge of your sleeve there," he pointed.

She tensed her arm toward her. It was there, a deep red stain, not very big but not small.

Freddie remembered the first night he'd gone to his apartment with a bloodstain on his shirt and more on his arm. Not his own blood. That was a stain he could see. But on that night, there was another stain. A permanent, invisible mark on his life. There was one of two things he could do about it: One, he could mope, quit, do something drastic—then again, that was when he started drinking heavily; two, he could stare at the stains, choose to live on with them as a symbol for what he meant to do every day on the job. He never thought of a better third option.

"Perfect segue, actually," Charlotte said.

"To what?" Wes passed a conniving stare at Freddie when he asked.

"My business."

"You a butcher?" He looked at Freddie again.

"She's a florist," Freddie answered. And when the two stared at him: "I can let her speak for herself."

"What Freddie said," Charlotte said.

Wes picked up his knife and analyzed it. "Does that tend to get bloody?" He placed it back down and waited for her answer.

"When you use the wrong tool for pruning." She motioned to a waitress passing by and asked for some club soda and a white linen napkin dipped in dish soap, pointing to her arm. The waitress was confused about the request until she saw all she needed to see. From there, it was like Freddie and Wes entered girl world where everyone lived by girl code. The waitress understandingly gave a sincere and almost apologetic "of course," though it wasn't her fault at all, and rushed off.

Freddie liked that Charlotte could make someone do that, that she could command the room without a hassle.

Wes said, "How does one get into flowers, Charlotte?"

She took a moment before she said, "In truth?"

"Always."

"I was always fascinated by poisonous plants as a child. I used to watch the rabbits in the backyard when I was bored." As she spoke, Wes intertwined his hands and leaned against them, intrigued. "I watched them eat plants my mother warned me about. I'd watch from a distance. We got other animals too, but I felt the sorriest for the rabbits. Eating plants is in their nature and I didn't want to deprive them of food. I'd watch them eat poisonous plants and end up saddened when I'd find them dead somewhere near the house. I've loved flowers ever since. I do wish it hadn't turned out so badly for the animals."

Freddie wanted to ask her how she could like flowers knowing they left animal carcasses in her yard. His stomach turned at the sight of roadkill, and he'd seen other dead things.

"Wow, Charlie," Wes said, "if I may call you that." Her grin became mischievous, and Freddie knew why. Their little secret since he'd forgotten to mention she didn't like that nickname. "Don't tell me you're as sick as this boy here," he said pointing at Freddie.

"How am I sick?" Freddie demanded, slightly on the defensive.

"You've both got a little darkness in you, don't ya?"

Charlotte said to Wes, "You're a homicide detective. Wouldn't you say you carry a share of darkness?"

"Sure," Wes said.

"I think everyone does," Freddie jumped in. "Some more than others." Freddie was surprised neither of them appeared to be uncomfortable yet. If Charlotte was, she did an excellent job at hiding it. He certainly was uncomfortable, and to hell with hiding it.

"Well," Wes broke the silence, "let's get it all out on the table before we order. Back to the papers…Do we think it's the same guy—"

"Or gal," Freddie said, Charlotte looking at him sharply then.

"—or do we think there's more than one fucker out there?"

"You're certain that this is a murder case?" Charlotte asked. "The papers haven't said."

Wes was annoyed to have his train of thought ruined. "Well, unless a bear's the culprit—which has happened once in my time on the force."

"It's a bear of very refined taste, if that's the case," Freddie said. "I think there's more than 'one fucker' out there."

"Dan, you think it's a single woman doing these things?" Charlotte was interested now, like she had a stake in the matter.

"I don't know what her status is, darlin'."

"I think she meant *one* woman, Wes." Freddie had to give Wes credit for acting like a clueless old-timer. He played it well, unless it wasn't an act at all and he'd aligned himself with an utter idiot. He was a character, nonetheless.

"Don't see why not," Wes said. "We're not sexist no more in this profession. Well, I'm not. I count the ladies in as much as I do the men."

"Why a woman? It could be a man killing other men."

Freddie listened hard, straightening his posture. But they had a long way to go and he was on a *date*. A good hang-out with friends, or enemies, at the very least. Regardless, it felt good talking about murder. And he had a feeling this…whatever *this* was…was going to end badly.

Wes said, "Opposite sex. It's common for men to kill women and women to kill men. Out of spite, anger, or jealousy. With motive, of course. That is, if we're just talkin' about bad eggs and not the criminally insane."

"Why would a perfectly sane woman have motive to kill a man, Dan?"

And before Wes could go off on one of his rants: "Maybe he did her wrong," Freddie interrupted, just as the wine arrived to the table. He hadn't even heard Wes order amid all the murder talk. "Or he's in the way of her getting what she wants."

Wes ignored him and spoke to Charlotte. "Do go on, darlin'. I'd love to hear a woman's perspective when she's not handcuffed."

Freddie reached for the wine glass before the waiter could finish pouring.

Wes continued when he saw Charlotte would remain silent but interested. "A man kills a woman because he's angry for something she has. Another man, money, whatever."

"You say you don't discriminate sexes. A woman can kill for the same reasons," she countered. "Another woman, money…"

"True," Wes agreed. "Go on, Fred, tell her."

Freddie slid his wine glass away. "It's bad to stereotype, I know, but you see it enough. It's just a pattern."

"What's the pattern?" Charlotte asked.

Freddie let out a sigh and leaned back in his chair. "Usually, men kill out of greed, women kill for love. Or jealousy out of love."

"Greed and love."

"Usually," Freddie pressed.

"Bingo," Wes agreed.

"That's going to need explaining to me," she said, looking at the detective with her big brown eyes.

"You said it yourself, darlin'. You let those rabbits die because you loved flowers. The rabbits, male, no doubt," he said with an evil grin, "ate your flowers out of greed. Basic, selfish need. Instinct."

"A man would kill his wife for life insurance or to boost his ego," Freddie went on. "A woman kills because she found her husband in bed with another woman."

"A man can kill his wife for the same reason. Cheating," Charlotte said.

"I did say *usually*."

The waitress came back with club soda and a lightly soaked white linen napkin. Charlotte let the napkin absorb some of the club soda, then started dabbing away. Lo and behold, the stain was becoming less noticeable. If she kept going at it, it would be nothing but a damp spot on her sleeve.

"Now that we got that out of the way," Wes said, "let's order! Just not the rabbit, eh?"

Wes used his phone to order a ride back to, where Freddie guessed was, Homicide; he knew an addict when he saw one. Apparently, Charlotte did too. They watched the detective leave.

Finally.

But now came the awkward walk back to Mystic Place. They couldn't walk back pretending the dinner didn't happen. They could, but that would make things more unpleasant.

Even walking to their homes was awkward. Freddie felt it was futile to accompany Charlotte to her home, considering it was roughly a thirty-second walk between 666 and 668 Mystic Place. They walked along their street together past his house anyway, silence between them. Freddie wanted to whip out a metal detector and search the sand for his unbreakable steel charm, because all night he had wondered, where the hell had it gone?

He pushed through his lockless back gate for them to walk on the beach to the Tudor. At least the waves would add some noise and ambiance to the sad, lonely street. The motion-sensor light shone against the pool as they walked past, ridding some of the darkness. "Anyone could come through here, couldn't they?" he asked, helping her down the old stairs that paved the way.

"No one really comes to Mystic Place unless they live here," she said. "It's such a small street, most people don't know it exists to trespass."

A convenient fact, he thought, how the area was typically misty, discreet, secret from dusk to dawn.

Freddie looked up to the sky, something he'd become accustomed to doing since his move; he could see sky instead of trees and buildings. He chose this. The view, to be alone. No one leaving, no one dying. But that night, the sky wasn't visible. No indigo, almost black skies above. The clouds and mist were thicker than usual. Before he could say anything about it, he noticed Charlotte was also taking advantage of the view. They watched the fierce ocean with mist hitting their faces in the breeze. Yet, everything around them was calm.

He asked, "Why 'Mystic'?"

"The mist tends to give this area an eerie feel, especially during nights and winter. At times, it can be difficult to see anything outside just a few feet away. It gives a supernatural impression. That's what people have said, anyway." After a moment of looking at the water: "It's something, isn't it?"

More mist kissed Freddie's face. "Yeah, it is." He watched Charlotte without her noticing; if she did notice, she didn't care. She continued to look out to the water like she was being taken away, the same way he felt when he would look out to the view from home. He recognized her expression. She was somewhere else. Hypnotized, dreaming, wanting something she didn't have. It was a trance of hope or letting go. He knew because he commiserated. But why would she feel that way?

Then he took advantage of the moment, maybe not the way most men would. "Makes me wonder how many people can just disappear back here."

Charlotte half nodded with a smile that came short. "Being in Homicide make you a brooding guy?"

"I just mean it's a nice place to come out and think. Or not think. Besides, you're the one who went on about poison earlier."

"Ah," she said with a shy smile. "The conversation had nothing to do with a wacky detective joining us for dinner."

"I'm sorry about that," he said. "I will find some way to make up for that, if you let me."

She took a few steps closer in her home's direction. She crossed her arms and strolled beside Freddie once he caught up. "I like Dan." Freddie wasn't convinced. "Really. How'd you two get so close in such a short amount of time? He seems very…attached to you."

We talk about you, mostly.

"He's an old friend of a friend back home."

"So you said at dinner. You don't see this place as your home?"

"Not yet."

"What do you think it's going to take?"

Freddie let a pause intervene. He shrugged and shook his head. "A reason to stay, maybe. Haven't found it yet."

"You're not thinking about moving back already."

"It's just a thought. Seems more reasonable now that we're questioning a possible killer on the loose."

Was he ruining the mood? Was he a boring, less-than-average Joe, and was she thinking he was a guy who couldn't talk about anything else? And were his chances to make up for it with a kiss—a hug?—gone for the evening?

Then he thought, *Who gives a fuck?*

Then he thought, *What am I doing here?*

Then he looked at the woman in front of him who he'd found beautiful and smart, middle of an odd date, and thought, *What AM I doing here?*

She said, "Why are you so absorbed by the details anyway? I would imagine detectives enjoy leaving the job."

Chances were gone for sure.

"Sounds like you have trouble letting things go," she said.

"Oh, really?" He gave her a little nudge as they walked side-by-side with little grins. Maybe he was getting some of his social game back. "One dinner is all it takes for an analysis. I should introduce you to my therapists." He let that slip, but who didn't have a therapist these days?

"Therapists? Plural."

"You caught that," he said unsurprised. "Like you said, I have trouble letting things go."

"I didn't mean anything by it," she said, trying to console him. "Out here, people have therapists for their Chihuahuas. I won't criticize." She wore the same expression she had during their run-in at the beach.

"Yet you have more to say," he said, and they both stopped their stroll.

"It seems like you care about it a lot, everything going on. Maybe too much."

Was that a warning?

"I care about a lot of things," he said.

With all his flaws, at least Freddie McAllister knew himself well. And yes, there he was, diving into things too soon and too deep like he knew he always would.

"I can tell," she said amiably.

Freddie tried to figure out which one of them was stranger: him for always talking about work, or her for going along with it all by asking questions?

Charlotte eventually said, "It was good company tonight with you and Dan."

He nodded. "Mostly. You were good company."

After some silence but the waves, she said, "See you around."

The catchphrase. Now he was hypnotized.

Say something. But he didn't.

She gave him a smile and began walking further away toward her home.

Had he waited too long? He thought for sure he'd read the latter of the evening right.

But it was a productive night. He did need a reason to stay, and he had one, even if everything inside him was telling him he needed to stop, to take a step back. But he was in it, the high he had told Wes about. Now that he had it, felt it boil beneath his skin, signals moving up to his brain, there was no going back. He was an addict.

9

Maneater

Date night. Had it been? Maybe Freddie had had too many dysfunctional relationships, in general, that the one with Charlotte was difficult to classify as a good one.

Or maybe it had been as bad as he'd thought it to be.

"Knock, knock."

Freddie's neck snapped like a rubber band as he turned around. "Ow," he said, touching the pain.

"Careful, old man."

Veronica. Who else?

"Always narrate onomatopoeia?"

"Look who's been catching up on his writing."

"Trying to find a hobby, like you told me."

"How's that going?" She dusted off the chair next to him and sat. He looked around. "You're hopeless." She lifted her sunglasses. Her smile was as bright as the daylight and Freddie was a little too aware of her skin. She studied Freddie's face a little closer. He could feel her body heat and wanted nothing more but to feel her flesh against his. Her face showed a hint of worry and it made his thoughts scatter. "You look tired," she said.

"Don't you love when people say that?"

"Give me a hard time 'cause I care."

"I'm fine," he said, touching his neck again. "Date night last night."

"Already?"

He shook his head finding her smile contagious. He didn't want to talk about last night. The bag hanging from her hand caught his attention. "What's in there?"

She forgot she had brought a brown paper bag for a moment. "My reason for visiting you."

"Please tell me it's a decapitated head and you need my help."

"Sorry to disappoint." She took a plastic bag out of the bigger paper bag. "Mom and dad took a trip to the mother-lands and shipped me some produce from back home." She handed Freddie the bag. "Potatoes from Ireland, apricots from Armenia."

He opened the bag of apricots and took a whiff, triggering his hunger. "They've outdone themselves." He took two out and rubbed them against his shirt for an instant clean. Then he tossed one to Veronica and she caught it, luckily not giving it a juicy squeeze, as it was very ripe.

"What can I do with potatoes and apricots? Other than eat them, of course." He clearly hadn't done much cooking other than grilling or roasting vegetables in a pan when he wasn't ordering takeout.

"Don't burn down the house. I trust you with my life unless food is involved."

He kept an apricot and placed the bag beside him. "Give Mr. and Mrs. Dorian my best. Things good with them?" He bit into the apricot.

"They're excited right now, waiting for me to be home. We'll be in the same state. The commute will be okay. I'll give their excitement a few weeks. They'll hear me curse per usual and wish I was sweet Ronnie on the other end of the phone."

"When's the move?"

"About a month out." She thought about it, then checked her phone's calendar to confirm. Doing so showed a little bit of her hidden excitement.

"Given your work notice yet?"

"They've known for a while," she said, putting her phone away. "They keep telling me they'll put me in a nicer house if it means I'll stay."

"I'd take it." Freddie threw the pit into the bushes somewhere.

Veronica watched him and his ungraceful ways. "No you wouldn't. Always on the go, you."

"Leaving me again, you."

"You'll be fine," she said, patting his shoulder. "With everything else you've been doing, though…"

"What does that mean?"

"Nothing." She was over it and changing the subject, eyeing the house next door. "I love a good Tudor, don't you? The seafoam green beams. Photographs well. Good vacation home."

"Except someone has permanently occupied it."

"Nothing's ever permanent, Fred. And sometimes that's a good thing. Even if you're setting roots."

Freddie missed the home he had cleaned out and left behind—the townhouse, not his crappy studio apartment. He didn't feel the same adoration for the scrap in the townhouse he was abandoning as he'd packed up what was left before moving to the West Coast. He'd thought about family vacations, which had resulted in coming back to a happy home each time, back when it was the three of them.

"Do you ever miss the days parents took us on vacations, everything paid?" Freddie asked.

"You'd really want to be in your thirties and on vacation with your mom and dad?"

Freddie scrunched his nose as he looked up at the sun and kept quiet.

"Sorry, Fred."

"Everyone's different, I guess."

"Mr. and Mrs. Dorian would love to have you vacation with them."

"Thanks for the offer."

Veronica got up and fixed her crinkled skirt.

"You're off?"

"Just wanted to bring that by." She picked up her purse. "Slowly getting rid of things at home." She gave him a little wave with her fingers as she looked back at him over her shoulder and walked to her car.

He was alone again. Not completely, though. He had the water as his very own sound machine to sooth him. He also had a preoccupation that made the rusty links in his head start turning like they used to.

How long could he stay in the same spot, doing the same thing, watching the waves? He needed a change in scenery; the challenge of how long he could last out there was starting to feel like a chore and he hadn't had an alcoholic drink. Maybe this dreadful feeling was what getting clean felt like.

Getting clean.

He took a shower and dressed up for whatever the day held for him. At least that would make him feel human. He opted for a gray T-shirt, dark jeans, and one of many sneakers from his collection. Dressed, he decided to stand out on his bedroom balcony and let the natural heat dry his longer curly hair as he watched some surfers in the distance, their heads looking like grains of black pepper floating in the distant blue.

He walked around the house aimlessly but was aware of his surroundings. Charlotte was right; he didn't have much. The place was bare. It needed a homey touch. He dusted the two living rooms for fifteen minutes, making sure anything with glass was spotless. There wasn't much in the kitchen to tidy up; he hadn't been using many plates or anything that didn't involve plastic and paper from past nights' takeout. He'd even taken out recyclables that had been piling up. He looked around again. The villa was well-furnished but still lacked something.

Flowers. It needed flowers.

He knew where to find some.

Charlie's Nursery was in the middle of a shopping center on PCH, shared with a laundromat, pet grooming salon, and bistro with a rustic setup and view of the canyons. He parked in the first available spot he found, just a few away from the front of the nursery. He had no plan, only dignity he could lose—this continued to surprise him despite the increasing evidence to support the fact. Freddie didn't even know what kinds of flowers existed, other than roses and succulents (if succulents were flowers?).

Good, this question could break the ice.

The door didn't have a bell and no one was around. He walked over to the counter and dinged the bell there. He waited a few moments. Still nothing.

He tried to come up with an excuse for his visit while he looked around. Christmas was months away. Valentine's Day had passed, and he knew Veronica was very allergic to anything living.

"Freddie?"

He turned around startled, expecting her to look just the same. But she smiled, looking good in a light blue button-down summer dress, like she belonged nowhere else but out on a warm day near the sea, hair light with the sun shining in through the large glass windows, and her skin tan. In one hand she carried an old bucket of dark red roses. She had pruners in her other hand, which made him think about Wes and them at dinner.

She placed the bucket on top of the counter. "Looking for something?"

You.

"I was doing some cleaning this morning and felt like my place was missing something. Everything is so one-dimensional. Even outside is so white and blue, and I'm on no Greek island—"

"Looking for something with color?"

"Long story short."

"I can help with that," she said very surely. She brushed past him toward the plants near the window. He could smell her sweet scent. He debated between vanilla or coconut before she said, "Any other reason for your visit?"

He felt himself take a gulp, the room too quiet for it to go unnoticed. "That should do it."

She stared at him a moment more. He tried really hard not to gulp again, but his throat started to feel like his passages were closing in, and he was afraid it would turn into one of those cough attacks that would go on for five minutes.

Charlotte walked further alongside the window to show him some options. He cleared his throat.

She said, "I have some orchids on this side of the shop, all different sizes, colors, patterns. They last a long time, but they need good care. Like any good relationship."

Was she flirting, leading him on, or just doing her job?

"Anything for a guy who's never owned a pet, let alone a plant? I'm a new homeowner and I'm just glad I have a drought-resistant lawn."

"Too much responsibility for you?"

"Just a guy from a studio apartment in New York City. Growing up, my mother had a planter of something by the door. I used to walk outside and it would miraculously always be alive."

"Well, you're in California now. A desert, mostly. Maybe something that can sustain hot weather. A cactus? That's a manly plant, right?"

"You're the expert."

She led him to the other side of the store that had a selection of cacti and succulents.

He remembered to ask, "Are succulents flowers?"

He could do better at small talk, and she thought this too. But she was the professional and it wasn't totally an out-of-this-world question.

"A succulent is a plant. The more they grow, the more likely they are to produce flowers. If you want color and easy care, that would be the plant for you."

"How often do I need to water?"

She smiled at him. "Don't tell me you'll forget to water a plant that requires minimal care."

"It's a possibility."

Second meetings were about attraction and the little quirks. *Right?*

She motioned an arm at the display for him to take his pick.

He said, "What if I do want to put a little more care into it?"

She turned to another area of the store and Freddie brushed his chin.

"This is no succulent, but it's the Venus Flytrap."

"I don't like the sound of that."

She smiled. "They're carnivorous. They mostly eat insects. It'll help keep your place clean of bugs."

Freddie examined it closely, viewing their closed flaps and some of the wide-open ones. They looked like they had teeth. "I've only seen something like it in my nightmares, but bigger. I'm being eaten alive and can't use a gun on it."

"Because guns solve everything."

He gave her somewhat of a wicked smile. "I won't get political with that one, though I do remember you mentioning you practice your Second Amendment."

She leaned against the counter. Freddie could see her eyes sparkle in the sunlight. "Maybe something else for you, then." She looked to the orchids again.

"Well, hold on a minute," he said. "I want to know more about the trap plant thing."

"The Venus Flytrap."

"Yeah, that."

"Not your typical plant. I happen to think they're exotic."

"Uh-huh." He stared at the plant closer, his knees bent so that he crouched. "How'd it get the name?"

"If you haven't guessed already, the Flytrap part comes from the fact that they eat insects once they land in the mouth. They close the flaps and wait for the prey to decompose as they digest."

A little gnat landed in the mouth of the plant just then. Freddie got excited, waiting to witness the monster in action.

Charlotte noticed and said, "These plants don't waste energy on something so small. They need something bigger to stimulate them."

Freddie processed the information, his face away from Charlotte's. Her words made him wonder again if she was trying to make him sweat, trying to turn him on, or if she was just delivering the facts.

He kept staring at the plant, fascinated and trying to rid his fear that haunted his dreams.

"You were saying about the name..."

"You have Flytrap. And Venus, because...I don't really know, other than Venus, the goddess of love. Some say it's because the inside of the flaps reminds them of the female reproductive system." She paused while Freddie was still crouching down to study the plant up close. "Specifically, the uterus or genitalia."

"Oh." He balanced on his feet, standing up-right again.

She pulled her hair over her shoulder and folded her arms. "Surely a homicide detective has heard worse."

"Oh, sure. Rapes, mutilations, all kinds of things," he said, brushing his chin again. He contemplated asking the next question, but in all fairness, he had his mind there before she even explained the name of the plant further.

"What is it, Freddie?" she said, already knowing what the questions would be.

He parted his lips to ask but stopped himself. He felt like he was in the fifth grade again getting The Talk. How all the boys laughed in one room and all the girls blushed in another, then gathered together outside to talk about it.

"You want to put your finger in there, don't you?" She was still smiling yet completely serious.

"I kinda do, yeah."

"Nothing will happen. All you might feel is a little tickle."

"It's not a maneater?" He was having fun now.

"You'd need your finger in there for a very long time to feel even a small amount of pain."

He stood up straight again. "I think I'll go with a succulent."

"Wise choice." She took her time for a moment to select a nice-sized succulent that had potential for his botanical needs. She picked one up and inspected it for approval, then handed it to him. "Read the label," she said.

He picked the tag out of the damp soil, little white rocks falling out as he did.

Fred Ives.

He smiled. "Now *that's* the name of a detective."

"Are you having an identity crisis?"

"No, no. This is a little embarrassing." He analyzed the plant as he tried to find the right words. "I've been writing recently." Charlotte seemed amused but didn't comment. "Nothing serious, but it's been a good distraction for me. A memoir type thing about life after Homicide. It's a joke, mostly."

She kept her smile. He had all he needed from the visit.

"It's my last pot of Fred Ives. Meant to be."

"How much do I owe you?" He reached for his wallet.

She shook her head. "A housewarming gift. I'm glad you made it. I was about to head home to transport some of the older stuff to my place. You might've missed me."

There was that weight in the back of his throat again. "Older stuff?" he said.

She nodded. "I hate getting rid of them. They're like babies in a weird way."

"Don't want to throw away any babies."

"I advise against that at all times."

"How many do you have? Plants, not babies. Unless you've got those too."

"Uh, maybe ten? Plants, that is." She flashed a smile again and Freddie stood there somewhere between mortified and mesmerized. "I can only fit three or four planters or boxes at a time, so I usually make two trips," she pointed at her car in the lot.

"No delivery van?" He realized he hadn't seen one parked outside the Tudor either.

"It's been having issues lately. I don't like using it knowing it's unreliable."

Or maybe she uses it to transport something other than flowers.

"I can save you a trip," he offered.

"You don't have to do that. It'll leave traces of dirt in your car, and I'm sure detectives hate that."

It took Freddie a second. "Was that a detective joke?"

"A bad one."

It got a chuckle out of him anyway. "Really, I don't mind. Show me where they are and I'll load them."

As Charlotte led Freddie to the back, he couldn't help but think that showing up at her shop was that progress he liked so much—the joy of something good, even if it wasn't necessarily good: the taste of alcohol to an addict, love in a toxic relationship.

Helping her at her shop wasn't just progress; it was involvement. *Involvement.* So as Freddie followed her, it wasn't alcohol or any other toxicity on his mind. It was an investigation he'd created in his head, and now he was warming up to someone he'd categorized as a suspect. Involved. He thought, *Aiding and abetting.*

At the Tudor, Freddie carried the heaviest planter behind Charlotte as she showed him to the home office, where she had already arranged the planters she'd brought in. He had broken a sweat by the time she affirmed the rug was a suitable place to set it down, near the window to the left of the room, the rest of Mystic Place in view outside.

He dusted the dirt off his hands, then realized that probably wasn't very polite. His face let it show. "Easy clean with the vacuum later," Charlotte said and dusted off her hands too. "I like that you see plants from the living room when the door's open. I hardly ever come in here. I'm hoping it'll be a welcoming touch walking in."

Welcoming for you and who?

Freddie went from feeling like this should have been a second date, to feeling like this was more awkward than a first date, to suddenly feeling like they were moving in together.

He eventually said, "Sorry about Wes the other night," and leaned against the executive desk in the middle of the room.

Charlotte watched him apologize, standing near the doorway from when she'd checked out the planter's position. "I had a nice time."

Freddie furrowed a brow. "Really?"

"I did. He's, um…"

"A pain in the ass?"

"I was going to say flamboyant."

"There's a word for him," Freddie said. "He has a mind of his own and decided to tag along, so sorry. It was weird having him there. Less like that date I'd asked you on."

"A date?"

Freddie thought about that too, how he'd felt like he'd messed that up. "Not a very good one, is what I think I'm trying to say. To be honest, I don't know if now is any better. I'm starting to think I've lost my game or something. Not that I have *game*, you know, picking up tons of women. I don't, usually. I don't."

She dropped her eyes to the floor for a moment then said, "Anyone ever tell you that you use bullshit as a defense mechanism?"

"Again with the analysis."

"Tell me I'm wrong," she challenged.

"I'm just a spaz." He was half joking.

She walked over to Freddie, who was half sitting against the desk in the middle of the room. He uncrossed his arms, letting her get as close as she could. Close enough that he could smell her scent again, though this time he was sure it was of coconut.

"Now's good," she said.

This was it, his chance for redemption. Because of Wes and his stupid clumsiness, and Freddie's own behavior at the flower shop earlier. Time finally seemed to slow down for Freddie without feeling its control drag him down. He hadn't felt calm or settled like this since he thought he had found The One.

He tucked some of her loose hair behind her ear—something he'd been wanting to do since he saw her tie up her hair before all the carrying. Her eyes were still calm. He kissed her once, tender and long. He still felt calm, safe, and she seemed to feel the same. Charlotte's hands held Freddie near his elbows as he made his move. Secure, trusting.

They went for it more fervidly this time. Freddie felt it was going well. Charlotte's fingers were digging into his sides and then his shoulder blades once he lifted her onto the desk. Luckily, nothing fell over. The desk was clean—nothing but a laptop, lamp, and phone, all well-spaced out—nothing to knock over and make a scene, though he thought they were still making a good one.

But she stopped. "Is this all because of the Venus Flytrap?"

He stopped to look at her like she had ruined some of his best work.

She couldn't help but laugh. It made him laugh. He'd lost the mood, but he was still there and very much enjoying the company of his neighbor who was no one more just a few days ago.

"Sorry," she said, her hands still around him, his still leaning against the table with Charlotte in between his reach.

Sorry? What could he say to that? It was fine; he needed to cool off, get back to the reality of things and walk out of there dignified, redeemed like he wanted.

"Don't be," he managed.

They searched each other's eyes before she kissed him like the first time. Freddie carried her back to her feet. She fixed her dress and put her loose hair back behind her ear. Even this little move of hers was attractive. Even her nervousness. Charlotte, like Freddie, was trying to navigate the awkwardness one step at a time. He found it endearing.

Everything was imperfectly perfect. Until Freddie got an uneasy feeling, one like he was being watched. His eyes went to the long, thin plant by the window he'd failed to notice before. Each spike had an eyeball, resembling the ones children use in arts and crafts. He nodded at the plant on the windowsill. "What are those?"

She hesitated to turn to where his eyes were set, but when she did, she let out a light chuckle. "That's a White Baneberry. Also known as Doll's Eyes because…well, they look like eyes."

"We didn't bring that in, did we?"

"No, it's been there. One of my exotic plants." She could see he disagreed. "I like them. They're like something out of someone's imagination come to life."

"Remind me to not purchase that from you. Ever."

"Something tells me you won't need a reminder," she said. "Don't like being watched?"

The guilt was back. "Not particularly."

After a moment she said, "Thanks for helping with the plants."

"Any time," he said.

The brief walk to front door was in silence. But what was another awkward moment for them? Charlotte opened the door for him and said, "Things are much more interesting without Dan Wesley around."

He turned around. "Are they?"

Her calm eyes—which were far different from the Doll's Eyes—were a little playful now, and Freddie liked them just as much as any other expression her eyes could give him.

"Maybe we can do it again sometime."

"You mean, exactly? Because that would be fine, but I might start to get the wrong idea."

She shook her head with a smile. "I meant a do-over without your detective friend around."

"It's a date." He leaned in and kissed her cheek. He made it out the door feeling good, but then he stopped. "Can I ask you something? It may be a little odd."

"Thanks for the warning." She leaned against the entryway wall giving him the look to go ahead.

"You didn't happen to leave a note on my doorstep, did you?"

"A note?"

It wasn't an immediate No or What are you talking about?

Maybe he needed to rephrase his question to be more direct. "Have you left anything at all?"

She shook her head, her eyes appearing lost now. "No. It seems I have more immediate access to you."

After a smile, he said, "And you wouldn't know anyone who would."

She shook her head again. "Got anyone trying to hunt you down?"

Was it her? With a question that specific, she knows something.

He said, "I guess that's what I'm trying to figure out."

He gave a boyish smile, acting to the best of his abilities, and gave an understanding nod before he left.

As he walked home, he was cautious, alert. There weren't any eyes watching him, human nor plant. But there were things left unanswered, much to do, and he didn't want to be seen while seeking the answers.

10

Wild Wind

Their third date was an afternoon picnic on the sand. An obvious choice, but it meant less pressure, no game-playing. But they were playful, like two young teenagers experiencing their first love. They held each other close, then walked at least a foot apart trying not to move too fast. After years of Charlotte being in an abusive marriage, Freddie understood her having any hesitations, even if she never admitted to them aloud. And with his history, he had some hesitations of his own.

The mood was light enough for Freddie to ask her about her marriage, and Ted Finley and for how long they had been together. But after countless moments of inward deliberation on whether or not to open the door to the past, Freddie decided he would rather eat sand.

Then days passed.

Freddie decided to execute the dirt move in the Men's Handbook, known as giving a woman some space. Mostly, he wanted to see if she would call any men to the Tudor, or any other strangers. But he wanted the space too. He had a taste of the single life for the first time in a long time. Now that he had acquired an appreciation for it, he wasn't fully ready to give it up yet.

Days became weeks, almost a month. He had hardly seen Charlotte, and if he did see her, he'd take a detour or wait it out in his car. He didn't like the idea of ghosting her; it was never part of the plan, not that he really had one.

Charlotte didn't seem like she had much of a plan either. She went on like she was fine. She never called Freddie for a casual check-in or to question his whereabouts or argue. And he never saw anyone strange nor familiar show up on her doorstep.

Craving a drink and new ambiance, he met Wes at The Reef around 8 p.m. It had become their usual. They sat in the same seats during each visit. The detective had promised to deliver some information, something to lift Freddie's spirits. Still, Charlotte had been on Freddie's mind, and the alcohol was going to make sure Wes knew it.

Wes said, "And you don't give her a call because...?"

Mr. Mixologist also seemed to be accustomed to their routine and placed two shots of tequila on the counter. Tequila Tuesday. Freddie took in the place. Wes hadn't been kidding when he said underage girls hung around to drink. All Freddie could think about was taking them in to a station to call their parents and cite the place; but then where would he be a regular?

Freddie took back his shot and asked, "Any of this discussed within the department?"

"You and your love life?"

"Whatever it is you have for me."

Wes turned around and scanned the room before he said, "I've got bigger fish to fry, son."

"So, what've you got?"

"Remember, this is all under the table as long as I'm giving you names."

"I'll take it to the grave."

"Careful what you say. This line of work?" Wes took his shot and slammed the glass back on the counter then obnoxiously sucked on a wedge of lime. Mr. Mixologist didn't like any of it. He flipped the towel over his shoulder and walked away.

"I'm—"

"Retired." Wes said. "Whole fuckin' town heard you already."

Freddie downed his shot and didn't bother with the salt or wedge of lime. "Start with the victims."

The detective adjusted himself on the barstool, ready for the conversation. "No broken bones, some bruises here and there, but no major lesions."

This was happy news to Freddie. "You found the bodies?"

"Fuck no!"

Freddie tried not to roll his eyes, wondering whether Wes needed another drink or already had one too many. He was becoming impatient, and alcohol usually gave him more patience. "So, no bodies still. Where does that leave you?"

Wes let the suspense build before he said, "Oh, I still think it's murder. And I still think it's a woman. *That* clean to be undetected? Only a woman would think of a backup, and then another to cover tracks like that."

"A man can be a neat freak," Freddie said, wiping the dribbles of tequila Mr. Mixologist had left on the counter.

"You don't say."

Freddie tossed the cocktail napkin aside. "Any other links?"

"The persons have been patients at the city hospital over the last year. In there for different reasons. We know Ross suffered of a sudden cardiac death. As for the missing, one guy had anxiety-like symptoms, felt like he was having a heart attack, not to be mistaken for SCD. Another one actually did have a heart attack and had recovered. The third seems to be clean of medical history as far as we know."

"Heart-related issues," Freddie said skeptically.

"Yeah," Wes agreed. But then he played devil's advocate. "Everyone's got heart issues. I get a heart attack sitting in traffic."

"I imagine there's a reason for yoga being big around here." Freddie took his next shot, then asked for another. "Back to the bodies. Where are you searching?"

"We've asked for any tips, obviously, and have our team searching any dumps, ditches, cliff ends, all that."

"What about the hospital morgue?"

"What?" Wes said absently, as he jiggled the empty glass at Mr. Mixologist.

"You said they all have links to the hospital. Have you checked the morgue?"

Wes adjusted himself again, this time to face Freddie. "Now, listen. What was one of the first things I told ya when you came stomping around the precinct? 'Don't tell me how to do my job.'" Freddie remembered, wishing he hadn't had that last shot. "I ain't gonna go sniffin' around in some morgue where families are losing people, and the ones I've got breathing down my neck want answers and call us pissed-off any time we're not looking in basic areas. Am I clear?"

Freddie held his shot glass tight in his hand. After a moment, he said, "I'm just saying, if there's a common link there—"

"You don't think I've checked? Then triple checked? Then did another round? Ain't no doctors or nurses they shared and the *morgue*," he said in a lower voice, "is of no help."

Freddie didn't like the idea of Nathan being in the clear, but this information from Wes didn't completely rule him out either. If Nathan had stooped so low with a license, Freddie could imagine what he was capable of without one.

"What about Tom Coaster?" Freddie finally said.

Wes was confused. Where did this name come from? "What do you know about him?"

"I know Coaster took care of the Finleys."

"Yeah, he was a friend to the Finleys and Ross. They knew each other through business."

This was news to Freddie. "So you've interviewed him? Coaster."

Wes looked at him skeptically for a few moments and said, "I revisited some people in that circle, but remember, Ross' death is still ruled of natural causes, so family and friends have nothing to be cleared for and they don't have any additional information. Our focus is figuring out what we can do with the three who are missing."

Freddie thought of something to do for his own investigation. His secret project. He slapped some change onto the counter and got up, ready to give Veronica a call about getting Tom Coaster's number (he didn't trust phone numbers found on a basic web search). With his luck and diligence, maybe he could be the retired detective who solved this case.

"Oh," Freddie said before he got too far. "Almost forgot. I've got a little name for your case."

"Oh?"

"Operation Venus Flytrap."

Wes silently mulled it over. "Sounds kinky."

Freddie chuckled and showed him his phone with the plant's bio page lit up. And as the detective read: "You think it's a woman..."

Wes nodded. "A real pretty one who likes to trap men."

"There you have it."

Maybe with one more tequila shot, Wes would be on the news by morning with Operation Venus Flytrap crossed off his checklist.

"Here's a real tip for you, son, if you still want it."
Freddie stepped closer, but it didn't help much; the crowd
was happy and unafraid to express it. "We detectives live
very decorously, righteously, and precisely. The good ones,
anyway. Truth is, no matter what we do to put an end to the
bad shit going on out there, bad shit's gonna happen. And
when it does, sometimes there's nothin' you and I can do
about it."

Freddie nodded, trying to determine if that was it, and it
was. What a touching moment it would've been if the wis-
dom wasn't coming from Dan "Wes" Wesley, flamboyant
detective with a tequila-filled belly.

On his way back home, Freddie remembered that the bottles in his fridge had disappeared, and not as a result of a
break-in. He needed to revisit the liquor store he could never recall the name of but knew it by its bright sign in the
deserted parking lot.

He placed a bottle of red and white, whiskey, rum, and
more of that lager on the checkout counter. No one else
was there on that Tuesday evening, except the one tired-
looking kid at the register. *Kid,* Freddie silently teased himself. The phrase was contagious.

"Big party tonight?"

"Huge," Freddie said, thinking that if he kept up with
Shitfaced By the Shore, he'd get a reality TV show.

"ID, please."

Freddie mentally strangled the kid as he pulled out his
wallet. He was at an age where the request neither scared
nor flattered him. But he was a law-abiding citizen. He snif-
fled, hoping he was only triggered by the chilly, misty
weather and not getting sick with a cold. "Thanks for asking
for ID," he said. "As a former cop, I appreciate it."

The kid was in disbelief. "You're a cop?"

"Detective," Freddie said, but heard the same disbelief in his own voice. "Former," he said again. He gave his nose a quick rub and decided to practice the kid's Don't-give-a-fuck attitude. He paid, gave the guy another dull look, walked out carrying his load in a couple brown paper bags, hearing the bottles clink with each step.

At home, he stocked the lager in the fridge and placed the remaining bottles on the counter nearby, then admired the new load of work he had to finish. *Shitfaced By the Shore* needed to earn its title.

But what about the other chapters?

He needed something more, and it was right next door.

Freddie tucked the bottle of rum under his arm, ready to make his way down the sandy slope. But he remembered the book. He secured the bottle of rum in the sand, then rushed back inside to scramble through the table by the couch. First thing to stand out was the notepad with his memoir title and the hidden warning he had received just a few pages behind. He didn't give it much thought, knowing it wasn't going to be a riddle solved that night. He gave the drawer a rushed shove and continued searching for Charlotte's book. He hadn't flipped through it since his first attempt to read one night before falling asleep in the study with no whiskey left untouched.

The study! he remembered.

Freddie snatched the book from the otherwise bare shelf and gave it a good sweep with his hand to dust it off as he returned to the bottle he'd left in the sand, feeling like a lucky pirate. As he walked to the Tudor, the wind had grown stronger, and its roughness somehow accentuated the fact that the villa was dark and grim compared to the Tudor's bright living room. It was nearly 10:30 p.m. and Freddie wondered if it was too late to show up unexpectedly. Charlotte was on her couch with a book. The sight pleased him, and he was glad to be returning one of her books since she seemed to like them so much.

The screens had been fastened, but the chilly wind crept through to the deck. The ceiling fan was whirling slowly to the gusts, also swaying the lit rustic lights across the white wooden ceiling. The couch and chairs were set with cushions, pillows, and a throw blanket, like she had recently been lounging out there.

The door was open, so he knocked on its frame as he peeked inside past the screen door. Charlotte relaxed when she saw it was only Freddie. Her demeanor told him everything that had come before had been left undone. Even more so when he saw she wore a light gray sweater dress that made her skin and hair look sun-kissed.

"Didn't mean to scare you," he said. "I come with a gift, if it's not a bad time." He shook the bottle of rum in his hand as she met him there. She smiled gracefully. God, he had missed that smile.

She held the door open for him. "I'll get us glasses."

"Figured alcohol's always a good way to warm up." He could think of other ways. "The rain and mist will be setting in again." Now he was one of those people who talked to themselves at home *and* made small talk with people about the weather. To quit the small talk, he scanned the books on botanicals decorating the ottoman. "Can I help with anything?" he asked. A book titled, *Deadliest Plants in the U.S.* caught his eye.

"Nope," she said. "Feel at home." She caught him browsing. "Like anything you see?"

He watched her reach for two glasses, her dress rising with her reach. He wished he hadn't seen it when his eyes met Charlotte's in the kitchen window's reflection. He felt dirty for it, though they were dating. Seeing each other?

Had they stopped? He wondered if she was another girl who'd friendzoned him. But he remembered their first date; standard as could be, minus Detective Dan Wesley.

Then there was that kiss in her office and their day on the sand. He was allowed to look at her that way and not have to feel weird. *Right?*

His brain hurt. *This is why I brought alcohol.*

"Reminds me, I brought this back," he said, raising her book in the air. He placed it on the ottoman.

Charlotte clutched two glasses and walked over to the coffee table. She poured about half a glass each and handed Freddie his. "What did you think?"

"I liked it." A lie, of course. Two, really, considering the fact that he hadn't read it. How easy it was for the truth seeker to tell lies.

She said, "We can sit in the back if you don't mind the cold."

"You call this cold?" He nodded toward the screen door and she led the way out to the deck.

They sat on the couch facing the ocean. Everything out there was dark. Monsters could be throwing a silent disco and they wouldn't know it as they sat under warm-yellow lighting and looked out into the black.

He listened to the waves again. It was perfect, being sheltered while feeling the wind, ready for rain to fall at any moment. "So many different views from my place," he said, "but I don't think any of them look or feel as good as this one."

Charlotte sat on her knees and touched her fist to her cheek as she leaned against the couch. "So," she said after some dead air, "It's a rum kind of night."

"Usually is for me."

"How're you feeling about being out here?" He looked at her. "The move. You weren't sure about it a while back."

"No complaints at the moment," he said. "Maybe ask me again after the drink." He took a sip.

"Meet any interesting people?"

I've met a nice detective who has a file on you.

"What's in it?"

Did I say that out loud?

"What?" he asked.

"What is it?" she said. "You seem a little off. Any pre-visit rum beverages?"

"No, none of that." He chuckled nervously.

"You know, I didn't know what to think about your weeks of silence."

He looked down at his drink, his go-to nervous tic if he was allowed a glass. "You were silent too," he said.

She nodded. "That's what we're doing now."

"What?" He sounded more drained than he meant to.

"Blaming each other. Playing the You-did-it-first game."

Freddie put his glass on the table across from him and got comfortable on the couch to look at her. "I don't mean anything by it when I ask this—"

"So then just ask it, Freddie. You clearly have some things you want to get off your chest."

Sharp Charlotte was out to play for the evening.

"Do you ever get lonely out here? Living alone in this house? No mom, no dad, no benefactor lady. Just you and the water."

She was looking down at her glass, rubbing the rim with her middle finger when she said, "Changing the subject?"

"No. I just want to know something else about you."

"Why?"

That was an odd question but perhaps sound. "I'm still getting to know you." Plain but true.

And when she saw he wasn't going to say any more: "I like my privacy." But Freddie wasn't convinced it was that simple and Charlotte knew he could be the prodding type. "The way I grew up and where I am now, they're two very different places—literally and figuratively. Being on my own has never been a problem for me."

"Different places how?"

"A lot of people don't get second chances, Freddie. I know I wouldn't give many people more than one. I took my second chance. My business and this house are what I'm proud of, and I got them on my own...and with a bit of luck. So, no, I don't mind being out here with just me."

That may have all been true, but still no reason to be in juvie.

"What about guys? No one who's valued your privacy enough to stick around?"

Charlotte smiled. "Are we talking about my exes now?"

She kept answering with questions.

"I can tell you all about mine." He hoped this would get her to talk if the alcohol didn't. "I've got some weird ones."

"That's why they're exes, I imagine."

He thought briefly about how he could put his failures so delicately. "I've been engaged twice before, to different women." It wasn't the best he could do, but he tried.

He watched her smile with her eyes before she said, "How scandalous, Detective."

He smiled, mostly embarrassed. And the sound of her calling him detective was agreeable to his ego.

"I know, I know. Fool me once...right?"

"Yeah, but third time's a charm," she said. "How did you end up engaged twice?"

If he could ever feel a specter's slap, that moment would've been it.

"Just didn't meet my standards in the end. We weren't on the same page. Morally, politically...That about hits all the points of letdown, doesn't it? The second time, I thought I was closer to all the good things. I almost married a fellow detective. Figured if that wasn't right for me, then…I don't know."

"Careful. Someone might think you have a problem with commitment."

"Not with work," he admitted.

"Maybe it's a sign for you. That you should go back to the life you miss."

"Or," he offered, "I love love, and there's my problem."

And for the moment after, Charlotte watched him the way she had since they sat for their drinks, until of course, Freddie couldn't stand the silence anymore. He interrupted it with, "What about your marriage? What happened there?"

Charlotte's eyes sharpened and her body tensed up, just enough for Freddie to barely notice her fidget. She watched him more, this time with a stare that showed bitterness. "How do you know I was married?"

I know more.

They were still in close proximity to one another, almost sharing personal space. But now she was less relaxed. She sat straight. "Never mind," she said. "I should've known. Comes with the territory of your type."

My type? Detective, he figured, but asked anyway.

She leaned over to set her glass down, almost empty now, then reassumed her comfortable position. "You sound like you're baiting me. Why?"

"I'm not baiting you. I'm just trying to get to know you."

"*Why?*" she said again.

Freddie would've liked to think that it was the rum giving her all the liquid courage, but he knew she could stick up for herself regardless. He watched her battle with herself between choosing to be comfortable and uncomfortable, having words of accusation and skepticism make her blood boil but still let on that she was cold and calm.

"I don't know," he admitted. "But I feel like I'm the one confessing, and I'm not used to that. I've only watched others do it."

"Have anything else to confess?"

"Do you?"

She didn't respond and wasn't going to.

He nervously rubbed his scruffs and wondered if he had lost control of the whole situation. But there was no backing out of this conversation or pretending like it wasn't happening.

"I also know you *did* spend time in juvie. You broke a man's nose in a one-sided fight at your childhood home." He tried to deliver this with confidence, wary of the fact that she could very well break his nose.

She lowered her fist from her cheek and played with her nail. "He had it coming." She showed no regret. She even had a little curve at the edges of her lips. "Details of that incident aside, I'm a new person now. Being locked up like that after everything, with other girls who have done what you have or worse, it changes you. I had a lot of time to think things through. And learn to fend for myself."

"Charlotte Walker, reformed prisoner." He meant it, yet it sounded pompous.

"I'm not a bad person." She had years to practice that line to perfection. "You say you're still trying to get to know me…I don't think you ever will." She paused for a moment before saying, "Do you remember the night of that dinner?"

"You mean the one with Detective Daniel Wesley tagging along? How could I forget?"

"You said anyone could disappear back here at Mystic Place."

"Yeah, I remember saying that."

She let out a heavy sigh, sitting there with him now less perfect than she'd shown before. "And tonight you asked me about whether I mind being alone out here. I don't. Isn't that why you moved next door? Listen." And they did, winds getting heavier as the night passed. "Look around. This is what people come here for. It's why I moved into a house with a superstitious address, tranquil by the water. I was tired of moving. I wanted to grow roots somewhere but have the option to lay low or disappear without actually going anywhere. I was tired of running."

He understood, and he couldn't think of anything else to say or do.

"I'm not a bad person," she said again. "I'm just trying to move on." She reached for the bottle of rum resting on the table, poured a quarter glass, and took a drink. "What else do you want to know?"

Don't push, Fred. But his job consisted of pushing people over their limits. That's when the good stuff was said for the record.

"Why'd you break the guy's nose?"

"You dug into my past and that didn't come up?"

"I'd rather hear it from you. In the spirit of honesty," he said, raising his glass to her.

"I didn't like what he said to me, or about me to my mother," she said very simply.

"I'll keep that in mind."

She let a smile show. "Anything else?"

He set his glass on the table. "What about your marriage?"

She let out a sigh. "He took me for everything I had. I lost a lot of money. And pride. Younger me really knew how to pick 'em."

"At least it was one engagement before the one wedding," Freddie said, letting Charlotte and him share an almost laughing moment.

"It's been a lot to unpack for a fourth...whatever this is. And you wonder why no one's stuck."

The wind persisted, with the sounds of thunder and maybe a flash of lightning if they didn't miss it in a blink. They sat in silence listening to the sound of rain hit the roof and watched the screens shake to the wind.

"We should go inside before we get blown away," she said.

She sat up and reached for the bottle to take back inside, but Freddie took her by the arm. He held on tightly, maybe more than what he meant to. She gave him worried eyes for a moment until he stood with her.

He said, "I don't think you're a bad person."

Maybe it was too brash of a conclusion. He thought for a moment that maybe his lips just did the thinking for him. His brain very much still doubted her. But under some of the full moon's light, and with the rum, he was willing to let judgment take a break and just live like he'd been advised to do so often.

He went in for a kiss. She didn't pull away or hesitate to reciprocate. He pulled her closer from her waist, drawing her in. She loosened up, feeling less tense or on guard like she'd been. Much less tense that she eventually fell over him, both of them vertical on the couch. Things were heating up, with Freddie's face in Charlotte's hands, until they slid down a little behind his head, close to his neck. Even this tender touch made him act on instinct to protect himself, and it was not missed.

Charlotte pulled away from him. He felt clumsy for someone sitting with a beautiful woman on top of him. "It's a trigger from the job," he said reluctantly.

"Any others?"

He shook his head, then kissed her again before his body did something else he didn't want it to do.

He lay her on the floor, knocking down the bottle of rum as he did. "Shit," he said, wanting to laugh. What he really wanted to do was clean the mess. But he felt better as Charlotte laughed and told him to leave it.

He kissed her neck, tasting ocean salt and smelling the rum, which had inched its way to her on the floor. She didn't seem to mind the liquid meeting her body as she lifted Freddie's shirt off and reached for his belt and zipper. Freddie lifted her dress—now partly soaked in alcohol. She clasped onto the foot of the couch to keep herself from sliding on the smooth, slippery wooden floor.

They had stopped talking.

While Charlotte was upstairs rinsing rum out of her hair, Freddie cleaned the mess he had made on the deck. He couldn't help but look at it as a crime scene before he kneeled down to start rubbing away with a towel he found hanging on a hook by the kitchen sink. He could see the traces of her body in what was left of the rum puddle. Then he followed the roars of the mild storm out on the beach. Now when he looked at the puddle, all he saw was a mess, just a puddle. He pulled the towel off his shoulder and got to it, stopped after a couple quick wipes to pick up the condom wrapper and find a trash bin again. And again, it was like ridding evidence.

He remembered when his mother found a wrapper in his pants pocket when he was eighteen, an adult. An adult whose mother still did his laundry. College for the fall semester was approaching, his clothes everywhere as he packed between the high school parties he didn't know he'd never miss once he stopped going and the girls he'd see on the side. His mother picked up his pants from a pile of clothes he hadn't cared to pick up for days. She checked the pockets like she did during any other laundry day. She found a wrapper crumpled up in the front pocket, went out to the living room, flung the pants then the wrapper at him, and told him to do his own laundry from then on. A few months later, he moved out and into a dorm, and he never shared a roof with his mother again.

Now, Freddie picked up his pants from the floor and finished dressing, then cleaned up the rest of the spillage. As he was at the kitchen sink wringing the towel, Charlotte descended the spiral staircase wearing a white cotton bathrobe. She had another towel in hand as she dried the bottoms of her hair.

"My floor out there has gotten a good polishing," she said, smiling and sitting on the couch's arm.

As he wrung the towel again: "Makes me wonder how many others you've had out there." He said it without thinking, obviously. It had to have been all the memories of on-and-off girlfriends he'd had the summer before college. He closed his eyes tight, knowing he couldn't retract any of it. How could he let that slip? He was always a thinker, a measurer. His job required working with strategy, structure, and scheme, like a Shakespearean sonnet.

Charlotte looked down, more disappointed than embarrassed. "That's convenient for you to say. Didn't seem to bother you when you had me pinned to the floor." She looked back up at him.

Was he going crazy, or was this what jealousy felt like? What if she made the other men go crazy, somehow drive themselves to their death with a jealous, self-conscious mind and a full moon controlling them like it did the nighttime tides.

"Sorry," he said, throwing the towel at the sink and walking to her. She stood up at his approach. Freddie pulled her in from the knot tied above her navel. "I am, I'm sorry. I'm an ass for saying that."

Charlotte said, "There's no one else, if that's what all the questioning earlier was about."

"What about Nathan?"

"Nathan?"

"I don't think you ever told me how you know him," he said.

"Is this you asking?"

"It is, yeah."

"You want to have this conversation right now?"

"I think now's as good a time as any." And he didn't want to find out through his usual methods.

She nodded. "I told you about my time—you found out about my time in juvie, and I've told you about my time volunteering…"

"You can tell me," Freddie said, trying to make up for moments past.

"Once in a while I also see a support group. I used to go more often, but now it's only when I'm so deep into my own head that I think hearing someone else's experiences would be helpful."

"A support group for what?"

"For people with criminal offenses," she said, and watched him carefully when she was done.

"You're not ashamed of going, are you?" he asked profoundly.

But she responded with, "No, I'm not," and it was as confident as he hoped she'd be about it; he wished he could feel and appear the same way about his addictions.

Then he understood. "So that's how you know Nathan. You know his history," he said surely.

Charlotte nodded. "I take it you do too."

"Occupational hazard," he said sheepishly. "What about that night in front of your house?"

"He came over angry. He was upset I hadn't been going to meetings. He started accusing me of things—mostly of being a hypocrite—but regardless, he can be delusional when he's not on his medications. That's all I told him to do, was to keep to his routine that worked. He got angry and a little violent. Then you showed up."

"Why you? Why show up at your place?"

"It's hard opening up to a group of strangers. It's hard enough doing this now with you," she said. "But some of us work harder at things than others, and differently. After my time in juvie, I was still lost, trying to get my life together the way an adult would. My timing always felt off. Falling for the wrong men, not being able to have kids with someone I thought was the right one. Divorce. Going back to school, having a record expunged, starting a business very slowly while people in my life came and went...When timing always seems off, you start to think *you're* off and ask yourself what you're good for, even if you know to think better things. There's a certain limit you give yourself with people about it all. Lucky me to be that person for Nathan."

Again, he understood, but maybe it was the pride that wouldn't let him tell her that. "I used to go to AA," he said, sending himself into instant indignity. Yet he felt okay.

"You don't need to tell me anything, Freddie. It's taken me years to be able to talk about any of this."

"I just want you to know that you're not *wrong*. At all, in any way. I want you to know that I think that."

She was in silent appreciation until she said, "It's not about what others think. No one else can get rid of the damage for you, even if you want them to or let them try."

He had some self-help to catch up on.

She inched away from him. "Suddenly, I wish we still had that rum," she said. "Anything else we need to get out of the way?"

Freddie weeks ago would've wondered if that's what she asked before she killed. But now: "No one else?"

"Not unless you count helping Earl with his trash."

"It's a dirty service." Freddie lifted her so that she was sitting on the couch's arm again. He held her cheeks in his hands as he kissed her gently. "Fuck Earl."

"Odd choice of words."

It didn't stop him.

"Forget Earl," he said.

"Forget Earl," her voice echoed in a near whisper.

They kissed again. Freddie gave it a little something extra this time as some form of an apology. Freddie lay her onto the couch, untying her robe. He lifted Charlotte's satin slip and kissed her thighs as he continued higher. No arguments, no fuss. None except for the wild wind making a mess outside.

Wild is the wind, he thought, before all sounds vanished except for her breaths.

With a clearish head—alcohol still remnant like an endless hangover—he thought about the roller coaster of a night he'd had. He had almost screwed everything up. Despite it all, Charlotte had found it in her to forgive him for his unexplained behavior. She was forgiving when they'd made it to the bedroom too.

Freddie started getting dressed, ready to make the shift back to his place when she said, "You don't have to leave."

He looked back at her as he put on his socks at the corner of the bed. "I know. And I don't want to give you the wrong idea, but...I don't really know what the right or wrong idea is here."

She scooched toward him and kissed his bare shoulder. "We don't have any kids, no one else to report to. No rush."

He liked the sound of it, the holiday he envisioned all along until he was stuck on work practices again. He turned around to her on the bed.

"And I know you can't use work in the morning as an excuse," she added.

She had him there, even though he could think of several excuses to leave, and several more to stay. He really wanted to stay, but he was thinking of the different reasons to make it out the door.

You know how you like your privacy? I like mine. Maybe she would think that was fair. *I'm ready to hit my bed and call it a lucky night.*

He opted for, "I've had some trouble sleeping lately. I'd hate to keep you up all night. Not that our waking hours haven't been fun." He kissed her and hopped off of the bed to grab his pants and look for his other shoe. When he couldn't spot it anywhere on the floor, he took it as a sign. What else was waiting for him at the villa? What was better than this?

Charlotte watched him. "Change your mind?"

"You make it easy," he said and climbed back into bed.

The wind was subsiding and had cleared the fog, displaying the dark night. They fell asleep in one another's arms with naked flesh and naked souls, very much in the present and not the past.

At the villa, Freddie kept his laptop resting above his legs stretched flatly across the bed, sitting up against a couple pillows. He could work—research properly now that he was in his own home under his own sheets. He opened his browser but didn't know why he bothered. He had nothing to search for. This was uncharted territory.

Everything was good in his life. He wasn't thinking about his ex and his almost-marriage, his former job, not even about giving Wes a call.

There it was. He needed to check in, the way an addict did with a sponsor to keep from using.

He reached for his phone on the nightstand and checked the time. It was nearly 4 a.m. It didn't matter.

He called Veronica. She picked up before what was probably the last ring.

After her sleepy hello: "That thing you're calling me on has a clock."

"Giving the bling a break for a bit. My wrist was starting to hurt."

"You better be dying or in desperate need."

"I was hoping to catch your voicemail, actually."

"Oh, great. I'll hang up and you can talk to it as much as you like."

Freddie had a smile on his face, but the laughter wouldn't come. He didn't have the energy.

"I need a favor, Ron."

"What kind of favor?"

"Can you give your man—" he began, but that wasn't right, "—Coaster a call?"

"This could have waited until normal hours, Fred."

"You know how I can get," he said. "I want to meet him. Interview him."

"Are you back on the force?"

"No."

"Then no."

"I need Coaster's number, Ron. You know I'll keep asking."

She was quiet for a while. Freddie thought maybe she'd hung up. But Veronica was used to the random phone calls at random hours. She knew it meant something was on his mind.

"Hey, Fred?"

"Yeah."

"Tell me, how're you spending your time these days?"

Think of a white lie, one that has some truth.

"I've been bicycling." He was glad they were on the phone. She couldn't see him blink or twitch to give the lie away. "Veronica, *please*. You don't have to call him, just give me his number."

"Fine. Can we hang up now?"

"Thank you."

"Fred?"

"Yeah?"

"I want you to know I'm being nice and not actually being manipulated like you think I am."

"I don't know what you're talking about," he said, though they both did. They had followed the pattern: he asks, she resists, he gives an alternate explanation, she caves, he's grateful, they let it go.

"I'll text you his contact info."

I love you, he wanted to say, but said, "Sleep tight."

She had already hung up.

His phone was buried somewhere under the covers, and his mug on the nightstand was filled with what was now cold tea. He sat up and searched the sheets for his phone. He found it, lit it up, and noticed a text from Veronica, time stamped at 9 a.m.

It was past noon now, but at least he had Tom Coaster's contact info to start his day.

Freddie responded:

Thx. Any reservations about telling him you referred him to me?

Freddie put his phone on the nightstand and drank his cold tea to wet his dry throat.

Veronica texted back:

He should hear my name every now and then ;)

Then another one.

Don't tell him I said that.

Freddie chuckled and didn't waste any time. He pressed the phone number and the line began to ring.

"Coaster."

That's douchebaggy.

Freddie always answered his mobile with "McAllister." A formality of the job. Any time it rang, he picked it up hoping for information from the forensics team or a tipster.

"Tom? Tom Coaster?"

"Yeah, who's this?"

"This is Freddie McAllister, we have a mutual acquaintance, Veronica Dorian. I'm—" he debated the next word, "a detective. Got a minute?"

"*Detective*? What's your name again?"

"Detective McAllister. I just have some questions for you about a house you sold a while back. Any time you can possibly meet today? All basic and for background."

"I know how that story goes. Nothing's ever just information with you people."

"Really, twenty minutes of your time, tops," Freddie said. He was prepared for an ambush if it came down to needing one.

"When and where?" Tom sounded put out already just over the phone.

"Drink coffee?"

"I do."

"Pick a coffee place in Malibu along PCH. In an hour? But I'm flexible." He tried to make it difficult to hear a refusal.

Freddie heard other people's mumbles until Tom Coaster broke his silence. "Beach Bistro, one hour."

Aside from being cursed at while walking on the lower streets of Manhattan, this was the shortest conversation Freddie had ever had. At least it worked out in his favor. But what was it about the bistro that seemed familiar? Freddie half debated writing it down or just memorizing it, but he'd seen it before. By the time he realized he knew exactly where it was, Tom Coaster had already hung up, and Freddie was too lazy to call him back to suggest a different place.

Freddie walked over to the living room window to sneak a peek at the Tudor, but the curtains were closed. So he left to check out the meeting spot before Tom's arrival.

11

Avalanche

Beach Bistro was in the same shopping center as Charlotte's flower shop. Going there had been the first plan he didn't overthink. Maybe even the first solid plan he'd had in a while. He parked closer to the bistro, early and anxious for meeting Tom. He glanced over at Charlotte's shop with his sunglasses on, a pathetic attempt at a small disguise. He walked toward the hostess before meeting his odds of a run-in to explain the reason for his whereabouts. At least there were several other parked vehicles with either bikes or surfboards mounted to them to distract from his car.

"Table for two," he said at the counter.

"We require your entire party to be present," she said chirpily.

"I'm thinking somewhere a little more private than standing here," Freddie said, ignoring her unnecessary cheerfulness for following restaurant policy.

"A date?" asked the hostess.

"Sure," he said mechanically.

Freddie ended up at a table in the back and near the wall, private enough, though the place wasn't busy to begin with. While he waited, he put his fingers to work, texting Veronica for a photo or description of her douchebag of an ex. After wanting to hit Send, he deleted what he had composed. What was he thinking? She wasn't going to answer, out of spite or just being busy, planning her new life that wasn't so far away anymore. He tried the next best thing to stalking: social media, because it made stalking permissible.

Freddie didn't have any social media profiles. Rather than spending his time searching through Tom's, he scrolled through Veronica's old posts, soon wishing he could unsee them. He wanted to puke at the lovey-dovey ones, but there was more to his icky feeling; he hated that they were an attractive couple.

His face was somewhere between awe and nausea when he saw a man in the parking lot getting out of his convertible car. Freddie couldn't get a good look at his face from where he was sitting, but everything seemed accurate based on the photos he'd been searching through.

Tom Coaster had light hair and a receding hairline that wouldn't make him suffer any actual hair loss until well into his late seventies. He swung the car door shut and stood by, dug his hand down his pants and adjusted his sack.

Jeez, Freddie thought, *this is what the wild winds blew over.*

This was going to be a hoot. He never wanted to gift a stranger a pack of tighty-whities before—or whatever would stop Freddie, or anyone, from seeing that again. *This is the guy who used to be with Veronica,* he kept thinking as he watched. He didn't feel so bad anymore.

Tom didn't make eye contact as he walked over. He either punched at his phone or looked at the empty tables. Freddie had already hated Tom just from word of mouth; his hatred was 100 percent confirmed now. He was dressed like he belonged in an East Coast frat house. He wore khaki pants, a pastel pink polo shirt with a navy blazer, and a pair of those reflective pilot glasses that screamed douchebag. If Freddie had to guess, Tom thought he was the same hotshot as he thought himself to be back then.

"Thanks for meeting me here on such short notice, Tom," Freddie said, careful not to extend his hand for a formal introduction. "How's it hanging?" He smiled stupidly at his own cleverness he was internally celebrating.

"I'm on a tight schedule, so just tell me what you need from me."

Freddie imagined that was one of the last things he requested from Veronica. What did she see in him?

Freddie needed to get down to basics: establish a rapport with Tom. He took his turn to look around the place and said, "Nice suggestion." The hostess brought them a menu with a congratulatory gleam in her eye. Sure, Freddie had told the hostess he'd be on a date, but he wasn't going to explain their relationship and he wanted her to go away, and fast, so he could get to work. Tom's tight schedule meant Freddie was on a tight schedule. "We're actually going to just do coffee, please," he said, showing a hand to Tom for him to order.

"Espresso," Tom said.

And after he and the waitress looked at Freddie: "Make it two."

"So much in common," she said, then took the menus and walked away.

Tom watched her as she walked away, checking her out at first, then pulling his eyebrows together as if in horror. Then to Freddie: "People out here get dumber every day."

"Let's not speak ill of her until we get our coffee," Freddie said. "Come here a lot?"

"It's a nice place for meetings, business and personal."

"Bring any dates here?"

Tom reached for a sugar packet and started smacking it rapidly against his fingers until he saw Freddie focusing on it, annoyed. He stopped, but it didn't make him appear less nervous. He was jittery before the shot of coffee.

"You want to know if I brought Veronica here," he said matter-of-factly. "You want to know if she's a psycho before you get in her panties?"

Freddie kept that on file for later.

He wasn't nervous like Tom was, yet he squirmed in his seat. He was a level higher than anger. He let out something like an irritated chuckle as he stopped squirming. "I've known her long enough to know her psycho tendencies pretty well. We're not here to talk about Veronica. We're here to talk about you and what you do."

"Me? I'm a realtor."

"I know," Freddie said getting comfortable again. "I live on Mystic Place. I believe you sold my current home to its previous owner."

"That doesn't narrow it down, man."

A waiter brought their two espressos, less chatty and nosy than his female co-worker helping another table a few sections away on the other side of the room. Unlike her, he didn't want to be there. Freddie silently empathized.

"I'll take the check," Freddie said. Whatever would get him out of there the quickest. He was with Tom again. "Six-six-eight Mystic Place. Great private beach view. Previous owner was a grandson to the woman who lived next door. Ring any bells?"

"Oh, yeah! Yeah, I know the place. Great property. You like it there? You'd be crazy not to."

"It's great," Freddie said, before Tom went on, taking away his chances at jumping in. "Do you remember the people who used to live there, in my place and next door at Six-six-six?"

Tom didn't need to think about it. "Grandmother-grandson duo. I remember. They had a close relationship. Weirdly close, if you ask me—"

I didn't. Freddie tuned the rest out, silencing the wanna-be frat boy like he did his alarm every morning. He tuned in again, practicing that good selective listening.

"—She'd met a young woman, hoped to feed her to her grandson, I think. She passed away, the older lady, and I helped get the property ready for the transfer of the deed."

"What happened to the guy in my house?"

"Why do you want to know?" Tom was giving Freddie attitude, acting even more put out and inconvenienced.

"I've got a feeling my house is haunted," Freddie said, hoping it would work for the duration of their meeting. "Just want to dig out any dirt."

"It's the house next door that's haunted, if you believe that sort of thing. That's the house the grandmother died in. I thought it would be a tough sell, but didn't need to worry when I learned arrangements had been placed and that the chick was moving right in."

"And the guy in my house?"

"Moved away. His grandma died. Pretty sure she was the only thing keeping him in L.A. He moved closer to other family, last I heard. Then again, I only pay attention when they're moving in, not out."

"Always know so much about your clients?"

"Oh, well, you have to, especially in this area. It's competitive. You need to know what your clients want and don't want."

"Did you ever get to know the girl at Six-six-six?" Freddie said.

"No. Wish I did, though. You've seen her, right? A buddy of mine got dibs on her. He, uh, died, not too long after they stopped going out."

Coincidence or murder?

"Sorry to hear that," Freddie said. "How'd he pass?"

Tom shrugged. "No one really knows. They said it was heart related, but he didn't have any prior issues. We might not always understand science, but it doesn't lie. It was one of those instances when you just say it was his time."

Freddie was positive this was the only smart thing Tom Coaster would ever say.

"Why are you asking anyway?"

"Veronica mentioned someone she worked with passed. I was curious, considering recent events."

"What, are you looking into it again now that there's people missing?" Tom leaned back dramatically as if he'd been shot.

If only.

"So that *is* what this is all about?" Tom said.

"I'm not done asking questions," Freddie said frankly. He wasn't about to confirm or deny anything. "The man in my house, was he still dating the woman at Six-six-six when his grandmother passed?"

"I don't know. He didn't seem attached when he left, obviously, or she probably would have moved with him."

"How'd she take it? The breakup, him leaving?"

"She got over it quickly." Tom was taking time to think before he spoke, but not overthinking. He wanted Freddie to fill in the blanks rather than do the talking.

"If you wouldn't mind elaborating," Freddie pushed.

"Once the guy left, there were new guys hanging around with her a lot."

"A lot?"

"I don't know, man. Never counted. Enough for me to notice while I was at your current place setting up for an open house, or when I checked up on her with her transition. Just friendly stuff."

Friendly, sure.

"And you never went out with her?" Freddie asked again.

"Me?" Tom laughed. "No, not my kind of woman. I like to be the shark in the water, know what I mean? Besides, she went out with my friend, Hudson. The one who passed."

"You don't seem to be grieving about the other missing men," Freddie stated blatantly.

"I was friends with Hudson. I'm devastated over his death. Like I said, it was unexpected. But the others in the news were more acquaintances through Hudson. And no one's confirmed murder. I guess I'm still hoping they're alive and well."

"Are you afraid for your safety these days?"

Tom didn't break eye contact for the longest time since they had sat down. "I wasn't," he said.

Freddie kept quiet for some time, finally drinking his espresso and wishing it was a shot of tequila instead. He took it down with a burn anyway, pushed the cup aside and said, "Keep in touch with anyone at Mystic Place?"

"No, don't really have the time for it unless there's a property on the street I have to deal with." He checked his watch rather obnoxiously. "Look, man. I'm meeting someone here soon, for a *real* meeting. You think we can wrap up whatever this is?"

But I haven't gotten in my twenty minutes yet, he wanted to say, all worn-out like Tom was. Instead he said, "Just one more thing. How's the housing business with the news about the missing and deceased circulating?"

The missing and deceased. He told himself to remember that title for later. He was tempted to reach for his phone and make a note, but he didn't want to lose Tom.

"I'm curious as a new resident too," Freddie continued. "Keep reading up on the details and figured I'd ask someone who knew the scene well, like you."

Maybe the flattery would get him to loosen up, gain that trust.

"Read all you want," Tom said. "Things, business is still okay. People with money think murder can't get to them."

An odd thing to say, but true.

"Is that a general observation?"

"I'm just saying, this is considered a good town and the people are eager to buy new, updated property after the fires, floods, and mudslides. I've lived in this town and worked here for years. Things are more than okay for me, and I'm not planning on leaving."

Freddie couldn't help but notice Tom's defensiveness. The defensiveness of an arrogant prick, not so much of a resident sticking to his moral ground, believing that a potential murderer should be the one driven out of town.

The coffee seemed to have put a temporary halt to Tom's withdrawal jitters. Or was it the frustration?

What else was Tom addicted to?

He was a typical frat boy living his good life in his good, obnoxiously transparent bubble. Of course he thought things were more than okay. Or maybe he was like Freddie: making things appear that way. For all Freddie knew, Tom was like him, a man who watched people through their windows waiting to feel some type of purpose again.

Tom scrolled through his phone, checking his watch, life behind his eyes disappearing into his empty head.

They couldn't be the same type of man.

"Thank you, Tom. Talking to you has been...well—"

"So, you know Veronica."

Here it comes. Right when Freddie thought he could walk away somewhat gratified with the outcome of his time with a moron.

"Does that mean I'll see you at the party she's throwing?"

Freddie looked into Tom's eyes with scorn in disguise, but it was more toward Veronica. *You invited the bastard?*

"You just might," Freddie said, putting money on the tab that had magically appeared sometime during their conversation.

"Thanks for the coffee," Tom said. Before Freddie could give him a snarky retort (and did he want to with his Big Apple detective attitude), Tom was already tapping at his phone in one hand, a sugar packet still in the other.

Freddie left him there; he'd had enough. In the parking lot, all that he could confirm was the fact that Tom Coaster was a prick who used the word man a lot to fake intimacy. Freddie tried to determine which convertible out of several was Tom's, now that he could scan more relaxed. It was easy to confirm which was his; license plate HWZCSTR stood out.

Freddie made sure no one was around to identify him later for what he was about to do. He went around to all four tires, unscrewed the valve caps, and pocketed them. His hand had a mind of its own for the last one. It stalled, wondering how guilty he'd feel about it when he would stash the caps in a drawer, only to find them years later. Maybe he'd get a good laugh, and for all he knew, stashing a good laugh for down the line didn't seem like a bad idea. "Sorry, mom and dad. Sorry, McKinney," he said, and let them go in his pocket.

A homeless man crossed Freddie's path, interrupting his moment of justice. "You hear the voices too?" he asked, watching Freddie's stupid smile and hoping for a response.

"The voices, the voices." He scratched his head and then tugged on his ear.

Freddie realized he was the odd one, standing there completely paralyzed.

"Got love?" asked the man.

Freddie could feel the caps weighing down in his pocket. Hands in his pockets now, he rolled them with his thumb, thinking about how their quantity was less than the amount of times he had wronged Veronica in some way. He said, "Too much."

"Got food?"

Freddie always appreciated a bum who asked for food rather than money. And this bum was like a godsend to him. He slipped a twenty-dollar bill out of his wallet and handed it to him. "And, uh, you look like you've been on your feet. You can rest in this convertible car," he said, patting the trunk like a used-car salesman.

"God loves all," the man said, making himself comfortable in the backseat. "And God loves you."

I'm going to hell.

It's beach town. People are laid-back, Freddie tried to make himself feel better about Tom being pissed to find a man in his car.

Then he thought about how he got Tom to meet him at Beach Bistro on a random day at a random time. Freddie's lies were starting to pile on, just like his learned information. He couldn't help but think both the lies and facts would eventually tumble down like an avalanche. Then he wondered how many lies he would let himself believe until he just believed and lived.

12

Might Be Wrong

Tom Coaster had taken over Freddie's otherwise silent drive home. No music, no podcasts, just Tom's voice in Freddie's head. What did Veronica ever see in him? Sure, he had boyish charm, a bulletproof smile, and above-average clothing. If you liked that type.

Thinking about Veronica and Tom as a single entity made Freddie aggressively throw his wallet and keys into their rightful drawer—the table by the east window, synonymous to Charlotte's window—then looked out to the pool, thinking about how he hadn't taken a dip in a while. His eyes shifted to the beyond, the great big blue, the grander choice.

But he ditched the idea completely and went upstairs to nap for a few hours. Several hours, actually. He saw another one of his recurring nightmares he'd had for some years. He'd close his eyes and wake up unable to open them, like they were glued shut. That got him to open his eyes and leap out of bed to go downstairs again.

The ocean was starting to cause trouble as the sun fell into it. Freddie picked up the landline to give Charlotte a call, unsure about whether it was the thought of trouble or the beauty of the sun's dive into the ocean that prompted him to do so.

She didn't pick up, and before he knew it, he was leaving a long, rambling voicemail, one he would later question repeatedly with some liquor. She answered about halfway into whatever he was saying—some small talk about the weather that had yet to become inane enough to let him down.

"Hi," he said when he heard her voice. He could see her in her living room from his own.

"Your place looks nice at night with the lights on. Haven't seen it so bright in a while."

"Yours looks like a castle."

"Maybe you've forgotten what it looks like on the inside."

"I remember well."

"No need for a refresher?"

He wanted to ask her about the deceased realtor. Victim No. 1. Why hadn't she mentioned him after all the opportunities that had presented themselves for telling the truth?

His eyes felt glued shut again. He stepped away from the window and rubbed his face roughly. The nap failed to keep him from clearing his head of the shitty conversation with Tom Coaster and how horrible he was for simply the way he *talked* about Veronica. But it wasn't Freddie's responsibility. He wanted to try things Charlotte's way: swimming in the ocean for mental clarity, to focus only on the waves taking him under and making him forget. The way rum and whiskey did.

Then he imagined her wet body against his. "How do you feel about a night swim?" he finally said.

"I love a late swim."

They met on the sandy hill between their homes at 9 p.m., like clockwork, both dressed as if they belonged in a high-end fashion catalog with their turtlenecks. Chilly L.A. evenings had Freddie wearing a sweater when he was missing the boroughs.

Night swimming had been the plan. They never made it that far. After each of them talked their nonsensical, charming patter back and forth, they fell into the dark and didn't go inside his villa until after another two hours of lying on the sand.

Charlotte spent the night at Freddie's this time. Freddie fell asleep quickly once he felt Charlotte's body loosen, feeling heavier against his arm, her breaths becoming long and even. Soon after, he sank into the ocean.

He woke up at 3 a.m. on the dot, everything still in darkness, with Charlotte's arm around him, holding his abdomen tight to calm him down. He'd had one of his nightmares, one of being shot and bleeding to death. He had never chased someone while on a homicide case; detectives in Narcotics did all the time. But he ran a lot in his dreams and they often led to being shot. It always took some seconds for him to snap back to reality. Now he was wide awake, but seeing Charlotte made him wonder if she was only in his head too.

You're my secret, he thought. *I'm my own secret.* He wondered if she'd heard him say anything of real conversations in his sleep. Secrets, truths…they had a funny way of making themselves known.

"Was it the killer plant?" she said. He lightened up to the sound of something familiar to just the two of them. She noticed the smile he was trying to hide with his cheek muscles working hard to avoid it. It made her smile. She kissed his cheek and lay next to him again. He felt her cold hand against his ribcage, and after a while, he sank back into the ocean.

Freddie had stored away the memories of leaving the precinct, his shit-shack of an apartment, and everything else in his urban life.

What he had diligently forgotten was the part of his life filled with romance. He had missed romantic bliss, unaware he'd been missing it until he realized his head and heart were stupidly acting as a team. In his experience, and according to an innumerable amount of record-charting love songs known to man, love made you do stupid, uncontrollable things. And in this way, love was a lot like murder.

Despite the lies or half-truths between him and Charlotte, he had been blind to the analogy as of late because he didn't need to count his breaths to the waves. The binge drinking had become reduced to social drinking. This is what he'd missed out on when he had decided to distance himself from Charlotte weeks ago. This is what he'd missed out on before retirement. It wasn't quite happiness, but it was close, attainable. All the bad now seemed to be a pretty picture in the rearview mirror. Why tamper with that by asking more questions?

The rain usually meant he didn't want to go out, and if Charlotte was with him, she didn't want to go out either. Their nights concluded in the bedroom, his or hers. No alcohol dripping down their bodies, but they felt intoxicated enough in something else that resulted in the sheets being pulled off the corners of the mattress. Freddie had become familiar with everything that was Charlotte. He had become just as familiar to every sound in her house—and his—now that he was spending more time away from the chair. There were the crackling noises through her bedroom ceiling or from downstairs; he was almost certain it was the wind, though previous conversations came to mind about a haunting in the house.

During a quiet night out on the sand after sundown, their voices feeble unlike the tides, Charlotte wanted to know if she could ask about his drinking habits.

"Sure, but yes-or-no questions only," he said, trying to lighten the mood before the actual hard part. He hated questions, at least being on the receiving end.

Charlotte considered it. "We talk, Freddie, but I think you know more about me than I do about you."

He nodded. "I know. And I've buried things under the sand...metaphorically speaking. That would scare me if it were the other way around." And it did. "Does it scare you?"

She stared at him for a moment and said, "I don't know."

They waited in silence for a moment until Freddie continued. "Something tells me you'd ask me questions anyway, no matter how I answer or if I choose not to."

She thought about that. "Are you calling me nosy?"

"No," he said with a chuckle.

"Then what *are* you telling me?"

"Keep asking me the questions."

She didn't understand the request.

"Rather than me telling you. I'm more likely to answer you honestly and wholly than tell you on my own." Another flaw Freddie put out in the open.

"Okay," she said and sat up next to him. "You quit going to your meetings and therapy, right?"

"Yes," he said, then took in some air and let it out. "I quit the meetings and I haven't been seeing my therapists."

"I don't want to make you upset," she said carefully.

"You're not."

"Do you regret quitting attending your meetings?"

"No," he said. "Going did its job in its time."

"Is that how you feel, or felt, about being a detective?"

"You're not bad at the questions," he said impressed.

"You're bad at answering them," she said, returning a smile.

"I don't know if I'll ever feel done being a detective." This was honest but incomplete.

"Why's that?"

He shrugged. "Might be a personality thing."

"Which is what?"

"These aren't yes-or-no questions," he said, but her patience with him deserved a response. He took another deep breath, wondering what he'd gotten himself into, then let it out. "Obsessive? Compulsive? I don't know." But he did.

"Is that why you drink? Because you're obsessive and compulsive?"

"Yes," he said. He caught her eyes just after, noticing the concern, the curiosity, the sympathy. Everything that told him she was good. He, on the other hand, appeared to be a maniac. "Just not the way you may think," he added.

"Tell me," she insisted calmly.

"I don't drink because I'm obsessive or compulsive. Not in the sense that it drives me to drink. I drink to make those feelings go away." She wore the same look of sympathy. "And because it makes me feel like a kid," he added.

"Did you abuse substances as a kid?"

"No. That's not what I meant." She waited for him. "The feeling I get when I drink takes me back to being a kid. Or just younger."

"You're not old," she said, trying to understand.

"Thank you," he said, trying hard to cover his flaws with poor humor. "It makes things simple like when you're a kid. Takes me back to a time where I didn't need to worry about money, or what I was going to do with my deceased mother's body. Or what I'm going to do tomorrow, whenever tomorrow might really be; five, ten years from now…literally tomorrow."

"A lot of people drink to feel numb."

"That's just it, though," he said. "I hate feeling numb. I drink to feel *something*. Ironic, isn't it? The cop who preached to underage alcohol possessors about how alcohol is a depressant and how it would only bring a temporary thrill. I dedicated years of my life to AA meetings."

"But you're in control of yourself now. You're better," she said, hopeful that she was right.

Better was good, but better didn't mean great, or resolved.

Charlotte wrapped her arm around his and leaned against his shoulder, deciding the questions were enough for the night. They let out some built-up nervous laughter as her scarf flew right into her face during a gust of wind. Freddie moved it away and drew her in closer. He kissed her hair and that was that.

It had been a while since one of Veronica's random visits. Freddie felt her absence any time his eyes came across the empty chair on the patio.

He sometimes visited Charlotte at the nursery, and when he didn't, he worked hard at staying sober, or at least maintaining the reduction to social limits. Night swimming alone after drinking marathons had ceased, and not just because he was too lazy (or cheap) to heat the pool. What if he needed the money for another long-distance move? Instead, he made Charlotte dinner—anything that involved grilled vegetables and slab of meat on the stovetop, since that was pretty much all he knew to prepare. The latter of their nights were spent on the couch with a bottle of red wine. Some nights they listened to the sound of unusually long rainfall, hard and heavy all around the villa, and all the internal chaos would temporarily wash away.

It wasn't unusual for Charlotte to return to her shop after dinner when a long romantic evening wasn't in the plans. He had visited her there once in the late hour, somehow feeling frisky while watching her prune buckets of roses. He told her how cliché it would be for him to bring her flowers at home. They laughed about it and eventually cleared the countertop for non-work purposes.

So, it wasn't unusual that one night after dinner she told Freddie she needed to go run errands for the shop. He checked his watch, knowing it had to have been late enough for him to feel tired while also feeling the sting of desire (for alcohol) excite him.

"It's almost ten-thirty," he said. "What errands could you possibly run at this hour?"

It was his natural-self doing the talking; the detective that never clocked out, not that it was ever a typical nine-to-five desk job.

"You have your secrets, Freddie McAllister," she said, then leaned over the breakfast bar to get closer to him, "I have mine." She gave him a quick peck, short and sweet, but one he'd think about for at least thirty minutes after she was gone. She snatched her bag off the corner of the chair and wrapped a scarf around her black knit sweater. "Some of my vendors don't sell mulch unless it's late and raining. Something about the weather that keeps it fresh."

It was absurd enough to possibly be true.

"Drive safely out there. The rain's as bad as the tides on a full moon. Forget the tides—the crazies out there on a full moon." She watched him gingerly, and he didn't blame her, considering he was behaving strangely superstitious. "Will you come back here?" he asked, hopeful as a puppy dog looking out of a small cardboard box on the side of a street.

She thought about it as she finished wrapping her scarf around her neck—something he had found inexplicably but increasingly adorable the more they were in chilly weather—and he helped pull her hair out from under the tight wrap.

"I'll see you back here in a bit," she said, and gave him another quick kiss before she left.

She hesitated.

Maybe it meant nothing, and she was already out the door on her way when he told himself not to dwell on it. He rinsed the pan and some dishes before loading them into the dishwasher, realizing he was performing these tasks roughly when he saw the flesh on his knuckles turn a pale yellow. He gently kicked the dishwasher door shut, then leaned against the counter. He was no gardener or nursery owner, but it seemed that mulch and rain didn't mix well. A little voice told him to get on the road and tail her. Another voice said, *She left five minutes ago; it's late. Who knows where she went for me to catch up.*

The sly detective, the paranoid boyfriend; he didn't know which one he was.

He drummed his fingers on the counter for some seconds before a sense of determination struck his stubborn head. He grabbed his keys and wallet—at least it meant he was going out—then patted his butt pocket to confirm his phone was in there nice and snug. Just as he looked up, he caught the light turn on in the Tudor. If he'd missed it, he would've thought Charlotte had left the light on earlier. No; someone was there now to turn it on. He froze and watched the house for the first time in weeks. *We're all entitled to our privacy,* he heard Wes say.

The light went out. A few moments later, Charlotte stepped back outside. Freddie's eyes followed her walking to her car, then she drove to the end of Mystic Place and flashed her break lights at the stop sign before turning right onto the main road. Freddie jogged to the street corner and saw her make a left onto PCH. That was it. He left the house as it was and hopped into his car, ignited the engine, backed out of his driveway, and just drove, ignoring all the tailing rules a detective knew to follow.

Where to?

Grocery store.

She passed that.

The nursery.

She passed that.

The pier.

The pier.

Charlotte removed her keys from the ignition but left the headlights on. Freddie looked across to where they shone, seeing the whites of angry waves and spots of hard rain pouring horizontally in the wind. Charlotte had a trench coat on—why she stopped at home, he gathered, which meant she had planned this.

Freddie killed the lights then drove over to the other side of the parking lot where he could see her walking down to the beach, balancing as she slipped down the hill in some of the sand-turned-mud, and eventually made it under the pier. He felt confident about his hideout spot and killed the engine. His eyes worked hard to see clearly through the rain. His brain worked hard too. His eyes were not deceiving him. It was Charlotte and she was still wearing that scarf. What was happening?

Everything had been so nice. Now all he could do was watch and wait in a stupor. At least the rain meant no footprints would be left in the sand. Freddie put his hood on, well aware that he would go home completely wet later, looking all the more suspicious than he had earlier.

This was no place to buy mulch; he could tell this much even with his hoodie and rain casting a dark cloud over his eyes. And judgment. He stealthily walked closer to see better given the conditions, and eventually barricaded himself behind the lifeguard station closest to where the deserted boardwalk began, trying to put an identity to the shadow figure she was with.

A little closer. Still too dark.

Finally, the face was in fact familiar. It was better than being a John Doe. Regardless, Charlotte had some explaining to do, because neither she nor Freddie was supposed to be there, and what was she doing there with Nathan Roberts away from a support group?

He couldn't hear anything over the storm and its beguiling effects on the water. Trying to pay closer attention, he could see Nathan yelling at her, either out of anger or simply because he couldn't hear anything with the weather doing most of the talking on the beach. This wasn't an affair, was it? No. Freddie had seen this many times before. This looked more suspicious than secret love or lust. This looked like it was part of a shady deal.

Even if it was, what could Freddie do? He didn't have a legal badge to flash anymore. He needed to decide between going down there to confront them anyway, or wait until his next moment alone with Charlotte to ask her point blank, when she could drop into her own deceit without being able to walk away from a lie.

He was suddenly aware of his soaking wet, very West-Coast coat: non-waterproof with a hood that served absolutely no purpose. He wiped his forehead with his sleeve as if that would dry the water on his face, thinking this was a good time as any to actually distance himself from following her, dating her…whatever, because, what the fuck was he witnessing?

Freddie was in trouble now that Charlotte was walking up the sandy hill, a short distance away from where he stood. He couldn't be seen. He couldn't slip into his car unnoticed and flick the nonexistent invisibility switch. One wrong move and Charlotte or Nathan could end up right in front of him. He watched them a while longer until his eyes shifted to his car, the only other car in the deserted parking lot. What a horrific sight it would be if they explored it, recognized it.

He waited by the bathrooms. Not optimal. The mixture of sewage and saltwater pierced his sinuses, and the disgust was gurgling in his knotted stomach. She was getting closer, and Nathan wasn't far behind. Freddie had to think fast. He gave them the slip by moving around the building he used as a shelter from the rain pouring sideways. Things would work out, he told himself, just as long as they didn't see his fucking car. At least it could pass as a patrol cruiser from afar. That was his only safety net, and he kept repeating it to himself inwardly. He prayed that they wouldn't see it, that the rain would divert them. He prayed for the first time in a long time. Maybe when it was all over, he would convert to a religion, something he'd abandoned altogether years back.

A nervous sweat built on his back and forehead. Already soaked, it was the perfect recipe for coming down with a cold. But he was too much in the fight or flight mode. His body would fight off a cold until he had the chance to relax, which he rarely ever did.

Freddie got lucky and had never been more grateful for rain. They had gone straight to her car. Charlotte was back behind the wheel. She ignited the engine and turned on her windshield wipers. Where was Nathan? The last time he lost Nathan, things didn't go so well. Freddie checked on Charlotte again in her car. This time, he found Nathan sitting in the passenger seat beside her. She reversed the car from the parking spot (though she could've easily driven away by turning her wheels all the way since the lot was empty). She followed rules, or habit; he couldn't tell which one. If she followed rules, could she be all that bad, the way he'd imagined in his head? Or she was a sociopath who couldn't be easily read. He did always like a woman with intrigue. But he'd suffered enough with that type. So why did he go back to it every time?

He didn't know the answer, or he wouldn't be in the middle of a parking lot, late night in the pouring rain, following two ex-cons.

He got back into his car once Charlotte drove out of the parking lot and back onto PCH. Instead of tailing her again, he turned the engine on but didn't shift the gear to Drive. He sat there with the windshield wipers swishing for nothing, because it was raining so hard and there was a dense white fog in the air keeping Freddie from seeing anything out there.

He turned on the radio, hoping that music or a DJ or shit commercial would distract him, make him feel normal (because happy was stretching it) for another second. But he continued sitting there, frozen. So many mental calamities in his head, but one distinct voice made itself known:

I might be wrong.

About the decisions he had made within the last six months. Doubting himself, proving himself right. That nothing was wrong, and that everything was just in his head. No matter how he thought about it, *I love being right, but I might be wrong.* About everything and everyone.

His head was telling him, *Get out of here, go!* But his body was completely numb.

Numb. He hated himself all the more.

Getting back to Mystic Place required leaving the parking lot, and he needed to beat Charlotte there. He was still frozen, and she'd driven out of the lot five minutes ago. With Nathan Roberts.

Where were they going? Why were they together? Could Freddie make it home before she did?

Freddie finally made the engine roar, able to hear the music now that the rain was mild. The radio was tuned to a classical station, the sounds of harshly played organs prompting him to make a funny face at the dashboard like the choice of genre was its fault, until he remembered he had set the station with purpose for his late nights on the road driving cross-country. He hadn't listened to music since then. What a depressing time it was if Freddie wasn't listening to music. Any kind. He was a fan of opera most of all. Or French pop tunes. They'd have him drowning in nostalgia or another mushy feeling he could never quite recognize. But that night it was classical music.

He picked up the end of *Toccata and Fugue in D Minor* and *Symphony No. 5 in C Minor* took over. He sensed a theme there. He never imagined himself racing home to a symphony, but life was full of surprises.

He left the pier. Of course, he just had to hit a couple red lights, feeling the panic weigh against his back with a small ounce of hope. Then he passed Charlotte's shop. Another red light. Fine, as long as he didn't pull up right next to them with an Oops-I'm-busted look on his face. The light turned green after what felt like it had been several minutes, time Freddie didn't have.

Mystic Place was foggy when he pulled into his driveway, rain stuck in clouds. Before he could open his car door, Freddie heard another open. Charlotte's front door.

The little hope he had managed to build up vanished.

He made a run for it before she made her way over. He made it to the backyard in good time, but—*The key.* He hadn't thought that far ahead. Luckily, he had it attached to his one and only keyring.

Charlotte had a key to the villa, and she had more keys than he did. Mathematically, not that Freddie was ever an expert at math, it meant he had some time to spare: Charlotte getting the correct key out, playing around with it until she would successfully open the door and see him sitting there soaked. *In lies, stories, inventions.* And compunction.

The key situation was his chance to see if every horror movie he had seen demonstrated some truth, or if his reality was simply that terrible.

What then?

It didn't matter. Getting in before Charlotte would be a step in the right direction. He watched her for a quick second, caught her walking past his car then make it to the front of the villa. She must've been playing with her keys, chunks of metal sounding as he made it to the back of the house. He lowered the hood from his head and went inside, closed the door, careless about how loudly he let it slam behind him. *Phew.* He wanted to wipe his forehead again. He was about to, ready to take the victory, until he turned around. His eyes met Charlotte's with that Oops-I'm-busted look he so desperately wanted to avoid.

The word "hey" never left his mouth as much as a breath. He was out of air, wanting to step out into the cool fog again. Right now, it was better than the warm shelter he called home. He felt like he was in the pit of hell, Charlotte the flames, slithering closer even though she was still by the front door across the grand room, probably cold like he was.

"What've you been up to, Freddie?"

His eyes were wide and showed trepidation like he had forgotten how to blink. He couldn't move while she stood before him calm, cool, collected. While he couldn't be certain about what was going on in her head, they were both caught, no way out.

"Where've you been?" she tried again.

"Went—" He swallowed whatever had built in the back of his throat. "Went for a walk." He took off his heavy, wet coat, feeling his neck tingle with sweat. He hoped Charlotte couldn't read him so easily. It was becoming a habit, lying to her. He felt guilty despite his anger. Dirty. He felt slightly better about it, though, thinking if he was dirty, then she was filthy.

"Your car was gone when I got back." She had guts for challenging him after where she'd been.

But he wasn't supposed to know where she'd been.

He shook his head and ran his hand through his hair, letting some droplets fly out of his curly traps. He would consider himself lucky if he were to slip on the puddle he'd created and knock out, sending him to the hospital. Normally, he loved this, taking great delight in being Mr. Know-It-All. But plunging to the ground followed by blunt force trauma to the head sounded like a good option, just so he could avoid the conversation he was in now.

"I had the car in the garage," he said. "Backed it out hoping to take my bike for a ride." He felt confident about it when he quickly rehearsed it in his head, until he saw she wasn't convinced.

"You're soaked." She showed a moment of genuine concern, then it faded back into an expression of having an inkling. "Where'd you go?"

"You know me," he said. "A walk in the rain is what a swim in the ocean is for you. Just wanted to clear my head."

"You seemed okay when I left. Where'd you walk?" She was sounding like a detective; with any other girlfriend, or even with Charlotte weeks back, he would have found this impressive. Cute, even. But now he didn't like it.

"Around," he said. "Didn't require going far to get drenched. It was pouring out there. Ten seconds'll do it." And after a moment of silence: "You get your mulch?"

She let the dead air collect more heat. Freddie finally hung his coat on the back of one of the chairs at the breakfast bar. "Yes," she said, "and it stopped raining." She twiddled with her keys. Then she walked toward him slowly. "Dropped off what I got at my place." He gulped, glad he wore a high-neck sweater that took the attention away from his Adam's apple. He felt a bit of a weight there, thinking maybe his sweater was choking him, but it was tension, he was sure.

She walked over to him slowly, watchfully. He was ready for the punch, the broken nose, the whole I-know-what-you-did speech. Instead, she wrapped her arms around him and gave him an adoring look—slightly devious but adoring. A distraction, at least. "I'm soaked," he said, feeling her warm body against his—warmth he wanted, but also fought off with shivers and a cold sweat.

"So take off your sweater," she said, starting for him and holding him from where his future love handles would be if he didn't quit drinking and actually start taking up walking and some more bicy—

His mind shut off when she kissed him. He kissed her back, half wanting not to, half wanting to relinquish all doubts. He put his hands against her back, holding her close and not wanting to give up that body heat.

Then she stopped. Freddie realized he probably wasn't being the convincing charmer.

"Anything you want to tell me?" she said.

He took a step back and brushed his face while she waited for a reply. He eventually said, "I'm going to change into something dry." He fixed the bottom of her knit sweater, damp against his fingers, then left her there.

Tread carefully, McKinney's voice said.

With each step up the staircase, Freddie's ambivalence dwindled.

13

Changes

Freddie pulled a charcoal-gray T-shirt over his head as he walked down the staircase the following evening. Charlotte was gone. This was what he wanted, yet there was something in him that expected her to be there. He needed something else to consume his time, something to distract himself from the fact that it had been his first night alone in a while, to stop analyzing the series of incidents over and over again.

The only way he'd stop analyzing is if he did something about it. He considered giving Wes information on Nathan but was interrupted when his cell phone vibrated, swirling on the glass coffee table. Veronica's picture illuminated. What were the odds? Veronica, always caring for him, warning him that he was being stupid, even when she didn't know it. He answered.

"Hey, Fred. Where are you?" She wouldn't let him get a word in, and she asked like she already knew the answer.

He took a deep breath, softly, hoping she wouldn't hear it and said, "At home. Resting."

This wasn't a lie. He was extra mindful that he was sitting on the couch. Yes, resting.

"You're in that chair, aren't you?"

"On the couch inside, actually."

"Now there's money well-spent," she said, her voice high, enthusiastic. He felt accomplished by it. But his hand was shaking, his tongue itching for the bottle of rum he kept somewhere behind a stack of clean dishes he had yet to put away. Maybe if he told her what was really on his mind, he would have an outsider's second opinion and the shakes would decrease. But she would know too much, making her involved. And Freddie knew that anyone involved in a detective's circle wasn't in a good place.

"Why? Where are *you*?" he asked.

"Driving home from the gym."

"Skip home. Come here. We'll take a walk on the beach and catch up."

"You want to exercise?"

"Don't be so surprised. You're a good sponsor."

All he could hear was the sound of the road until she said, "Fine. Only because I want to see you anywhere but that chair."

"See you in a bit." He hung up and placed the phone back on the table. Had he lied to her? He wanted that drink but didn't want to drink alone. That was a sign of progress, wasn't it? He had intended to have a beachside stroll with her, but the odds of that happening were slim.

Freddie tried to hide the shakes when Veronica arrived. He'd even changed into sweatpants for the artifice of wanting to exercise. After a small hug hello, Veronica placed her purse on the kitchen island and removed her sunglasses. He could spend money every day to see her do something so simple—give up the house and whatever millions he had accrued.

"So. Exercise?" She looked around the kitchen, and he knew exactly why.

"No," he admitted. "I called you over so we could go out, get a drink."

I need one.

"Fred, I'm happy to get you out of the house, but is something wrong with all that liquor?" She nodded to the glass bottles he never stored away from the countertop.

"Better to drink in public and with company, isn't it?"

"I'd be a bad sponsor."

"Good thing you're not really mine, then. Can we take your car?"

"Oh, God. What the fuck happened to yours?"

"Nothing," he said. "You have a convertible." That, and he wanted his car to noticeably remain in the driveway for a few more hours in case Charlotte felt curious.

"*One* drink," Veronica said. "And somewhere I won't see anyone I know."

He tried not to take that to heart as she chucked her car key at him. He caught it with one hand and said, "I know the perfect place for that."

Driving to The Reef had become a reflex, kind of like knowing his way around a gun. Driving to any bar, really. Reflex, instinct.

The place was crowded, but Freddie was able to spot a table past the several heads. At least sitting at a table was different than what he did with Wes on business. He started walking over, but Veronica pulled him by the wrist. "Let's sit at the bar," she said.

But that's where I sit with Wes.

He looked there. "Really?"

"I sit at the bar after work and get hit on by sleazebags. I want to sit at the bar and not have to worry about it. I've got a cop with me."

"I see. I'm a cop when it works to your advantage." He didn't put up much more of an argument. He had witnessed what she was talking about, maybe had been one of those men.

After a drink and another round, he had almost forgotten about how he'd spent the night before. Almost. He wasn't so tense anymore, but all the facts were still fresh.

"I miss drinking with you, Ron," he said, hoping that focusing on her will get things back to normal...for him, anyway.

"You just miss drinking." She sipped on her whiskey. Freddie had the same. Two peas in a pod, those two.

"No, really, I do. Shows your true colors, if I remember correctly."

She let her head fall back then leveled it again. "We had *one* drunken kiss, Fred. How is that memory appealing to you?"

"Just is."

"Alcohol on our breaths, foggy memories, weird lines crossed." She shook her head violently.

"Your voice getting huskier the more you drank," he said, picking it up in her already.

"Very attractive."

"Some may say."

For a moment, they were both careful not to move a centimeter, until he took a step back from the counter, hating that they were at the place, the awkward place, but glad it was all on the surface again. He pushed the glass away absent-mindedly, and Veronica picked up on it. "Are you going to tell me what's really going on in there?" she said, tilting her glass to his head.

He nodded a few times. Finally, he said, "I met this guy on Charlotte's property a while back. Wasn't going well with them two." He took a moment to make sure no one was eavesdropping, though the place was packed and loud.

"Last night, I followed her to the pier. I don't know what I saw exactly, but it didn't look good."

"What do you mean, 'it didn't look good'?"

"It means that she met this guy there and things looked…*off*."

They paused, both feeling like it suddenly got too quiet in their immediate environment. Then the obscure, nearby conversations filled their ears again.

"Who's the guy?"

"Look at you, asking all the right questions." He had the urge to put her in a headlock and give her a noogie, but she'd throw a fit. He clinked his glass to hers instead.

"Don't change the subject, Freddie. You followed your girlfriend. I wish I could say that's new."

"I'm not proud of—" Freddie rolled his eyes mid thought, then said, "Wait, yeah, prying was my living, so, yeah."

Now she knows more. Involved. More inevitable changes. He wished, sometimes, that he could prepare for them, but then they wouldn't be inevitable.

She ignored his sarcasm. "Anything can look suspicious when it's taken out of context."

"What's there to be misread? Regardless of what's going on, she's with me, right? So what's she doing sneaking off with this guy and not telling me? That in itself is suspicious to me."

"I think you're being ridiculously sensitive. And stupid."

The stupid idiot. An early chapter title?

"I'm a sensitive man, Veronica. I lost my mother without being there for her, I don't have a dad to turn to, I'm out of the force, my girlfriend is guilty of…something, I can't get murder out of my head, and all you L.A. people do is tell me to pull out my fucking yoga mat and breathe in and out. And now you're here trying to teach me a lesson on something you don't know anything about. So, yeah, I'm sensitive."

Alcohol had a mind and lips of its own. He didn't know what to make of her contemptuous but beautiful grimace.

"Are you done feeling sorry for yourself? Of course you're not," she said. "Still miss drinking with me?" He tried to keep a serious face but couldn't. She went on: "You and I are here together, talking about whatever narratives you have in your head. How do you think this would look to her if she saw?"

Fair point. But...

"Oh, come on! You warned me about her, remember that? 'Slimy fish on the shore' is how you put it, I think."

"Lack of sleep, blacking out, drinking, obsessing over your old job...none of it's good, Fred."

"That's, that's a different set of issues," he admitted hastily.

"I'm just saying, you're blaming her for something you can't even talk to her about. And let's be real here. You just can't stand the fact that she's basically you but maybe better at it."

"I'm onto something," he said, "You don't get it because this isn't your work, it's not your life. So unless you join a squad in the field of law enforcement, fuck off." It sounded crueler than he intended. Veronica's fist was going to meet his face, he knew it.

"This new detective friend of yours? I thought you just needed someone to feel like it was Wednesday night at the bar talking about all the different scenes and weird stuff that happened during the day. But it's more than that." She put a hand on his shoulder; he flinched as she did but was glad it wasn't that punch. "I'm *concerned* for you."

He shrugged off her touch. "Sorry I'm not Mr. Fancy Realtor Man—real asshole, by the way. This is it. This is what I'm used to. I can't give you another version of myself. I thought that's been clear for years now."

"I'm not asking you to be anyone else. And for the record, you're being the asshole right now."

Freddie took another drink and watched the people. Then to Veronica: "It is weird that she met the guy under the pier, though. Right?"

"I'll give you that."

"*Thank you.*"

"Listen," she said, all serious again. "Weird habits aside, I want to see you at my place in a week for my farewell celebration." He couldn't understand how this was a cause for celebration. "Bring whoever. It'll be a good crowd. Just *please* leave work at the door."

He bit his tongue but asked anyway. "Will Tom Coaster be there?"

"Mr. Fancy Realtor Man." She tossed aside the wet cocktail napkin that had lived under the glass—ripped in half as she did—then asked the bartender for another whiskey on the rocks. "Probably. I invited him."

"You're killing me."

"You met the guy *once*."

"One time too many."

He thought about Tom Coaster some more. A smile eventually invaded his face, made Veronica contagiously smile back.

"What's this? What's with the smile?" She took a sip out of her glass.

He chuckled. "I let a homeless man sleep in his car."

She almost choked and she set her glass back onto the counter. Once she cleared her throat, she let a smile show before it became a full laugh. "You're serious."

Freddie brushed the bottom half of his face, feeling to confirm whether that smile did in fact exist under his facial hair. "You know how I feel about a homeless man in a rich neighborhood. Gotta share the wealth."

"So you let him sleep in Tom's car? You may not think so, but Tom's okay. He probably drove the guy anywhere he wanted to go."

"You sound so fond of him," he said with sarcasm.

Checking out the crowd again, Freddie could see a man checking Veronica out and trying to read their relationship. Freddie, too, wondered what kinds of vibes they gave off. *Friends, first date, ex-couple?*

"Five o'clock," Freddie said with a discreet nod.

She turned her head subtly, remembering how they'd done this years back. When she faced Freddie again: "How do we know that's not for you?"

"I'd be flattered. But between the attractive lady in workout clothes, or tall, shaggy guy in sweatpants? I'd say he's looking at you."

"Don't get me wrong, because you need to do s*omething* about it, but the facial hair isn't bad on you."

Before Freddie could take the conversation about his appearance further, the man across the room had taken the space between Freddie and Veronica as a positive sign, because now he was standing there like the three of them were lifelong friends.

"Evening," he said.

"Yes, it is," Veronica said, and Freddie turned around for a restrained laugh.

"You look nice tonight," the man tried again. This to Veronica, and Freddie gave her a side eye as he sipped from his glass. "Bet you always do."

"You bet well," she said, avoiding eye contact, but being a smartass anyway. "Must be a good gambler."

Freddie fiddled with his glass. He knew how south this was about to go. She brought up gambling.

"Yeah, win lots."

"I hate gamblers," Veronica said, looking at him. This was true. She grew up with family issues due to toxic, addictive risks. It occurred to Freddie that maybe this was why she'd kept him around: some messed-up complex she had developed.

"What do you do?" the stranger asked her.

"Right now, I'm drinking with a friend, so if you don't mind, I'd like to get back to it."

"You two *together*?"

Freddie didn't like the confused expression that came with the emphasis. It wasn't good for his friendzoned ego. He pulled Veronica in from her hip, proud to have her, though he knew Veronica was the type of woman who would never really belong to anyone. "Yeah, we are," he said. "Ended our open relationship a few weeks back. Isn't that right, sweetheart?" He kissed her cheek.

She didn't falter to play along, holding him in a half embrace. "That's right, sugarlips."

They faced the new man and waited, only saw the same dumb look on his face until he eventually gave up and simply walked away.

Veronica let go. "Like I said, you need to do something about your facial hair," she said, rubbing her cheek.

"Sugarlips?"

"Open relationship?"

They both brushed it off.

A group in the back celebrating some occasion caught Freddie's attention, shot glasses all over the table, incapable of leaving space for anything else. Another crowd was eating tacos at the bar. The jukebox kept going even if no one cared to listen.

Veronica said, "Let me ask you, Fred. What are you doing?"

"I'm fine."

His default answer.

"No, not how are you doing. *What*."

"What do you mean? I'm here with you."

"I mean with this neighbor of yours—"

"Charlotte."

"Right, her. Are you dating her, using her?"

"Have you known me to use people? Glad you think so highly of me."

She sat on the stool and leaned in closer to him with her cheek to her fist. "Are you the detective trying to get close or are you the stranger in town shacking up with the girl-next-door type? Literally."

After trying to devise an answer, he said, "We've had a bit to drink, so I'll just ask. Where are you going with this?"

"The moment I saw you at that hotel on the Sunset Strip, I knew something was different," she said. "That things were going to be different." And when Freddie didn't respond, she added, "Complicated."

Whatever the hell that meant.

A new crowd was walking in, similar to a conga line, people back-to-back. Everyone was fine, happy, in conversation with someone else in the group. Freddie leaned back out of the way. The smiles and loud talking went past. Except for the one who wasn't smiling. The one who bumped right into Freddie's shoulder. He looked at the man with the serious face, the same face he'd woken up to in the hills. The same face that was on his sleeping laptop at home. Nathan Roberts.

Something switched off on Freddie's content, slumberous face, the glow he had started to regain since being out with Veronica was dimming, and she saw it happening. Veronica pulled him back from his forearm as he took a step forward. She called out his name in a Fred-don't-do-it tone. He followed Nathan's direction anyway.

"I saw you," he said.

Nathan turned around with the face of a confused little boy, still no smile. Freddie waited for it to show up, so he could hit it right off his face.

"Just an accident," Nathan said. Was this him trying to act normal, to rouse Freddie? He wasn't buying it.

"Accidents seem to happen around you a lot, don't they, Nathan? So many, they should redefine the word for you, start calling it premeditation."

"Hey, man. Not in here." This coming from Mr. Mixologist behind the counter, who had appeared for his shift out of nowhere, ready to put a glass aside and stop tending to a group of women, all of which had the sober look of anticipation, ready to watch a bar brawl. But it wouldn't be Freddie's best move, not with Veronica pulling him back again. But her presence wasn't enough to make him change his mind.

He closed his eyes for a second, and in that moment, a wave pulled him into the ocean. He wasn't in control. Next came the pain and headache, a breath knocked out of him. He wasn't in the ocean, so this wasn't drowning. He had expected a punch from Veronica after seeing her scared and furious before the darkness. But now he wondered why or how her hand felt so big and rough. He didn't understand the full scope of it all until he regained total consciousness in the parking lot.

After they sobered up the slightest bit, Freddie drove Veronica home, this time with the car's top up. Fun time was over. The two of them were silent, thinking about the people at the bar whispering—some of them drunk and not feeling so courteous to speak quietly—and pointing at Freddie's bloodied face while they were in The Reef's parking lot. Veronica didn't feel comfortable driving, not that Freddie's shape was much better. Typically, alcohol never made Veronica get loose or crazy; she just wanted to sleep. She was too angry to get behind the wheel. And if Freddie were ever to train for a marathon, it would be for boozing. So all in all, he was still okay.

Freddie pulled into the driveway, put the gear in Park and unbuckled his seatbelt. They still hadn't shared any words. No one moved and Freddie didn't turn off the engine; at least that produced some sound.

She was the first to break the silence. "Are we going to talk about what happened back there?"

"You calling me sugarlips, you mean?" he said lowly. His face was still stinging.

"About you telling a guy you're watching him, then getting punched in the face by him. You practically threatened the guy, Fred. And you tell me I don't handle my drink."

"*I* threatened him? He punched me. You saw it all, Ron. The whole thing was confrontational."

"You were looking for a fight."

"I'm fine not talking about it."

She let out a sigh, watching her house straight ahead of her, the lights brightening her front door. If a sign was ever going to present itself so clearly, this was it.

She unbuckled her seatbelt and said, "See you at my party thing, okay?"

But not before then?

"You want me there?"

"Yeah, I want you there."

"The way things are going..."

"The way things are going, I don't know if I'll see you again after I leave, so yeah, I want you there. But right now, I want to go inside alone."

His jaw tightened. She had her hand on the door handle, but her torso was facing him more than the door. She was giving him big, sad eyes that said, It's now or never.

He adjusted himself in his chair ever so slightly, enough to get her in direct view now. She was still giving him those eyes. He kissed her, not giving it a second thought, not thinking about the consequences. For a moment he felt her hand clasping his T-shirt at his chest, letting him. Then it became a push.

"What the fuck, Fred? *No.* No, no."

All he could think to say was, "You'd be good with a dog." All she needed was a finger in his face yelling at him again.

"Jesus, Mary, and Joseph."

Freddie hadn't handled rejection like this since the sixth grade.

"Jesus," she said again, "I sound like my dad when I say that."

"There's an image for me."

"What was that?"

"I read that wrong," he said, trying to downplay the humiliation of it all. It would have been worse if they hadn't been here before. Or was it worse now?

"No shit."

"I'm sorry," he said. He meant it too. "What am I supposed to think with you coming around unannounced, acting like no time has passed for us?"

If she wasn't under the influence and drained, she would definitely be the next person to punch him.

"I stop by because I care about you. I'm not in love with you, you *idiot*."

Veronica pushed the car door open furiously. Freddie mentally noted that her insults weren't the best when she drank. But she wasn't done yet. Veronica turned to Freddie once she'd stepped out.

"You're a smart, talented, good guy, Fred. But sometimes you make all the good things not matter."

There was the punch.

She slammed the door behind her without saying goodbye and walked to her porch.

So, something was missing, but at least the passion was there. It always had been. Freddie never wanted a one-night stand with Veronica; it would ruin what they had had for good. Freddie had been in love when things were different yet left unchanged. He always considered change as something important. Change made a case solvable. It made things move forward. Good, bad, just forward. With Veronica and his exes he'd almost made it with, they'd grown together. Not necessarily with so many years, but with whatever time brought their way. If the little things that were once insignificant were still there after the changes, like Veronica talking about the same hole-in-the-wall restaurant she loved despite the years and everything else that had come between them, then they would become significant. This significance told Freddie he was at home, settled, happy, ready for forever.

He'd have a chance to redeem himself, he figured.

He still had her car.

As he reversed onto the street to head home, he realized, Veronica was right. Things weren't just different; they were, dare he say, "Complicated."

14

Bloodstream

It was always one step forward then three steps back; with progress in a case, and with Veronica. To Freddie, Veronica was far more complex than a murder case. This time, they may have gone further than three steps back, onto a completely derailed path. He had crossed a line, and now he didn't know what was waiting for him on the other side.

As he pulled onto Mystic Place in Veronica's car, the lights shone over someone—a man, Freddie noticed as he rolled closer—sitting on the curb in front of the villa. Freddie heard the car lock with a *beep* behind him as he walked across the driveway to meet the man, who was now at the front door. Freddie was ready to return a punch to Nathan.

It was Wes.

"Is this a bad time?" he asked but didn't really care.

Freddie glanced at his watch. "Usually is with your timing." It was late for him to want company, and certainly not that of a snarky detective. But he couldn't turn Wes away, especially if he didn't know whether this was a social visit, or one for business. Freddie let him in.

"Hope I'm not interrupting anything," Wes said looking around inside, even up the stairway (Freddie took note of this with a smirk) until they made it into the living room and kitchen. "I've got some news for ya." Freddie dropped onto the couch, showing his defeat, and waited for Wes to sit. He remained standing up.

"I also have something to share," Freddie said.

"If you're alone, that is." Wes continued looking around persistently. "I take it your girlfriend ain't home."

Freddie confirmed. He wanted Wes to stop with the wandering eyes. It was making him nervous.

"Good news or bad news first?" Before Freddie could think about it: "Doesn't matter, does it?"

Freddie raised a brow.

"Listen, son. You're not gonna like it."

"Okay," Freddie said gingerly. "Let's have it."

"There's no evidence for me to believe your girlfriend is a killer. So you can rest at night knowing she isn't going to cut off your man parts while you sleep. It's happened. Several times."

"Thanks, Wes." He was only half serious.

"But let me tell ya, she ain't a saint."

"We knew that."

What's the catch?

Wes peeked out of the living room blinds and turned back to Freddie. "We need to bring her in for questioning."

"Why?" Freddie said. What was he missing?

"I'm only here out of courtesy. I've already told you too much, but I trust you'll do the right thing here. And that's to keep quiet and let us do our job."

This all sounded so courteous and friendly, but Freddie knew what this was: the good cop routine detectives pull during their initial visit to a suspect's home. It was filled with jokes, compliments, basic observations that came across as threats, and then some actual threats just as the detective would make an exit.

"I went back, interviewed the victims' families and friends some more. Brought up a name this time around.

Care to venture a guess as to who all of these guys had as a mutual acquaintance?"

Freddie's eyes went to the plant and back. Almost guilti-ly. Maybe because he already knew this information and had made it a point not to ask Charlotte about it for his selfish reasons.

"I told you, beach town can feel like a small town. She obviously has a type. The type that's been written in the pa-pers. Now tell me somethin', Fred. Did you know?"

Freddie perked up on the couch, deep in agitation with his bruised face. He said, "As someone who tells me to move on with my life, you sure do bring these case details up a lot."

"You're the one who came to me to look into her. You know what I think?" Wes didn't care if Freddie was pre-pared to hear it or not. "I think you think she's guilty. You want to do the right thing, but you don't know how since you're not with a badge anymore, and you're balls deep. I think you gave me a cry for help. And, well, here I am, at your service."

Freddie didn't move or change his expression. Not that he could with the bad eye.

"That sound 'bout right? I think so."

"I didn't know. I talked to Tom Coaster, the realtor. He mentioned the three victims, so to speak, were friends. They were friends with Hudson Ross, the deceased, too. Coaster told me Charlotte and Hudson had been seeing each other romantically, but it was brief. No other connections made."

"You interviewed Coaster?" Wes shook his hands at Freddie as if to say never mind. "What you do on your time isn't my business. For now. But you knew she was connect-ed to a dead man and his friends and didn't care to mention that? After everything we've talked about?"

"I didn't find out until after you and I talked."

Wes nodded, not exactly understandingly or with sympathy. But he had processed everything and it didn't make Freddie redeemable. "Like I said, son, just wanted to give you the courtesy warning."

"Thanks," Freddie said more than sarcastically, ready to physically show Wes the way out.

"I'm leavin', I'm leavin'." Wes began walking to the door but stopped in his tracks. He turned around and said, "You said you had information. Was that it?"

Shit. Maybe this could be the chance to clear his name early in the process. Or find out more about what the detective was hoping to learn from Charlotte.

"Am I a suspect or witness?"

Wes thought about it. "We can call this conversation background."

Freddie moved to the kitchen feeling both hyper and fatigued. If the high from the rush kept feeding his brain, he'd run out of oxygen and pass out. He was already seeing deep purple bubbles floating around.

"I followed Charlotte," he said, then waited, baffled that the detective didn't share the same countenance of shock. What did this indicate about Freddie being a suspect or a witness? Maybe Wes had already made up his mind about him and had evidence that painted a picture other than innocence.

"Where'd you follow her to and from?"

"From here to the pier."

"Did she see you?"

"No, I don't think so. I stayed behind, only followed her so far. The waves were loud, and it was dark and foggy. I got stuck waiting by the outhouse," he said with a shaky voice. How ludicrous it sounded out loud.

"What did you see at the pier?"

"I don't know. I couldn't make out words. Just saw enough where I knew he was angry with her and she was too. She yelled back. She'll do that, you know? She's not the type to stand by—"

"Go back a few steps and slow down," Wes said, "Who's the guy?"

"Nathan Roberts."

"And he is…?"

"It was never very clear how he ties into everything, but he's bad news, Wes. He has a criminal history with meds as a nurse." Freddie stopped pacing nervously and watched the detective to see if he could ascertain what was going through his head. It was pointless. "The whole thing looked bad to me and I've never been wrong about a gut feeling. I mean, *never*."

Wes put his hand on his belt, getting on the defensive side, having never seen Freddie on the cusp of madness.

"All right, what else did you see? I need details."

"When he touched her, she'd flinch. She wasn't enjoying the company." Freddie bit his tongue to keep from blabbing about his encounter with Nathan in the hills. He tried to pick up his talking speed again so the detective wouldn't notice he was refraining from disclosing certain information. "She told me she was going out to buy mulch and I followed her—"

"Wait," Wes said, crossing an arm, raising the other to let two fingers reach the middle of his eyes, tired. "Let me get this. Am I hearing that she told you she was getting mulch, which sounded suspicious to you, so you followed her, only to see nothing and have her go home with mulch, like she said she would?"

"Yes." *I sound crazy.* "Well, she said she did. I don't really know for certain."

"She's a florist, son. Why should I find that suspicious? I know it was late, maybe an odd time to want to buy work materials, and maybe she's two-timin' you—"

She wouldn't be the only one, he thought, the night he'd just had with Veronica flashing in his head.

"That's not why I'm telling you any of this," Freddie said.

"Thanks for the chat, Fred. Good talk. I'll write this up in a report, give the folks a good laugh," Wes laughed to himself. He caught his breath and walked slowly to the entrance, ready to leave Freddie with the echoing sounds of his hefty laughter. "Oh, Fred?" he said, turning around when he was halfway to the door. "Don't do anything stupid, like be a hero or rogue boyfriend or nothin' like that. Can you do that for me?"

Still frozen.

"I need to hear you say it, Fred. No taking matters into your own hands, or you'll be the first person I cuff if things get worse around town."

Was this the detective or McKinney's guy talking?

"Yeah," Freddie said. "No hero bullshit."

"My boy!"

For a moment, the idea of Wes leaving scared Freddie because it meant seeing Charlotte again without any logical excuses to avoid her. And she was going to be taken in for official questioning, making him aware that he was losing someone else to his old practices.

Wes left the way he came. Freddie didn't move until he heard the door close. He walked over to lock up. Now he had an immediate problem: His girlfriend was to be called in for questioning, and all he had done was shake up a detective in Homicide and piss off a batshit crazy nurse he already had physical altercations with, and all because of cyberstalking. And a hunch, one he relied on so heavily.

From Charlotte's living room windows, he could see her walk into her office. It brought some odd sense of comfort to him. She was safe and so was he. The current in his bloodstream could slow down for now.

But then he thought about something he'd found unusual: *Why didn't Wes mention the eye?*

After Wes left, Freddie returned Veronica's car. He took his bike out of the trunk, then hid her key under a pile of rocks that landscaped the front yard. He marked the spot with a cactus in a planter for her to find later. Returning the key to her in-person would've been simpler, but he needed to be someone greater to do that. And right then and there, with his eye and the puffy skin underneath feeling like it was going to pop and spit out blood from torn veins, he didn't feel like someone great.

Freddie rode his bike with the night's cold blowing against his face, rolling downhill effortlessly until he reached PCH. He was tired, and his left eye was swollen, impairing his vision, and the migraines were growing worse.

He iced his eye all night while he lay in bed listening to the water until he fell asleep, only to wake up in the middle of the night with the ice having melted, sending cold drops of water down his neck and to his chest. He didn't sleep thereafter. Another sting, another reminder of what a miserable night it had been.

The fucking eye. Why hadn't Wes brought it up while he had visited?

In the morning, a shower and clean set of clothes later, Freddie was back to sitting on the couch with rum and ice, using his eye as an excuse to day drink (and place the cold glass against his face). He needed something new to concentrate on to avoid the pain. And among the pain were questions that needed answers. Only one way to get them before it would be too late.

He walked over to the Tudor, knocked on the door. How was he going to explain the bruised eye?

Shit, he didn't think about that.

"What happened?" Charlotte closed the door and pulled him further into the natural light past the dimmed entryway. She made him sit on one of the chairs in the kitchen. With his head in her hands, she analyzed each side. "Did this just happen? It looks fresh."

This simple gesture felt like home to him. Then it didn't, because their lives were full of lies now. And another one: "I was drowsy the other night. Got out of the shower feeling like a baby going into a deep sleep. Big baby I am, I ran into the wall. Gave me this handsome look."

He had worked with Forensics enough to know that there was no way the injury happened by running into a wall. Someone would have needed to attack him to create a bruised abrasion of this kind, something she would know, given her record.

"And now you're better," she said, her coldness too strong to be left on the other side of the door. "Aside from the eye."

He stood up when she moved to the refrigerator, trying to not get used to the coziness of being with her again. She got him a plastic baggie full of ice and placed it on his eye. He winced in pain. Getting the ice and placing it to his face was a sweet, caring gesture, but had she pressed hard on purpose?

"Thanks," he said and kept it against his face more gently. "I'm okay," he lied, wondering why he bothered; he clearly wasn't okay and she clearly knew he was lying. And the lies kept coming more and more naturally. He walked into the living room brushing his face in nervousness before she could notice.

"Get to do anything other than rest?" She still had the same coldness, but he respected the fact that she tried to keep a conversation going, because the cold silence was bad too.

"Said my goodbyes to a friend moving out of state soon."

He noticed the open office door, wondering what she was doing in there. Bringing in more plants?

"That's nice of you. Did she do that to you?" She sat on the couch, adjusted the pillow behind her back, and waited for his response.

He had been careful not to use any pronouns, nothing to give Veronica away. "What makes you think my friend's a 'she'?"

She gave him a smile, one that was too confident for his liking. "I have windows, Freddie. And eyes. You're not the only observant one around here."

Freddie's mind was churning thoughts about his weaknesses he hated. But one of his weaknesses, particularly curiosity, was what made him a good detective; curiosity and his dark necessities he adhered to in times of anger, fear, and desire.

"What were you doing in the office?" His eyes would start growing roots there if he didn't look away from that direction.

Freddie wondered if he had developed a fucked-up sense of foreplay. McKinney had always warned him about the job getting to his personal life. Romance and sex had so far proven to be deteriorating for the future.

He nodded his chin to the door. "It's usually closed. Then out of modesty he said, "And I saw you go in there earlier from my place." He sounded more like a creep than someone modest.

"Do you do that a lot?"

"Stare at doorways? No." He knew what she meant, but there he was again with using bullshit as a defense mechanism. He adjusted the ice against his face.

"I mean watch. Do you do that a lot?"

They hadn't touched since Charlotte took a good look at his eye in the light, and for this Freddie was relieved. He was afraid they'd both feel how nervous and distant the other was. Even making eye contact was difficult now, but he finally gave in.

"Sometimes," he said. "Just to make sure you're okay." He hoped she couldn't hear his heartbeat like he could, throbbing in his ears. "Do you?"

"No. I just see what ordinary people see," she said plainly. Now she was the one avoiding eye contact as she played with her nails. Despite the inner pandemonium, Freddie was able to notice how her nails were smooth, clean, polished. She had to have worn gloves on the job to avoid the mess.

"So," he changed the subject. Yet all the passiveness was making him want to submerge into ocean water and yell where no one could hear him. "Why the office? You hardly ever go in there unless you're redecorating or rearranging the plants."

"I brought plants home from the shop," she said. "Come, let me show you."

He left the ice behind as she took Freddie's hand and guided him to the office.

The plants added much more color to the blue and gray room; now there were spurts of red, orange, and purple flowers standing out against the cherry shelves.

"It is nice," he said, rubbing her shoulders complimentarily. She didn't seem to mind his cold touch. She took his hand then, but all he felt were the Doll's Eyes staring at him from the windowsill, making him tense.

She asked, "Are you okay? Really, Freddie, your eye looks bad."

"Fine." He kissed her forehead to convince her of his lie, knowing it still wasn't working.

For a moment, none of it mattered, not when he could smell her all close, her usual smell of coconut and the occasional hints of sea salt, while she kissed him. He wore a content smile in between kisses. It was all a typical day in, all the ones he had enjoyed with her. This was how she was going to get him to break, to test him; see how far he'd go before he admitted to following her and lying about it. But she was giving him a look of appetite and, yes, he too had it. Did it matter if detectives were going to call her in for questioning? He had almost forgotten about that.

He lost the mood.

He grabbed her wrists tightly and zoned out for a moment, trying to figure out his next move.

"My arms, Freddie."

It took him a second to understand, then he finally let go. She rubbed his yellow fingermarks away. He tried not to perform a nervous tic: an eye rub, a headshake, a brush of the face. He walked to the living room and swiped the bag of ice off the glass table. Charlotte had already met him there. He placed the ice against the fading prints on her skin. "I'm sorry," he said.

"What's going on with you?"

You first, he thought, but he was the one acting unusual. "I've been feeling like blacking out from not sleeping. I'm not myself, I'm sure you can tell. I think I'm just going to call it a day." Then he clarified, "At my place."

She looked into his eyes intently before throwing the plastic bag at him, the most violent thing he'd witnessed her do. "So you're going to run away to your hideout and pretend everything's normal?"

He placed the bag of ice onto the kitchen counter peacefully to show her it could be done in such a manner, and said, "I'm going home."

"Why did you come here, Freddie?"

"I didn't like how we left things the other night."

"We haven't talked about the other night. And now you're leaving."

"I can't do much at the moment with this eye."

"Tough shit," she snapped.

He was taken aback for a moment, though this was exactly how he wanted to catch her. "Look at that," he said. "Is this how you got yourself into juvie? Starts off nice and small, little provoked chitchat, then you aim for the nose?"

"Where is this coming from?"

"Quit acting like you're so fucking perfect. You went out the other night to buy *mulch*?" As if the emphasis on that word was the part that mattered.

"That's what this is about? I go out to buy mulch and you feel the need to stop my blood flow?" She flashed a quick glance toward the office before meeting his eyes again to say, "You can take a look at the mulch. It's in the office you like to watch so closely."

"There you go again with the *fucking perfectionism.*"

"You think I think I'm perfect?" This was the first time he'd ever heard her raise her voice. "Freddie, I'm a thirty-one-year-old divorcée with prison time on my record."

"Expunged," he corrected.

"That doesn't change the fact that I did my time. It happened and I live with it every day. It's not exactly a conversation starter when I meet people. It's not a parting conversation either. Why don't you cut the bullshit and tell me what's really bothering you?"

"You want to talk about problems? Let's start with the fact that I'm an ex-cop and you're an ex-con. I mean, what were we thinking here?"

A knock on the door prompted them to forget all else and turn toward the interruption.

"It's probably Earl complaining about the yelling," she said.

"He lives closer to me than he does to you. No way he could hear us." And Freddie knew they would be expecting others.

Shut up, you know-it-all. He thought it, her face said it.

Charlotte purposefully ran into his shoulder on her way to the door, and maybe Freddie moved to the friction a little too dramatically.

Sure enough, it was Earl. Freddie didn't greet him, only listened. Earl had been on his daytime walk and did in fact hear their voices. Charlotte assured him she was fine, that Freddie was just mad about a bruised eye—one she still didn't know how he got, not really—and hurried him away as politely as she could before getting back to Freddie and their problems.

Being honest with himself, Freddie had expected this moment with her to have happened much sooner, but here it was, months into what he thought were part of a decent relationship until this point—no, the night at the pier. He'd ignored all the red flags; or he had regained hope, the most beautiful, dangerous thing in the world.

She returned to the living room and sat on the couch again, a sign that she was exhausted from their conversation. What could he say to her to make this slightly better, to reapproach it from a new angle?

"I'm sorry about your wrists," he said.

"I've dealt with worse," she reminded him.

"I know, but you shouldn't have to deal with it from me."

"Fights are healthy," she said.

He looked at her wryly.

"When channeled properly."

He sat next to her. "Ever think we get into them too much too soon?"

"This is our first fight, Freddie."

Fuck, had it felt like they'd had more. He tried to craft a response in his head to save himself from the risk of sounding like a complete asshole again. But he was saved by the bell—sort of. Again, there was a knock on the door.

"Earl," they mumbled together.

Freddie was about to get up, but Charlotte stopped him. While she went to appease Earl, Freddie relaxed on the couch and touched the swelling under his eye. Then he looked out her window where he had a clear view of his house. He was in his head again, that internal dimension no one else knew about. In there, he imagined himself running through the window, creating a Freddie shape above shattered glass. He shook his head at the thought, then felt a funny feeling, like a premonition was striking. But it wasn't a warning. It was a scary fact: Detective Dan Wesley was at Charlotte's front door.

Freddie turned toward the door, his eyes catching Wes's. The detective said to Charlotte, "This would be a lot easier with all of us. May we come in?"

15

In the Sand

Charlotte and Freddie had been confused about the *we* in *May we come in?* until both detectives made it inside and occupied the kitchen area. Funny how Veronica had never mentioned that an open-concept home was inopportunely a reasonable space for detectives making home visits.

They took their time teasing Charlotte and Freddie, building up the suspense by nosily taking casual glances around the first floor—the art hanging on the walls, the tattered mail left on the entry table, Charlotte's muddied boots by the door, the knife on the wooden cutting board resting on the kitchen counter, farsighted views of the photos in the living room, the view outside her large living room window. Freddie's house.

Once the detectives stopped snooping, everyone attempted to settle by standing in different zones of the living space, like someone was going to catch a disease if they moved any closer into someone's terrain. Wes stood in the middle of the living room while his partner stayed behind in the kitchen. Freddie took the corner between the window and the spiral staircase, Charlotte across from him, leaning against the office's closed door—a mistake, Freddie thought; as if she was guarding the room. Then again, his position made him look like he was guarding his property lines.

No one said anything for a while.

Wes finally smacked a folder onto the ottoman where Charlotte kept her books on botanicals. Charlotte and Freddie stared at the folder like they were examining a dead animal on the street, trying to get a good look without getting too close. Then it came to Wes and Charlotte staring each other down until the other cracked. Neither one gave up, which caused Freddie to want to crawl into a corner and sit in fetal position with his eyes closed until it was all over. *Coward,* he kept thinking.

Wes nodded his head over to the man at the counter and said, "This is my partner, Detective Acosta." A handsome man, probably in his early-to-mid forties. His hair was straight, flat, salt and pepper. The rest of his face didn't show any signs of aging or stress, and his dark hazel eyes made him seem vigilant. Good build; not short, but shorter than some of the men Freddie had seen around Homicide when he'd visited.

"Nice to meet you, Detective Acosta," Charlotte said, then sat on the couch to get more comfortable. This was better; she needed to show she had the upper hand. Then to Wes: "It's not every day I have two detectives in my home. To what do I owe the visit?"

To what do I owe the visit? Still so polite. That grace under pressure, she had it, even if there was a train wreck inside of her.

Acosta leaned against his arm on the counter now, and brought his hands together, looking like a '20s man at a speakeasy. "Sticking around, McAllister?"

Freddie wasn't expecting this, not from the otherwise stranger who was getting crafty. "Appears so," he said. It was a bold answer for the belittlement that had filled him since the detectives walked through the door.

"Ms. Walker," Wes said. "We got a call from a surfer stating there was something suspicious on the beach. Specifically, your backyard. With everything going on in the news around here, I'm sure you've heard, I've got a warrant to search the grounds."

"A warrant?"

"Now, it doesn't mean anything about you, not right away. But we gotta be the gentlemen who take a look around. We don't choose the coordinates."

Wes shot his partner a look for him to chime in. Acosta obliged. "The climate conditions at the beach can mess things up out here, tamper with potential evidence. So, I have a legal document here that lets me search the back of your residence."

"A surfer," Freddie said in disbelief.

"Got somethin' to get off your chest, McAllister?"

"You're here because a surfer—at least a mile away out at sea—saw something right back here?"

"Maybe you've seen something around here, Freddie. Around the pier, perhaps?"

Charlotte shot a sharp look at Freddie, which translated to, I can actually kill you. Sadly, he'd seen the look before; it was of pure disappointment.

Wes continued. "Beach goes for miles. You've got nice running routes and all."

"The pier is several miles and a long walk from here, detectives," Charlotte said.

"Ms. Walker, we know you're connected—acquainted, to our missing persons. Now, something suspicious turns up on your property of all places. Tell me I'm putting my curiosity on the wrong street, wrong house, wrong person. Or people."

"You have a warrant and a concerned citizen," she said. "Do what you need to, but I'm not answering insinuating questions."

Acosta tapped the counter before pushing himself off, eager to get to work. He walked out onto the deck and inspected where Freddie had clumsily made love to Charlotte. Not that the detectives knew what went on out there, but the memory was being invaded along with the house.

"Thank you, Ms. Walker," Wes stepped toward the door again and said, "You two sit tight in here, please. Just in case we need you. We've got a patrol car out front if you decide to get resourceful, which I know you both are." He joined his partner outside.

Freddie and Charlotte remained on opposite ends of the room, watching what was now a jinxed entry to the beach, then Charlotte moved to her office, probably to watch the detectives make a mess of where she called home. Freddie shifted to the window with the street view. He spotted the patrol car. Inside the vehicle, one officer typed away at the keyboard, squinting at the monitor, which meant Freddie and Charlotte were officially on a report involving potential evidence at Mystic Place. The other officer stood outside the car, monitoring the Tudor.

He heard Charlotte settle onto the couch. He didn't pay much else attention to her until he heard her say, "You followed me the other night."

He released his fingers from the blinds and met her eyes, keeping quiet.

She let out a sigh. "You did, didn't you? All that just now about the pier, you behaving weirdly that night and today. You followed me. And had a conversation with the detective about it."

"I—"

"It's a relief, actually," she said. "It's good to know that you're motivated enough to do something when you really want to. I was beginning to think you were completely lethargic, but again, good to know that you don't just stand idly by."

"Judging by the fact that there are detectives in your yard, I don't know you very well, Charlotte. Care to elaborate on anything while detectives search your property's parameters, or should we wait until they come back in to get all the questions out of the way?"

She shook her head and looked into dead air. "I don't like this, Freddie."

Which part? The detectives being here, or me following you?

"I don't either, but we should have this conversation in private while we can," he said. "What were you and Nathan doing at the pier?"

She watched the detectives outside, until they blended with the rest of the search crew.

"What were you doing there with Nathan, Charlotte?"

"I told you about the support group we go to."

"That didn't look like a support group."

"No, not a group, but he needed support. You've seen us away from the rest of them before. It wasn't any different."

"I've seen him angry and violent with you before, here. Why the pier?"

"He didn't want to meet in a public place with a lot of people. He gets stressed and anxious and crazy, in lack of a better word, and sometimes needs a quiet place. You could understand that, couldn't you?"

"In the rain?"

"Does it matter what the weather was like?"

"Still," he said, "way to make it look suspicious if a little chat was all he needed."

"Would you rather I bring him here? Or your place? He told me about your encounter in front of his house."

"Why would he come to you? What makes you so understanding from anyone else?"

"We all cope in our ways. He's had some emotional trauma from all he's done. I don't think he likes himself very much, and it's understandable. I shouldn't have to explain this to you. You know all about it."

"Have you ever helped him in any other way?"

"What's that supposed to mean?"

Freddie already had in mind that she'd warned the detectives she wouldn't answer any insinuating questions. At this point in time, he wasn't the exception. "I'm trying to understand why there are two homicide detectives outside with a search warrant."

"I don't know."

"But you meet with Nathan in secret, for who knows how often and for what—"

"I told you why."

"—and you know about his history poisoning people and drug abuse."

"So what? You think I'm helping him?" And when he didn't say anything: "You think I'm helping him, what? Get off on drugging people?"

"I have to ask."

"No you don't," she said. "Why? Because I have a past? Don't you? I'm not accusing your drunk self of any poisoning or—"

"Murder," Freddie said, and wished he could record this conversation for the detectives.

"How have you come up with all of this?" She stood up and paced around the living room. "How *long* have you been coming up with all of this?"

"You have the history, you have the access. You have the violent past, the connection to these men, to Nathan. And poison, frankly. Natural drugs. You nurture them for a living."

"So does every florist out there. This is all circumstantial and doesn't prove shit," she said somberly. She moved to the door to watch where the detectives stood in the yard making their calls and taking their pictures. "The only reason you're still here right now, Freddie, is because there are detectives here who won't let you leave."

Even in the midst of a police search, he was being put in the doghouse.

Freddie didn't move. He watched her for a few minutes. He didn't see her display any regret or fear. She just watched curiously. He did too, until he heard another patrol car pull up in front of the Tudor. The cop who had been standing outside was walking toward the front door. He knocked and entered without a word. By then, the detectives were back in the house.

"Find anything?" Freddie asked Wes.

"We found somethin', all right. Ms. Walker, we've found some remains in the sand. My guess is, around here, they don't belong to a bunny rabbit. And I also reckon there are another two dig sites around here somewhere. We've got Forensics on their way and some patrol cars keeping an eye on the street. Sound enough of an explanation to you, Freddie boy?"

Another hour later, the detectives had their own set of facts and were ready to do some more questioning.

"Take a seat and relax for a bit," Wes said, Freddie and Charlotte already seated, both of them ticked off at his unnecessary glee. Why had no one been taken in yet?

"Human remains," Wes confirmed. "Lots of sand crabs feeding. A bit funny, I gotta say, being used to maggots after all these years."

"How long have they been out there?" Charlotte was pale and petrified. Freddie couldn't tell whether she was a good actress or actually had no idea.

"You tell me, Ms. Walker."

She looked at Wes angrily. "I'm asking you, Detective. I wouldn't know how long a corpse has been in my yard, *buried*," she said with a shudder.

"Team thinks they've been there for less than a month," Wes said. "Which means, someone either held the victim captive for a couple of weeks before the murder, or moved the body after the initial crime. It's nearly preserved." His gaze had gone south and still, like he was entering hypnosis. "Years from now, teens in the neighborhood are gonna be lookin' back remembering how the police found mummies on Mystic Place." He zoned out for a moment, then came back with, "Waiting for more lab tests. In the meantime, Acosta's keeping an eye on the neighborhood. Specifically, this street."

Freddie said, "You mean this house."

"And yours, Freddie boy. We ain't here for the romantic view. But, now that we're all in the know, we had some props delivered to us before we came over," he said, looking at Charlotte. She waited for the point. "That folder my partner placed on your...whatever this lovely piece of furniture is here. Is it a table or a couch?"

"I think they call it an ottoman, boss," Acosta said casually.

"Right. Well the folder Acosta placed on your, uh, ottoman, has professional layouts of your flower shop." Acosta handed him the folder. Wes opened it and flipped through some pages, then finally pulled out a sheet. "You have a freezer in the back of the building." He waited.

"Florists usually do. I have a refrigerator section too."

"So do butchers. And I had a feeling you were a butcher of sorts the night we met, Ms. Walker. You even had a bloodstain on your sleeve. And you blamed it on using sharp objects."

She didn't say anything. Freddie felt nervous for her. "What is this?" he finally said. "You haven't arrested anyone and no one is on record."

"We're here on official business, Freddie," Wes said. "You know how it is. Everything is on record and don't you worry. Acosta and I follow procedures. We'll make sure this is all on paperwork. Before we do that, Ms. Walker, you can tell me why you have a freezer and what you use it for. Those can be two different things, can't they, Acosta?" But his partner remained calm and silent as both detectives kept their eyes on Charlotte.

"The freezer was conveniently there when I started renting the space. I place plants in there to keep them on a cycle. We don't exactly have four seasons in Southern California. The change in temperature helps their growth. Roses are stored in cooler temperatures, other flowers too, depending on the season or when they've been pruned."

"Use it for anything else?"

"No, but something tells me you have an idea all on your own."

Freddie nudged her arm. She ignored him like she didn't feel it.

"Not for preserving anything? Say, some bodies?"

Freddie wanted to interject, but this was a question he wanted an answer to.

"The freezer is used for flowers only. You can have Forensics sweep the place. You won't find anything but plants.

Maybe my own blood since I do prune·using sharp objects. There's really no other way to prune."

Freddie wanted to give her an Interrogation 101 course, thinking, *Never say that.* It was asking for another jinx.

"Oh, we will take a good look, Ms. Walker. And if you don't mind, I'd like you to come to the station to answer some more questions."

"I'll answer whatever questions you want me to, Detective," Charlotte said. "I just want to help. And move around for a while. I'm a bit traumatized just sitting here."

"That would be a mistake," Freddie said, unable to sit and watch anymore. "You won't go and you won't answer anything else."

"That because you're hiding something too, McAllister?"

Over from the kitchen island again, Acosta said, "We found what we're pretty sure are nearly two corpses in Ms. Walker's backyard, Freddie. One for sure and some remains we're still working on identifying. We're going to take her for formal questioning."

"I'll go," she said. "I'll just need a minute to get my purse from upstairs."

"Acosta will escort you up," Wes said.

Charlotte hesitated. "Is that necessary?"

"You'd be surprised by how many people have made it out a window when being questioned about murder."

Charlotte and Acosta exchanged a glance before he moved to the bottom of the staircase to watch her ascend.

"I'll be waiting outside," Wes said.

Before Freddie could absorb everything to process it all, he was standing outside watching Acosta close the car door for Charlotte in the backseat. The officer who'd been typing away earlier was ready to drive her away. He led the way, and the two detectives followed in another car Freddie didn't recognize; Acosta's, he assumed. Another cop escorted Freddie away from the Tudor. All Freddie wanted to do was to be a detective who could drive away. What a simpler time those shit-show days were.

16

Bottom of the Deep

In the comfort of his own home, Freddie sat on the couch shaking his leg and eyeing the built-in bar he surprisingly hadn't used. Beer could've helped him celebrate a new record of having lost the attention of two women in different, extreme circumstances.

No. It wasn't a good idea.

Beer was too weak.

Rum.

The idea of corpses next door and a load of professionals taking pictures and running tests, working hard to pack everything up and take sand samples with them to a lab had him feeling too nauseous to have a drink.

He stepped out to the backyard and watched the chaos from a new perspective, somewhere between shudders and reverence. The crane wouldn't let him admire the water. That and the perimeter of neon tape around the beach didn't exactly say, This is a quiet place. Anyone out there could catch little glimpses of yellow plastic shining under the sun.

The pot of Fred Ives was daunting him at the windowsill, making it impossible for Freddie not to admire it. It was so simple and good, a better version of a Fred. According to him, it had the better name too. Then he stared at the crane again.

Low budget, my ass.

That evening, Freddie's nap was interrupted by two distinct knocks on the door—the knocks of two different people. He made it to the door slowly, ready to yell at intrusive surfers trying to have their nighttime sea adventures on the private beach. He opened the door and saw Detective Acosta looking impatient as he leaned against the wall, his finger ready to try the doorbell. But he was alone. Then again, for all Freddie knew, Wes would jump out of the bushes and roll on the floor laughing after giving him a good scare.

Freddie wondered how long Acosta had been there. It was a warmer evening, high seventies, yet a chill managed to crawl up his spine. What if his Mirandas were to be recited right then and there? And there was always something about Acosta that rubbed him the wrong way, partly because very few people could make Freddie look and feel guilty simply for existing. His mother, for one; maybe Veronica and Charlotte; but definitely Acosta. Only he couldn't hide this feeling around the detective, as he had learned to condition himself, mostly with women, over time.

"Mr. McAllister," Detective Acosta said. "Freddie boy, my partner calls you, right?"

Freddie wished he wasn't himself, any variation.

"What is it now?"

"You like to get to the point. I like it," Acosta said and met him closer. "New developments. Our job is to find them and talk to the people involved. Thought you know how this stuff works."

"These new developments have to do with me?"

"My partner and I would like you to come in officially, help us get a few things straight. It'll help us out a lot."

Great. Charlotte had been called in for questioning, Veronica was angry with him, and he hadn't had an alcoholic or caffeinated drink in some hours. There had to be a window of recovery for all that right about now.

He could refuse to go for questioning; he had the right. But he knew how that would make him look: guilty, if not arrogant—another trait that would raise a red flag.

"Anything you can tell me before I go?"

Acosta thought about it for a moment, or pretended to. "I'd rather just have my partner do the talking," he said, followed by a shrug. "You know how it is."

"Yeah."

One partner always wears the pants.

Acosta and Freddie were silent during the elevator ride down to the interview rooms. Freddie felt nervous, and he could see it in his reflection. His pale, clammy face made the elevator doors seem even dingier. He felt knots in his neck, though they had probably formed before his big move. He tilted his head side to side, satisfied yet displeased with the cracking. Detective Acosta turned around and watched Freddie skeptically as he stood straight again. All Freddie could manage was a weary, dumb smile, which didn't help his situation with Acosta.

The elevator doors opened, and for a moment he forgot where he was. He could've been running errands for his next vacation. But the hallway reminded him of exactly where he was: a step away from Homicide. Just not how he hoped. The hall was depressing, more so than Homicide back home (and he thought, *It isn't home anymore*), but that was the point, Freddie knew.

He tried to hide his shoulders wanting to quiver, prompting another skeptical look from Acosta, who then motioned his hands toward the hallway, giving Freddie the silent After-you. Freddie gave a dumb smile again and let him exit the elevator to follow him to whatever realm of hell he was ready to enter. His beach house was suddenly that vacation in Hawaii he'd had his dreams set on. He thought about Charlotte, if she was still in a gray room under surveillance or not, but it didn't change the fact that she had been there, and that made him want to run to her. Because somewhere underneath all the mind games and silent accusations, he believed her. Or wanted to.

When they entered one of the rooms, he saw Wes sitting, waiting. He said, "You've been hiding something from me, Freddie boy."

Some plan was in play now and had been for some time. Freddie got the feeling he was about to play monkey in the middle; no tries needed to guess who the monkey was. His throat suddenly felt dry and heavy, and he wasn't even sitting in the chair yet. He jumped to the sound of the door close behind him, then Acosta made his way toward his partner. Freddie took a seat.

What could Wes possibly have been referring to? Nothing came to mind. He thought everything was crystal clear since they last spoke, not that he was thrilled about any of it.

"I don't think I have, Wes."

"Detective Wesley," he corrected, then began filling in the gaps. "Oh, but you have. See, your girlfriend and I were talkin' and she mentioned somethin' about a note that was left on your property."

Freddie tilted his head toward the ceiling as he remembered. His throat felt dry again. "Must've slipped my mind with everything. It's no secret." His voice croaked.

"I'm just tryin' to figure out if you lied by omission."

"It was an honest slip."

"There such a thing as an honest slip, Acosta?"

"Not that I've ever witnessed, boss."

Wes was enjoying the power trip. "Listen, son. Just tell me about this note. Make things a little easier for all of us."

"What did Charlotte tell you?"

"I'm more interested to hear what you have to say. On record. You willing to do that?"

No. He knew better.

"If I find you've had more than one slip, well…it makes you look a little unusual, wouldn't you say?"

Freddie shook his leg again like a kid waiting for the last school bell to ring. He had told Charlotte not to go, and she was guiltier than he was (he questioned, was he guilty at all?). Yet…

"Yes, fine."

Detective Acosta left the room. *Why?* Freddie remembered Wes's comment on budget cuts, but surely they had some other detectives watching the monitors.

"State your name and date for the record, please."

Freddie did so.

"Okay," Wes said. "Let's start with the note Ms. Walker mentioned you have. Simple, right?"

Freddie chose his next few words carefully. He tried. "I had just moved in. This was a couple months ago, maybe? I fell asleep on the patio. I was there all night. I woke up late morning and found a notepad I had used the night before under my chair. I picked it up to take it inside and I saw there was a note written on there, one I didn't write."

"Why all the mystery around a notepad? What did it say?"

Freddie hesitated at first. "'She's going to get you too.'"

"Who's the 'she'?"

"I don't know. Like I said, I woke up and the note was there."

"Just like that?"

"Just like that." Then Freddie backtracked. "Well, I thought about writing on a notepad before I fell asleep. But there you have it. I fell asleep."

"What were you thinking about when you fell asleep? What did you want to write down and get out?"

"Just some thoughts," he wanted to keep it at that. "Creative thoughts."

"Creative thoughts?"

"Literary thoughts. Just some random book notes. I still have no idea what the note I woke up to is."

"You a writer now?"

"I found the notepad, didn't think anything of it at the time, and took it in the house and eventually did get my ideas out. That's it."

"So you took in a suspicious piece of evidence into your home and did in fact write on it? Putting your DNA all over it. Completely okay with the concept of a stranger being all up in your business and personal space. Do you hear all of this playin' out?"

"Like I said, I didn't think anything of it at the time."

"Not your handwriting?"

"No." Though it could be.

"Had you been drinking?"

Freddie hesitated. Not a good move. "What does that have to do with anything?" Not a good response either.

"A lot," Wes said. "The alcohol could make you forget you wrote it. Alcohol could make your handwriting sloppy, make you think someone else wrote it."

"I was sober." He thought he had been. But don't all drunk people say they're sober?

"Sober, tipsy, drunk, passed out are all different things, Freddie."

"I had some beer, but I was sober. In my right mind."

"Some beer," Wes repeated. "Okay. Who do *you* think wrote the note?"

"I don't know."

"Do you think Ms. Walker wrote it?"

"I don't know. I don't see why she would, but I guess I can't rule it out either."

Some silence until Wes eventually said, "I was telling Acosta that I think there are two people involved in these murders, and as it turns out, they've done a good job at pickin' a murder method that makes their hands look clean." And when Freddie didn't say anything: "We know your history, Fred. We know you're an idiot when you're in love."

"Who isn't?" This from Acosta, behind Freddie now.

I get called an idiot quite a lot these days.

"And being an idiot can mean a lot of things. Murder being one of them. People do crazy things on a daily basis, but heart- and gut-wrenching things can push a person off the edge," Wes said.

"You're investigating *premeditated* murder, and you think me being an 'idiot' has something to do with that?"

At the moment, Freddie preferred to be shark bait, his head between layers of teeth rather than sitting in the stale-aired room under shit lighting that was giving him a migraine that would last all week. At least being shark bait would get climactic quickly. This was slow and painful.

Wes leaned back against his chair exhausted, or pretending to be, and looked up at his partner. "I think I've reached an early dead end with the notepad."

Acosta walked around the table, just to send spikes of nervous pain across Freddie's back as he moved past and sat beside his partner. He said, "How've you liked living on the beach, Fred?"

He saw the detective wasn't going to let it go. He answered, "It's great. Very peaceful."

"I want to get a place that makes me feel at peace, with our line of work. Mystic Place good for that?"

Freddie knew what this was: the first phase of getting buddy-buddy with a suspect with casual talk and mutual interests to establish an empathetic relationship. The You-can-tell-me-anything, trusting vibe.

Freddie looked up at the camera, the red light next to the lens. He quickly looked away, mad at himself for looking at all.

"Can you confirm your address is Six-six-eight Mystic Place?"

"Yes, that's my address."

"And can you confirm you were a detective in New York City's seventy-third precinct in Homicide?"

"Yes."

"Why the drastic move, Fred? New York's got its murders and beaches."

There he was, thinking of an autobiography title again. *Murders and Beaches.*

He said, "I wanted to move away from where I grew up."

"Why's that? Still getting into fights with old schoolmates?" Wes interrupted. Acosta gave him a look that said, I got this. All part of their usual skit, surely.

"Violence isn't my thing," Freddie said.

"Clearly, if you chose to leave Homicide," Acosta said with a chuckle, and got more comfortable in his seat. "A homicide detective in Brooklyn, well-ranked in his class, who *doesn't* like violence? Rare breed to find these days."

He had expected Wes and Acosta would dig through his records, but it still bothered him. "I wanted to leave after my mother passed away."

"Sorry, Fred," Acosta said, almost passing as empathetic. "Were you two close?"

Freddie's eyes cringed a little. *Stop slipping.*

"You can say that."

"That's nice. Again, I'm sorry to hear that. How'd she pass?"

"Cancer."

"It's going to get us all. Best to just live life at its best. Detective Wesley here can't quit smoking for that reason."

Freddie kept quiet.

"Any relationships before you came out here? Girlfriend, boyfriend, whatever label you want to give it?"

"I've had girlfriends."

"Ha," Wes interrupted again. "Our guys need to beg people in your seat for that kind of admittance."

"I'm a one-woman-at-a-time kind of guy."

"You mean monogamous?" Acosta clarified.

"Call me old-fashioned," Freddie said, but his countenance and tone said, Duh.

"I see. So, any *one* before you moved out here?"

"Yes."

"I'm sure she'd be losing her mind if she were behind that mirror," he pointed.

"She was a detective too, so I guess she's used to this."

"I take it she didn't move out here with you."

"No, she didn't." The disappointment and heartache were coming back to him as he said this.

"Have you been in communication with her?"

"Is this really relevant?" Freddie said, showing some real agitation now. "My walk down Memory Lane." He tried to act calm, wondering just how much anger he'd been bottling up and for how long; it was only a matter of time before his cap blew off, and all things considered, sitting in an interrogation room was a reasonable time for it to happen.

"Just answer the question," Wes said.

"I don't tend to stay in touch with my exes. I find it's less stressful."

"Understood," Acosta said. "Any other relationships since you moved out here? Romantic or platonic."

Freddie knew where this was going. Obviously, both detectives knew the answer.

"Yeah. I've met a real son-of-a-bitch detective, I've got an old friend, and a girlfriend."

A smile stretched across Wes's face, one that told Freddie to watch it, but also showed him finding humor in the mockery as his eyes were fixed on the notepad he hadn't bothered to scribble on, pen in mouth. When he lowered the pen: "Sounds like you've got your hands full with just those three. This friend of yours...from college, high school, best friend since pre-k?"

"We met in college."

"Good to meet new friends then. Little more established," Acosta said.

Freddie kept quiet again.

Wes said, "She a pretty young lady? 'Bout your age?"

"She's a woman, about my age, yes."

"And you've got a girlfriend?"

"Yes."

"Have they met each other?"

"No."

Freddie could see the detectives found this detail strange.

"Do they know about each other?"

"Yes."

"Any hints of jealousy between them?"

Freddie was starting to lose interest with the questions, and Veronica wouldn't appreciate being dragged into this.

"I don't see why there would be if they haven't met each other."

"They popular with the boys?"

"I don't talk to them about their sex lives, if that's what you mean."

"You want both of their approvals, sexually?" Acosta asked, like a therapist.

It was the first time Freddie wished he'd never given Veronica so little as a touch to her hand. "I didn't say that. Again, I'm a one-woman kind of guy." He thought about that kiss with Veronica.

"Okay," Acosta said, "so any men for you to be envious of?"

"No. Envy isn't in my nature. I like to work with what I have."

"Do you?" Wes asked.

"Yes."

"You can confirm that Charlotte Walker is your current girlfriend?" said Acosta, like he was throwing Freddie a bone by asking an easy question.

"I thought we're past that."

"For the record, Freddie," Wes ordered.

"Yes."

"How'd you two meet?" Acosta asked.

"We're neighbors."

"Can you confirm her address number for me?"

"Six-six-six Mystic Place."

Wes laid out two satellite pictures from a manila envelope that had been on the table, Acosta still doing the talking. He said, "You live right next door to each other?"

"Yes."

"Are these your houses?" Acosta pointed at the two photos with a pen he took out of his shirt pocket.

Freddie glanced at them for half a second each and confirmed. Acosta asked him to identify each one. Freddie did, scrunching his nose, trying to tolerate the pain from his eye—the migraine and the wound. He wondered if he was being a wimp about it; the punch was hard but not the worst.

Wes caught it and laughed. "I've been starin' at that eye and haven't brought it up. Ms. Walker give you that?"

"No."

"No? Your neighbor, Earl, said he visited Ms. Walker's home this morning before we dropped by. Said he saw you with the bad eye."

This had been a long day.

"So?"

"He also said you were in a heated discussion, an argument, when he showed up."

"Even if we were, that's not really anyone's business, is it?"

"It is with this eye of yours, and what we found today."

"I got this eye last night at a bar fight." Another part lie. It wasn't much of a fight at all if Freddie couldn't get back at him.

"Thought you said you're not violent," Acosta said.

"I'm not."

"Which bar?"

"The Reef."

"That's not really known to be a bar for confrontations," Acosta said. "Have you seen the clientele? Youngsters with friends, family gatherings, those sorts of things."

"Yeah, well, it happened there."

"Time, best of your knowledge?" Acosta said, reading over Wes's shoulder as he took notes.

"I don't know. A little after six?"

"Know the guy who gave it to you?"

"Don't be a sexist, Acosta, you know better. Could be a woman."

Freddie reminded himself, *It's all an act. Everything, from the minute you walked in.*

"Who gave you the eye? Do you know?" Acosta asked as if he was helping Freddie out. The good cop.

Freddie let out a sigh. "Some guy named Nathan Roberts. We've met before. Don't think he likes me much."

"So, Ms. Walker didn't do that to you?"

"Why would she?"

"Self-defense," Acosta said.

"Nathan Roberts did this," Freddie said firmly.

"Why?"

"Because he's a violent guy. You should interview him instead of asking me all these questions."

Wes said, "You mentioned before that this Nathan Roberts has been pushy with Ms. Walker, physically. I'm wondering if he did that to you because you assaulted Ms. Walker."

This got Freddie red and angry. "I have never! I *would never.*"

"I hope you're right," Wes said, "and that there are witnesses who can vouch for you at the bar. Were you with anybody?"

"With a friend. Veronica Dorian." He was sinking into self-loathing. "She can vouch."

Wes scribbled the name in his notebook. "Before we move on to her, I'd like to know more about you and Ms. Walker," Wes said. "And if you two are as normal and cozy as you say you are. I'd like to know how it all started."

"How what started?"

"You two, together. Love at first sight?"

That was never the case for Freddie; it would be too easy.

"We ran into each other at the beach and got to talking. Couldn't keep away since." That sounded normal and cozy. It was the most couple-like thing he'd ever said about them two, but even now, he said it with a fake excitement in his voice.

"That was your initial meeting?"

"Yes."

"That's not what she told us."

Freddie looked at Wes like a helpless deer in headlights.

"I'll give you a minute, if you'd like to try to recall." He let a chuckle slip. "Glad you've only been dating for less than six months. After that, these little details and the anniversaries, they start to matter."

"Before that, boss," Acosta said.

Freddie sat tenser now, at the corner of his seat and leaning in toward Wes.

"Okay, Fred. Ms. Walker said you two first met at her place. Want to tell me what you were doing there if you claim you hadn't met her until a day out by the water?"

Freddie leaned back again remembering the whole thing. "I was sitting outside. I'd heard a noise. I thought there might've been people on the deck, but there was no one around. I went down to check it out, she came home then. That's when we met."

"You like to spend a lot of time outside on your property?"

"I enjoy the views, like anyone living on that street would."

"Which view, would you say?"

"Any view."

"But you have a favorite spot, don't you? A house like that's gotta have more than one nice view. What's your favorite? Most popular?"

"Don't have a favorite."

Wes wasn't happy with the response. He went for another try.

"You mentioned a couple times having just moved in. And this beach chair you like to sit in. Where's it located?"

"I didn't mention a beach chair, Detective." Not during interview. Charlotte must have brought it up when she was being questioned.

Wes stared blankly, probably upset he'd made that minor mistake. It also meant he was getting a glimpse into who Freddie was. This wasn't a game between two drinking buddies, built on theories and silly accusations. This was an interview with Detective Freddie McAllister, former top dog of Homicide.

"We know you've got a chair out there, son. We have pictures from different angles of the dig site. For the record, please."

"On the patio."

"Up front, side of the house, toward the water...?"

"The patio goes all around the house. One of the perks," he said to Wes. Then to Acosta: "So my realtor says." And now it looked like Freddie was trying to buy himself time.

"Which side is the chair on, Fred?" Wes asked again, now standing with his hands on his hips, next to his relatively calm partner.

Acosta said, "Even if you're not that good with directions, take a crack at it. Feel free to show me in the pictures, if you'd like."

"East side," Freddie said.

"What's your view from there?"

"My backyard and the beach."

"That's it? Based on these pictures, and I did a full three-hundred-and-sixty-degree satellite view on this too, you can see Ms. Walker's house well."

"Charlotte is my neighbor, so she sees my house and I can see hers."

"Is that how you saw her—" Wes returned to his notes, "—deck? From looking from your patio?"

"Yes."

"So you've been keeping a close eye on your then-just-neighbor, now girlfriend. That right, Fred?"

"Depends what you mean," Freddie said. He knew he was in deep shit now. "I like to keep an eye on anyone I care about."

"But you've been keeping your eyes on your now-girlfriend," he said matter-of-factly. "Working extra." Freddie didn't like the smile that came along with that last sentence. "The way Ms. Walker put it when we had word with her, was that she's known for a while that you've been watching her, and that it worried her for some time until she got to know you more intimately. She said she recently confronted you about it, asked you if you'd always watched her, since you moved in."

"She didn't *confront* me," Freddie said a little more than just slightly pissed-off.

"That's not denying the fact you've been watching her."

"She asked me earlier today if I'd ever noticed her next door, and I obviously said yes. And she asked me because *she* noticed something going on in *my* place. So, I guess, what Ms. Walker conveniently neglected to tell you, is that she's been watching me."

"To recap," Acosta said, "you've been watching your neighbor, Charlotte Walker, since you moved in."

Freddie was silent. No answer was going to save him now.

"It's a simple yes-or-no question, Fred."

More silence.

"Let's try somethin' else, partner," Wes said to Acosta and sat again.

Acosta nodded without looking over his shoulder and said, "You had been going to a support group during your days in Homicide. How'd that make you feel?"

"Are we in therapy now?" Freddie asked. He started shaking his leg again.

"Humor us," Acosta said.

"Okay. Going to the meetings made me feel okay."

"Go on."

"You know how it is. Cops are required to see a police psychologist for critical incidents. Homicide is full of critical incidents. I had to do more therapy given recent events. I didn't want to, but I had to." He quickly regretted that. That made him sound like he wasn't in control. "It was good for a little while. Then I quit and moved out here to not think about the old stuff at all."

"I get it. Everyone comes to L.A. for that."

"Or to be a *star*," Wes added with some heightened pizzazz.

"You were diagnosed with PTSD while attending these meetings," Acosta said.

"I have certain triggers. I haven't been officially diagnosed."

"Right, okay. Ms. Walker said you two grew close talking about therapy." Freddie didn't see the point in reacting to a personal and inane fact. Acosta continued. "One of the reasons you continued going before you quit work was because your mother passed away? From cancer, you said."

Freddie wondered if they had gathered this information from Charlotte or McKinney. It was as if Wes knew exactly what he was thinking when he said, "Yeah, we talked to your pal," he admitted. "Told us how he wasn't able to attend the funeral because there wasn't one."

"No funeral, Freddie?" Acosta asked.

"There was a church service with several of my mother's respected friends and acquaintances, and there was a private burial. Just me."

"Why the fuck would you do that?" Wes leaned forward after asking, ready for an absurd response.

"She was all I had left," Freddie said. "I never wanted her money or any of her other forces. My dad passed away long before she did. My uncle is an alcoholic, and I didn't want to be near him. I never got along well with her friends either. It just made sense for me to have a more private parting. People can pay their respects for the rest of their lives whenever they want. She's buried, it doesn't mean she's forgotten."

"Forgive me, Freddie, but I need to ask," Acosta said. "Are you sure it was cancer?"

After a moment's pause: "What?"

"You're certain you're telling us the truth about her passing away due to cancer?"

"Aside from that being a ridiculous question, Detective, yes, I'm sure. I know how my mother passed away. I'm sure her death certificate can confirm."

"You moved away to a nice spot, considering you were still a grieving man when you came to L.A.," Wes stated, pulling in his chair closer. "No trouble spending her money, what was left of her."

"What am I supposed to do, sit on a pile of cash just because I'm grieving? She wouldn't have wanted that," Freddie said. He wasn't close to his late mother, but he knew she would want him to live well, that was made certain by her unremitting hatred of his and her husband's careers.

"So you wouldn't do anything to her for an extravagant amount of money?"

Freddie rubbed his eyes, frustrated, on the verge of yelling, maybe even crying.

"Sorry, Fred," Wes said. "Didn't mean to make you upset with that eye bugging you and all. But you and she hadn't spoken in a while. With recent events, I just wonder if you conveniently made her go away and used her cancer as a cover."

"No, no, no," Freddie said, heat rushing to his face. "I didn't plan for my mother's death. In any way. Hence the private burial, the grieving, and the sudden decision to move."

Wes and Acosta weren't sloppy, Freddie knew this much. He knew they would have done their research with obtaining his mother's death certificate. Were they trying to get him to admit to something false? Why would thorough detectives want a false confession? Or was someone setting him up?

Acosta interrupted his thought. "Is that why you broke off your engagement?"

"Oh, yeah," Wes said to his partner. "Freddie here loves proposing to ladies. Just can't get past that."

"Eh," Acosta said. He deliberated his partner's words over a sip of coffee. "Some people aren't meant to get past that," he said, placing the paper cup back to where he had picked it up from. "So, moving out here, maybe you needed something else to think about. Something, or someone, else to keep your focus on from broken relationships. Sound right?"

Freddie kept his intense stare. For asking a bunch of yes-or-no questions, Acosta was getting a lot out of Freddie. And for that, Freddie feared him.

"Sound right?" Acosta repeated.

The way Freddie saw it, he was only guilty of finding his neighbor attractive—and suspecting her of murder based on sheer nothingness. At first.

"Too much focus can lead to obsession, son," Wes said. "I'm just thinking about whether you and Ms. Walker being together has put an ease to the obsession or only made it worse. Say, worse enough to kill Ms. Walker's ex-boyfriend and his equally fine friends out of too much built up rage and untreated trauma."

Freddie thought about his and Charlotte's dinner with Wes. The topic of murder, the news in the papers, everything. She had been so calm and the right amount of curious. She didn't show the least bit of discomfort, not even enough to squirm in her chair like he was now. How did she pass their first round of questioning?

"You'd know how to do it," Wes continued. "You know how the other side lives and thinks. Your father was a detective in Homicide too, wasn't he? You could be traumatized, even obsessed from that. You can be quite the little fucker of a sociopath." Wes spoke and Acosta kept his stare into Freddie's eye. "On top of that, Ms. Walker says you've been blacking out, feeling tired, falling asleep," he snapped his fingers, "without much warning. Who knows what you've been up to? You may not even know."

Where's your proof? he wanted to ask. Instead he said something he should have said the minute the interview began.

"I'm not saying another word without my attorney present."

Wes let out a little laugh. "Funny. Ms. Walker had the same look when she said that too. You know what they say about couples: They start to look and sound alike after a while."

Acosta stood as if Wes's speech was his cue, the chair screeching backwards as he did.

"No matter what I ask," Wes said, "something leads to you, Freddie boy. What I see is a traumatized detective with mommy issues who doesn't know how to spend his time other than being a creeper."

"We done?"

"We'll be in touch," Acosta said and opened the door.

Freddie slowly stood from his chair and tucked it under the table. Acosta held the door open for Freddie to lead him back to the elevators and escort him out. Freddie tried to hide the shakes as he walked, feeling Acosta watching him from behind as they walked toward the elevators.

"Oh, Fred?" Wes called out after them in the hall. Right when Freddie thought he was off the hook. "Do me a favor and don't skip town or anything."

17

Beneath the Flowers

Everything was a haze, distant and unclear, as Freddie drove through a mix of L.A. fog and smog to get home in stop-and-go freeway traffic despite it being past 8 p.m.

He glanced at his rearview mirror once he was on the I-10 West with Beverly Hills and Culver City on opposite sides of the highway. As he reached closer to Santa Monica, he noticed he was sharing the busy road with another driver who'd been reluctant to take the exits. He watched his rearview mirror and the road interchangeably. The familiar vehicle was still behind him, but the night made it difficult to really take note of the car model, make, and its driver. Maybe the car would change lanes and disappear as the freeway ended and became PCH. This was L.A.; a driver would tail you until the next chance to manically squeeze between two other vehicles in the lane over.

Through the mirror again, he saw the handsome face under the lights that looked like they were turning on and off as they sped past. A handsome and a creepy presence. Detective Acosta had been tailing him in an unmarked vehicle. The scare tactics were working.

Miles later, when he approached his home, he glanced at his rearview again and saw the detective pull over behind him. Freddie stayed in the car. He'd just left the detectives. Home was supposed to mean peace, sanctuary. His thoughts of unattainable desire were interrupted when Acosta walked past the driver's side and gave Freddie a little salute as he walked toward the beach. It wasn't just the beach anymore; it was a dig site. Acosta eventually ducked under the tape and stepped into Charlotte's backyard. There was only one thing Freddie found to be true, something even he couldn't miss: All his life he'd lost the important things, important people. He was going to lose something again, and whatever case Operation Venus Flytrap had morphed into, it wasn't going to end well. Just how, Freddie was on the ride to find out.

He wanted to sit in the cold breeze and watch the sun dip into the horizon, and stay there in that moment forever. He wanted to lay under the sky and beneath the flowers in his childhood yard. At home.

Home. Wherever that was.

He tested himself with some sleep, wanting to see if he could enjoy some before the next load of folly would strike.

He slept and dreamed. He was at his father's funeral again. After isolating himself from the guests at the wake and his Uncle Harry, he had trailed off to find his mother. When he spotted her, he tapped her on her black dress and said, *I want to go home.* Confused, she'd replied, *We are home, Freddie.* He didn't see a way out.

He woke himself up mumbling. Then, in a near whisper, he said, "You are home, Freddie."

As he sat up trying to clear his head of sad memories, he realized he needed to warn Veronica of the latest developments with the detectives, aware that the timing of this call would look peculiar on phone records if there was ever a need for the detectives to examine those.

Had he jeopardized Veronica's move? She would never forgive him, and the reasons for her not to forgive him were becoming extensive. That was all Veronica needed: a detective showing up on her doorstep, Freddie bringing her into his world, inviting her in. The idea of inviting Veronica in was pretty, like following the colors of a rainbow; like it would be splendid and not an utter waste of time. But this was more like forcing her in.

Thinking about Veronica wasn't helping. He was preoccupied with what Charlotte was admitting or keeping. He couldn't picture her in a small room with a two-way mirror and ugly lighting. He wanted her to be perfect. And even if he loved her looks, the little bad she had in her, and all she was with her past and present, he didn't want to know her as ugly.

He thought a drive to Santa Monica would help him release some steam, this time, as a therapeutic drive without a detective tailing him.

It didn't work. The drive was useless. He made a left turn onto Mystic Place and wasn't any calmer. He sat in his car for a while. Suddenly, the sound of a bullet made Freddie duck in his seat without any time to embrace the fear or the reality of it being a tap on the window.

Wes leaned against the car with his hand propped against the roof. Freddie rolled down the window since Wes didn't bother to move away from the door.

"A little shaken up, Fred?"

"Yeah, Freddie boy's seen better days," he said honestly, avoiding eye contact.

"I hate to be the bearer of bad news, on top of this bad day you're having." Freddie waited for it. "We're going to need to search your house, which is why my partner and I are here. Searching the yard will require daylight, but I'm going to need the notebook tonight."

"How long will it take? I'd like to ice the eye," he pointed at it. "Preferably with some liquor. And preferably without you in my house."

"We take the notepad and we'll be on our merry way."

At the moment, Freddie could drive back across the country without a care while Mystic Place burned.

Freddie stepped out of the car and handed Wes the keys. Wes dangled them up high for Acosta's attention. He had already been watching them from the villa's front steps. Acosta came over coolly and Wes handed the keys to his partner without another word.

"Can you—"

Acosta looked back at Freddie annoyed.

"—lock the car door, please?" Freddie pointed out the car key on the ring.

Acosta gave him a grimace. "Don't worry, a patrol car will be here soon. I think your car will be safe," he said, and walked ahead to open the front door.

Acosta checked out the built-in bar on his way in, but not for long since it was unused and wasn't decorated for the homey feel. In the kitchen, Wes pointed out the leftover booze on the counter. Now the empty bar made sense to Acosta.

Freddie led the detectives to the drawer, where he handed them the notepad, giving them what they wanted. Now they could leave and he could recover from his day.

Freddie's cell phone rang and buzzed, distracting both detectives. He took the call in his other, more private living room.

"Hey, Ron."

"Is this Freddie McAllister?" This was not Veronica, though it was a woman's voice. It was her tone that bothered him. He hadn't heard one like it since he was making arrangements to bury his mother.

"This is. Who's calling?"

"My name is Caroline, I'm a nurse calling on behalf of Ms. Dorian. She's busy with the doctor at the moment."

"Doctor? What happened?" He tried to keep his cool, remembering that there were two detectives in the house, but he was almost yelling.

"Sir, all I can say is that Ms. Dorian is a patient and that she was in an accident. I was instructed to notify you."

"Veronica doesn't get into accidents. Veronica is smart and checks the street four times before crossing." He kept going, his voice escalating. But if he continued, he'd stop making sense. He was exclaiming random facts about Veronica to a total stranger. Not a total stranger; Caroline, the nurse.

"Can I talk to her now?" he finally managed.

"You can visit her when she's done with the doctor."

"I need a quick word now."

"Sir, the doctor is with her now. I was instructed to call you and let you know, and that's it. I can't discuss more over the phone."

"Fifteen minutes," he said. "Tell her I'll be there in fifteen minutes."

Freddie didn't wait to watch the detectives leave Mystic Place. He even sped on the road, not wasting any more time to get to Veronica.

After an eternity of what was just half an hour, Freddie felt like he saw his entire life flash before his eyes—something that hadn't happened since a man started choking him on an empty street, causing that neck trigger he had. At the time, he couldn't remember how much time had passed as a man tried to take his life in that lonely alley. The report claimed patrol cars turned the corner approximately within the minute of Freddie making the call for backup. Thirty minutes compared to an approximate minute was an eternity.

Freddie finally undid his seatbelt and made his way. He studied the building as he got closer, unsure about what condition he was going to find Veronica in once he stepped foot inside. Whatever it was, it couldn't be good, or she wouldn't be there. He couldn't undo any of it—what happened to her and seeing her that way. These were all of his thoughts as the doors split open for him.

He checked in and stuck one of those tacky nametags that would peel right off any minute against his chest. Past the information desk, he walked around the aisle until he found Veronica's room, which she shared with another injured patient. He couldn't knock once he was in the room, the other patient separated by a curtain. He slowly pulled the curtain aside. She had an expression that made him feel like the world was a bad place but still complete and holy.

He sat on the chair beside the bed and reached for her hand, but she moved it away, grabbing the remote to adjust the bed. She sat up more comfortably and said, "They asked me if I have any family out here. I told them I don't, so I gave them your name."

"Again, it's 'cause I'm a cop, isn't it?"

"That's right. Couldn't bring a friend in uniform with you?"

"I know a detective in his late sixties who would find you delightful."

"I was thinking younger."

Seeing her with wires hooked to machines and an IV in her arm didn't make him feel tickled. "What happened?"

"Well, not too long after the detective showed up at my house, some asshole hit me with their car then drove off like I was nothing."

Freddie wasn't a good caretaker, as past events could support this statement. He didn't know what to do when anyone around him did something so small and human like cry. What the hell was he supposed to do with a grown woman in a hospital bed? He stuck to what he knew how to do: ask a bunch of questions.

"Did you see the person who did it?"

"No. The sunset was bright orange in my eyes."

"Where did it happen?"

"Right in front of my house."

"What about the car?"

"I don't know, Fred."

"Color, make?"

She shook her head. "I don't know."

He sighed, taking the moment to remind himself not to get frustrated. "What's the damage?" He eyed her elevated leg.

"I don't know, I'm on some pain meds at the moment, and they seem to be doing good things," she said. "Safe to say I won't be dancing at my now postponed party."

Her face had some cuts, and what he could see of her arms were bruised. Then he stared into her green eyes some more, until he noticed them in worry.

"Detective Wesley came to ask me some questions about you. He told me they took Charlotte in for questioning. And you."

"I've had a crazy day."

"Me too," she said.

Freddie tried to deduce when the detective had time to question Veronica. Maybe Wes was with her while Freddie had gone for a drive after being questioned himself. Freddie remembered Acosta on the road with him after leaving the precinct. "Your neighbors didn't see anything identifiable when the hit happened?"

"The cops got her statement, but she wasn't a witness. The rest claim they didn't see anything."

"What did the detective ask?"

"About you, mostly. Personal things. How we know each other, if I noticed you acting weird lately, if I knew your mom, your neighbor."

Freddie waited, but Veronica had nothing to add.

"And you said…?"

"I answered honestly. Good things, you idiot."

Again with the idiot.

"It might be the meds, but I'm starting to feel paranoid. It just seems weird that it happened after the detective's visit."

"It's not a crazy thought," he said.

"It's not your job anymore."

"How can you say that when you're here? I am sorry you're here. And for the other night."

"We're okay," she said. "Mostly."

"I'll look into this," he assured her and stopped there.

"What is it?"

He was about to spill the rest of what he never wanted to tell her or anyone aloud. "I'm afraid I might've done this to you."

"Fred, you couldn't have had."

"I've been blacking out. I've been driving to clear my head. I could've driven to your house and done this and wouldn't remember a thing."

She thought about it. "It couldn't be. Besides, I'd recognize your car."

"Not if you were blinded by the sunset and car lights." But as the thoughts and images of Veronica being hit played out in Freddie's head, he realized, the timing didn't make sense, especially if Wes tapped on his window when he'd returned from his meditative drive.

"Get out of here, will you? We both need rest," she said. "I'm leaving soon and I need to be better than this to do that. And since you showed up, consider your debt paid."

"My debt."

"Remember back in the day? We said if we ever got the strange phone call from the other, we'd drop all else and show up."

He chuckled with the memory coming back to him the way an old song would before falling asleep. "Ben was in on it too. We said we'd kill for each other. Can you imagine Ben? Talk about an inside scoop."

"It was a dumb pact made by three drunken college kids. Nonetheless, you followed through on showing up, so that's something."

Freddie wanted to put an end to this conversation. Talking about Ben and murder while Veronica was in bad condition was indecorous. "Get well," he said and left her in what privacy the room could offer.

Of course she would get better. She was Veronica Dorian and she had her mind set. She just couldn't set it on him.

Back in his car, Freddie's phone rang just as he turned on the engine. He reached for the phone in the cupholder and saw it was Charlotte calling. Was she finally ready to talk?

"Charlotte," he answered.

"Can you meet me? Just not at home. Not at Mystic Place."

"Where, the pier?" *Not the time to be a smartass.*

"No, the nursery. Tomorrow. Cops should be done searching the place by then."

He was silent as he contemplated the odd request at the odd hour.

"Freddie? Will you come?"

"Why?"

"Eleven o'clock tomorrow morning. Come in from the garden. I'll be out there."

She hung up.

On his way to Charlie's Nursery, Freddie tried to snap out of the relief he felt for hearing from Charlotte after both of them were questioned by the police. He also tried to snap out of the eagerness he had to drive over and see her.

As Freddie parked, he realized that he could be walking into his grave—a trap at the very least—and he was too late at reaching this conclusion.

Everything in the shopping center was closed except for Beach Bistro. Freddie foolishly searched for the HWZCSTR, half wanting to see a homeless man lounging in it, but the car wasn't anywhere in sight.

He was early, but as instructed, Freddie entered through the nursery's garden. He had never spent time there, at least not enough to admire its beauty. He had heard Charlotte on business calls or entertaining clients who would walk in inquiring about renting the space for weddings and other ceremonies. It was beautiful and seemed far larger than what it really was. On one side were plants and trees available for purchasing. The collection made the browning valley view seem more vibrant and flourished. And the lot was even more flourished across the way where a gazebo stood covered with blooming vines and more planters nearby, perfectly landscaped like a whimsical land straight out of a fairytale. He appreciated the sight until he heard Charlotte approaching him from the greenhouse. She wore a teal, embroidered blouse that protected her skin from the sun yet accentuated her tones. She had it paired with denim shorts and her usual ankle boots, topped off with a tan sunhat. It was the most stripped, as he liked to think of it, he'd seen her (aside from in the bedroom). She had that careless, perfect glow. With the greenhouse and her under the sunny sky and gentle breeze, the scenery was complete.

"You've never seen it in all its glory," she said. "It's difficult during the summers when there's no escaping the heat. A lot of plants left unsold die or go home with me, if I can revive them. Then there are things out of our control, like fires."

"You've done well with this place," he managed to compliment. "Cops left it in good shape."

"I wouldn't let them search back here," Charlotte said confidently. "It felt too personal. Besides, the dogs didn't sniff anything out."

"We know what happens when you think things get too personal." Maybe Freddie wanted to bruise his other eye to even the pain. He could feel her giving him a vindictive stare. After another moment, Freddie stopped taking in the view and turned to her. "Why the call?"

"I wanted for us to get things straight without any detectives around."

"I'm listening."

She adjusted her hat as it swayed to the generous breeze. "You don't have anything to add?"

"No, but I have questions. Where were you yesterday evening?"

She gave him a disappointed smirk. "I was here for a little bit after leaving the police station. I didn't want to go anywhere else."

"You weren't up in the hills?"

She thought about it. "No. Why?"

"Veronica was hit by a car. It was a hit and run. She's not doing great."

"I'm sorry to hear that," she said, almost passing as sincere. "Are you accusing me of this now too?" She tamed her hair flying in the wind. "I came here. Our homes aren't exactly inviting at the moment."

"Is that why we're here? What is this?"

"Goodbye, for one. And I got a lawyer. Thought you should know in case you need to make plans."

"A phone call would've sufficed to tell me that."

"I thought an in-person meeting would've been proper closure given our circumstances," she said and paused again. "I have never lied to you, Freddie."

"Except about your criminal record," he said in an obnoxious chuckle. "Was I an asshole for discussing your life with a detective? Yeah, okay. But let's remember you're the one with a criminal record."

"I was *fifteen*. What were you doing when you were fifteen?"

"I wasn't in a penitentiary."

"My record was expunged because I was a minor and didn't commit murder. I didn't then and I haven't ever. Even now I tell you the truth and you refuse to answer a simple question about yourself."

He shook his head ignorantly as if she was speaking another language.

"What were you doing when you were fifteen?" She genuinely wanted to know, as she always did every other time she had asked him a personal question.

He thought about it, hoping to find a better response before he actually answered. "I was thinking about ways to get out of the life I had. Of getting away."

"I was too, and we both did," she said. "I've learned to accept my fate over the years. You'd be surprised by the things you can come to terms with when you do."

"Being interrogated by detectives has been eye-opening," he said pompously.

"Good," she said in a reciprocated tone. "Now that that's settled, you can look around as long as you'd like." She removed her gardening gloves from her hands. "Take what you want and leave. It seems to be a part of your skill-set." She looked at him for what might have been the last time and left him there.

Freddie continued enjoying the garden until he heard Charlotte close the door behind her at the nursery, and it was mostly because he didn't know what to do, until a plant by the exit gate caught his eye. He didn't want to actually make it out with a free item. How pathetic he would be if Charlotte saw him walking to his car with a plant. But this plant was perfect for blocking the dig site at Mystic Place.

Freddie took the plant home without shame. It still wasn't as neat and perfect as the Fred Ives over at the kitchen window, but Fred Ives' flaw was that it couldn't do what this plant could. In its new habitat, it stood tall and unkempt, and the search crew outside was temporarily invisible.

Feeling slightly unperturbed, Freddie dialed his lawyer.

Calling his lawyer wasn't very helpful. The cops had already searched his property, and while they didn't find anything on Freddie's side of the beach, they had already collected evidence from his home.

To Freddie's dismay, his lawyer hadn't arrived to L.A. yet when he got called in for questioning again. And he hadn't gotten much sleep to not fuck it up. He'd thought about Veronica too much, her and her pain. How dare he be at home in his comfy bed and cushy house while she was in a hospital bed. How dare he self-medicate with alcohol while she was having pain meds forced into her system.

In the interview room, Freddie stated his name and date and the fact that he was there for questioning cooperatively. Then he cocked an eyebrow for the go.

"You've had trouble sleepin'," Wes said.

This again, Freddie thought.

Acosta got out of his chair, walked around the table, stopped midway and made himself comfortable, half sitting on the table before Freddie. "I don't wear makeup or anything, but my wife tends to use that concealer stuff when she's not sleeping. You look like you can use some."

"I'll add that to my shopping list."

"What time do you get to bed, if you get to it?" Wes asked from his seat.

"I don't know. Depends on the night. Could be eight, midnight, earlier or later. I couldn't tell you. I don't really have a pattern. Why?"

"Ever notice anything between the hours of ten p.m. and three a.m.?"

When most homicides occur.

"I called Charlotte one night, couple nights before the date you tagged along on. She sounded like she'd gotten a good workout doing something. Not sure what, but I heard a loud noise come from her place before I called. I always thought it was suspicious, but she claimed it was because some books fell in her home office."

"You're not convinced."

He could feel his brain turn to jelly. "I've told you everything I know," he said, hoping that would be it.

Wes gave Freddie a twisted smile, finding too much humor in Freddie's pain. "One more thing before we let you go. We collected that notepad for evidence, as you know. Mind giving us a handwriting sample to go along with it?"

Freddie said nothing.

Acosta said, "Hey, you wrote it? You wrote it. Doesn't add up? Nothing to worry about."

"Right," Freddie said. A handwriting test would help prove his innocence in the whole mess. He hoped. There was that one percent of doubt he had, the one that said, *What if it helps prove you're guilty?* It was the same amount of doubt anyone on a jury needed. He waited in the interrogation room, again, wanting to be at his old home, in his small backyard, low on the grass beneath the flowers where he could drift away to sleep without being seen.

He was thinking optimistically again. Veronica was going away soon. He thought maybe now that a case was heating up, a step closer to closing, he could go to a party clear-headed, drink with company, say a proper goodbye, a proper I love you. Anything relatively normal. He wanted to follow through like he'd meant to do years back, like he meant to do so many times before. He really wanted to. He felt sanguine. Because at the end of the day, that's all a homicide detective—a *former* homicide detective—had to hold on to in the midst of bloodshed (actual and metaphoric). But something in the back of his mind was shutting it all down. He knew the detectives weren't his friends. They weren't trying to prove his innocence. Wes wasn't a buddy anymore; he was old-timer detective in Homicide, what he was all along.

There were more whispers in Freddie's head.

To hell with optimism.

Then more whispers.

They said, *It's not meant for you. It would be too easy.*

18

Couldn't Get it Right

Operation Venus Flytrap went viral, only it wasn't really known as Operation Venus Flytrap to law enforcement, the courtroom, and press. Yes, the press; it was reported like small-town gossip. Even Freddie's longtime journalist friends he hadn't heard from in years called from out of state asking for comments. He hung up the phone each time and decided not to call them friends anymore.

Ben made the cut. Freddie needed someone from his college crew to celebrate moving into his new house—in the canyon, away from Mystic Place, none other than Veronica's ranch she had put on the market before hiring a stranger from a shady website to drive her belongings across the country while she planned to catch a flight to New York. Freddie had convinced her he'd be the best fit for the house by stressing that all the care she'd put into the property over the years would go to waste if she sold it to anyone else. That fucked-up karma they'd always lived around.

They shared the courtroom on a sunny but chilly October morning, about four months since Freddie had moved into the villa. Detective Dan Wesley, Freddie McAllister, Charlotte Walker, and even Veronica Dorian were all present to watch Nathan Roberts on trial with the hope that the former corrupt nurse would get hauled to prison for first-degree murder (and other charges the media didn't care to emphasize). But they loved to repeat the fact that Nathan had the guts to confess—to plotting and executing murders, attempting to frame local innocents (it was convenient that he knew Charlotte on such a personal level, and word had gotten out that Freddie was involved with her), and writing the note Freddie had found on his patio months ago.

Freddie still questioned the validity of Nathan's confession to writing the note, though he couldn't think of any other explanation if he hadn't written it himself.

Forensic experts from the crime lab's botany team took the stand to enlighten the jury and anyone else allowed inside about the plants native to California that could be poisonous to humans and animals, and aid in murder. They further explained that toxicologists found spikes of adrenaline in each of the bodies prior to post-mortem. It could've been due to the fight or flight response before the moments leading to death, but in this case, there were higher adrenaline levels due to the ingestion of poison found in plants, known for inducing heart complications, making the detrimental reaction seem natural.

This method of poison prompted the DA to bring up Nathan's previous violations and charges, all the headlines Freddie had found in his early searches. The jury was convinced this was enough to get Nathan Roberts locked up. This was the first case Freddie had seen in which the defendant's status and money didn't matter, but he wasn't going to start complaining about the verdict.

The entomology team confirmed that the bodies had been preserved before being buried in the sand, as there weren't any extreme cases of insects inhabiting the bodies. The narrative went on to say that Nathan had stored the bodies in the freezer police found at his home. The freezer was empty when they'd found it, and they didn't find any

DNA samples. Still, it was enough circumstantial evidence to complete their narrative for the jury.

Pathologists were on standby in case the judge had any questions, but no bodily injuries or intrusions meant they weren't of much help. They did confirm, however, that the bodies were wrapped in plastic and kept frozen before they were moved to the beach.

Freddie and Charlotte were puzzled by this fact. How could neither of them notice someone unwrapping bodies behind her home? But there had been busy nights in, away, or ignoring what may have been in the shadows or under pleasant rainfall.

The bodies didn't rot due to how deep they were buried in moist sand, safe from excessive heat. Because there were no intrusions to the bodies, they were less prone to decompose so quickly. Any bodily fluids that seeped out on hot days were absorbed by the sand. The rain, however, caused some minor erosion that brought one of the bodies to surface, the others not too far away from the premises of the first corpse.

Very few members of the press were allowed inside the courtroom. No cameras or recorders. The judge agreed to leak information to the press slowly to keep a storm from hitting the newsstands and all people involved, out of respect to the grieving families, and for the tourism and elegance that kept Malibu rich. So far, Nathan's name had been printed, along with his history and how the nurse was about to get "a taste of his own medicine." Other details of the murders were still unfolding to the public.

After the jury's deliberation on the last day of trial, Freddie considered approaching Charlotte outside of the courthouse. Instead, he watched her fade into the crowd with her lawyer, who served as her bodyguard against the newscasters extending their microphones. Once she was out of sight, Freddie found Wes standing around, appearing to have been waiting for him. Wes motioned his head for Freddie to walk over.

Outside, they stood against the wall and watched some jurors running late, latching their tags onto their shirts. Wes lit a cigarette in the shade.

"No luck quitting, I see," Freddie said. He tried to say it with a smile, but looked disappointed, not that he actually gave a shit about Wes's life choices.

"Yeah," he said raising his cigarette, "it's my tequila. Want one?"

"I prefer tequila."

He let out a sigh with his head hung low.

"It only gets worse as you go, son."

"Good thing I'm out of the force, right?"

That got a laugh-turned-smoker's-cough out of Wes. "Think about it this way, son. If you hadn't moved out here, maybe no bailiff would've taken Nathan Roberts behind closed doors."

Freddie was still mopey. Sure, a sense of happiness lived inside of him; justice had been served. But a part of him was depressed at the fact that he couldn't ever catch a break to have one good thing last. He couldn't get it right.

"Between you and me, Fred," he let out a puff of smoke, "somethin' don't feel right here." Wes kept the cigarette in his mouth and lifted his hat from his head, wiped some sweat away, though it wasn't particularly warm yet; still, standing in the sunlight made them appreciative of the cool breeze and aware of the humidity. He put his hat back on. "Forensics, every time I went over to talk to them, told me the bodies were in good shape because of the freezing. It drives me crazy that there wasn't any DNA in that freezer. And the fishing excuse Roberts gave us is possible."

Freddie agreed. "It *is* a coastal town. But some criminals are better at hiding their tracks than others."

"He's been caught before for milder crap. Who's to say he's better at murder?"

Freddie kept hush.

"Ms. Walker provided a blood sample. The only match was found on a pair of hedge trimmers she uses at her shop. Her freezer had nothing unusual. And Nathan wasn't sneaking around some random freezers either. No rentals, didn't spend time at the nursery. Just had the one we found in his garage."

"So? He cleaned it. Or swapped it out. Could be in a landfill or deep in the ocean somewhere, God knows how many miles away." Freddie stood straight from leaning against the wall. "Why are we still talking about this, Wes? He's convicted of murder in the first degree by means of poison."

"Yeah, but I've got that gut feelin' you love so much. And his confession? What was that?"

"He doesn't need reasons for doing the things he's done." Freddie took a deep breath, taking in the smell of Wes's cigarette. He wanted a tequila shot. "It's over," he said, trying to convince himself just the same.

Wes threw the cigarette butt to the ground and stepped on it, letting out the last of his toxic breath. "Yeah, you're right." He gave Freddie a playful shove and began walking to the parking lot.

"What was that?" Freddie teased. "I didn't catch that with your smoker's cough."

"Don't push it, son." After another moment, Wes said, "You should try that whole early retirement thing for real this time. Promise not to make fun of you for it if you promise to leave me and other cops alone."

"Noted."

Wes adjusted his hat in the sunlight and said, "I saw that nice young lady in there today. Ms. Dorian."

"She was there," Freddie concurred.

"For you."

"Yeah, maybe," Freddie said. "Or she was curious to see why a detective questioned her about her friend."

"Sure," Wes said, "but that's not the only reason."

Freddie tried not to let this meddle with his emotions.

"Nothin' there between you two? She seemed very protective of you when I interviewed her."

"Yeah, she's good like that. But she's made it clear she doesn't like detectives—me included—and I think I'm okay with our friendship."

"Just figured, you hadn't asked her to marry you, somethin' might work out."

Freddie nodded. "Very funny."

"Easiest case ever solved: Freddie McAllister needs to stop buyin' women rings. The end, case closed."

Freddie chuckled, a bit fakely, and thought, all his life he had been around crime and death. But at the end of the day, Freddie wanted something simple, something he could latch onto to take his mind away from it all. Charlotte had lived between other kinds of fights. Her fight was to simply live. She couldn't ever find a way to achieve that. That was how Freddie always saw himself after a day of work, even now. That was the only logical explanation he could think of as to why he was drawn to Charlotte from the start. They could smell the desire of hope on each other.

Now it was his end, the calm and normalcy he'd always wanted. Alone again.

But he didn't fool himself. He was always in the fight, the game, the crime…whatever he, McKinney, or Wes would call it. He was addicted to it since he was a teenager. He witnessed firsthand what trying to escape it could do.

But deep down, he knew none of it could leave him, no matter how much therapy or beach time he had. And just the same, he couldn't really go back to the force; he'd never truly left.

McKinney called Freddie to let him know he had seen him on television. Luckily, Freddie hadn't been bothered by the press, but he had been on camera in the background of a clip. "You're famous out there now too!" he said. "I have to tell you, it's not the type of fame I thought you'd have, but look at you on the telly. Grandkids taught me how to record it."

For the first time, Freddie had hung up the phone with McKinney feeling both lost and found. Lost because he somehow knew he didn't need the calls anymore, and found for exactly that same reason. Another chapter complete and time for another: *Canyon Life: The Valleys and the Peaks.*

Veronica's goodbye (celebration?) was his last chance to see her, make it feel old and nostalgic and new altogether. Bittersweet and more of that fucked-up karma.

Loading the last of his belongings into his car at the villa, Freddie could hear people—lurkers—outside talking, pointing at the crime scene, trying to cross taped borders before they would be taken down. More than a couple times, he'd stormed off outside toward the crowd yelling at them to fuck off. He reminded himself he didn't need to care about it anymore.

When he returned, he took a final look at the crane at 666 Mystic Place, which was abandoned and faded under the sun. It was good timing for a move. Another.

The drive to the canyons was jaunty. He even mentally mapped some biking routes. A good sign of what was to come, he hoped.

Mid-November. After a week of 80-degree weather, it was rainy again, reminding Freddie of his first day touring Mystic Place with Veronica. Only now he lived on a different street with a different view, one with mountain lions nearby. He had unpacked his dad's revolver (which he stored in a box deep into a cabinet near the bar Veronica had previously used as her workstation) on day one of settling into his new abode, ready for the mountain lions to pay his yard a visit, now that there were no seagulls or alcohol to help occupy his time. Well, there was alcohol, but only for the guests that were expected to fill his otherwise mostly empty home tomorrow.

Freddie hadn't been to a party in a long time, and Veronica's goodbye kickback came in a blink of an eye. He was excited and nervous. Or was it regret and sorrow making a new chemical concoction that would later require a different kind of concoction to help it all down?

The beach chair was in the backyard near the pool, with miles of canyon for a view. Every now and then, he could hear a car going 50 miles per hour around the canyon's narrow curves, sounds echoing, dogs peeved and making it known. Once they went silent, he could hear birds chirping. It was peaceful. He could catch glances of the ocean from the front and back yards of the house if he looked between the trees and other houses nearby. Then he could see bushes in the distance moving even without a breeze. The angry waves at Mystic Place were replaced by hungry wild cats.

The night of celebrating new beginnings and mourning partings was loud. Freddie had friends and acquaintances in his new home drinking, eating, laughing, and playing songs off a backyard jazz playlist; the music was indeed loud but not actually playing from the backyard. It had been raining on and off, and Veronica's intuition warned Freddie that setting up outside would bid the rainfall. He assured her his weather app had no indication that it would rain. November in L.A. years ago may have brought fog and rain, but now the month was the continuation of summer.

But Veronica had been right, as always. The rain meant the house was crowded. God forbid Angelinos experienced a little humidity.

With the people in his new home, Freddie wondered, was this what hipster beach life was? It couldn't be, not with Tom Coaster there. Annoying mongrel, yes; coastal hipster, no. Tom—in his fraternity uniform as usual, with those fucking sunglasses—popped open a bottle of champagne, bubbly foaming out all over. Old Veronica, the one who used to live there, would have caused a scene. Now she was all smiles, waiting for her glass to be filled without a care about spillage.

Somewhere in the background beyond the music and loud, tipsy crowd, Freddie could hear a cry, realizing it wasn't a cry at all. It was a mountain lion's keening echoing through the valley. He watched his guests drinking spirits, thinking what a terrible idea it was to have everyone in his new home. It should've been him and Veronica alone, sitting in matching beach chairs, toasting to their new endeavors.

He watched her socializing with Ben, the one journalist who refused to cover the story for his paper, giving the promotion to Senior Editor to a woman with whom he was in playful competition (as Ben proudly told Freddie and Veronica at The Reef shortly after he'd arrived). His conscience was clean, and he was happy to help his female counterpart with a promotion. *A win-win*, he'd said. It had felt like old times with the three of them.

Now, in the living room at the party, Ben asked Veronica how she was feeling walking around in heels. "I've been stuck in my hotel room after the accident. It feels good to be out of the boot," she told Ben, who kept eyeing her stilettos. "The sneakers will come out, just you wait. Give it another one of these"—she held up her glass— "and I'll get them."

Freddie flashed a smile at the two of them. He wasn't exactly in their conversation, but he didn't mind; they were both happy, a good sight to see, though he was unusually moody that night with another gut feeling he couldn't pinpoint. He could handle staying in with Ben and Veronica, especially if animal predators crashed the party. But having never been one for hosting, all he could think was, *When is everyone leaving?*

He wanted to step out for some fresh air (and not without grabbing a bottle of whiskey first, because the other bottles were all gone, consumed by the whats-his- and hernames they had invited), hoping his moment with Veronica would occur naturally.

Freddie remembered the revolver was stored near the bar. He had the bottle in one hand, reached for a glass, but instead pulled out the revolver and stashed it in his back pocket. He walked over to the sliding door slowly. No one in the living room was paying attention to the dimly lit bar area at the back of the house. He gently slid the door behind him and watched the periwinkle sky before it would become darker, seeing the sunset in the distance below. He sat on his chair and took back a big gulp.

Going to the liquor store will take longer now.

He took a drink back again and nearly spit it out, startled to the sound of the door sliding open. Could it be Veronica to let him have the moment he wanted?

He turned around, saw it was Tom Coaster.

It would be too easy, he thought again.

"Hey, man, sorry to interrupt. It's getting warm in there with all the lights and alcohol. Thought I'd come out for some air if the rain had stopped." The music silenced again when Tom slid the door shut.

Freddie nodded sympathetically. He got up from his chair and looked around as if he actually gave a shit before he said, "Sorry, I don't have proper furniture out here."

"No sweat. I won't be out here long anyway." Then Tom became distracted by the crying animals prowling around where Freddie now called home. "Woah, listen to that. It's a new view and everything for you, huh? You have to deal with all that wild out there."

Freddie didn't feel like pretending to find Tom personable.

Wild. A despicable word after everything he'd seen throughout his career and personal life. Talk about wild animals, Freddie had seen plenty. Wild animals he referred to as human beings.

"Yeah, I've seen some wild before, Tom." He walked closer to him on his way back inside. "Thanks again for everything. For helping me bring in some boxes, for bringing drinks tonight," he said, shaking the bottle in his hand at him.

Tom sat on a tanning bed next to Freddie's chair. "It's no problem. I like being on this side of town every now and then. New perspective on things, know what I mean?"

Freddie half nodded. "I do." They gave each other a brotherly handshake, something Tom Coaster still did after years of leaving his brothers and the frat.

They were both quiet as they felt the evening chill tickle their spines.

"You'd think it wouldn't be as cold away from the water," Tom said.

"Might be Mystic Place catching up to me."

"Glad you got away, man."

Freddie felt another handshake coming on. Thank goodness it didn't.

"L.A. weather, right? I mean, Jesus, it's colder than a freezer out here."

"Yeah," Freddie said with a light chuckle. "Still not as bad as New York this time of year."

"Speaking of Mystic Place and freezers," Tom said, and Freddie didn't like where this was going, "I was reading about it in the paper this morning. Local news is still covering it on TV. This Nathan guy had to be smart, but a mess of a guy, right?"

Freddie took a drink. "I'd really rather not talk about it, if you don't mind, Tom."

"Shit. I'm being insensitive. I'm sorry, man. Just thought after all that, who knew the freezer thing would actually work for as long as it did."

"Still talking about it," Freddie said, getting pricklier by the words that came from Tom. Yet, it was the silence that followed that got to him.

What was it? It was definitely too soon to joke about the case, or even bring it up as casually as Tom just did. It wasn't small talk. It was forced. He kept going, and he only brought it up when he was outside alone with Freddie, intentionally trying to piss him off. Something about the freezer actually gave him chills. The freezer.

The judge had agreed to release information to the press gently, gradually. Freddie had paid close attention to all details that the media presented. No freezer had been mentioned in the press yet, not in the papers and not on TV. Even as of this morning. Not even the fact that the bodies were moved from point A to B. Just that they had been preserved in the sand. Most of the information that made it mainstream had been about Nathan Roberts and his rogue history, that small town gossip everyone loved to spread.

Tom Coaster wasn't in the courtroom. Tom Coaster shouldn't have known about a freezer full of bodies.

Freddie's prefrontal cortex was still telling him to keep quiet and think things through before doing anything hasty. But his mouth...

"What was that about the freezer?" he asked.

Tom was silent now. Again, on purpose, his face going long.

"Always like to be the shark, is what you said, right?"

Tom was overconfident now. It was out of the bag. No going back, and now he was going to boast about it. He stood up from the tanning bed.

"Knew it the minute I met you, Freddie. Nothing gets past you. So for us to be out here is a little embarrassing for you, isn't it? I read all about you during your detective days in the Big Apple after Veronica told me you'd moved into Six-six-eight. You're not as good as you used to be, so why don't you give me the gun you have behind you?"

"I don't think so, Tom," Freddie said gingerly. He set the bottle down by the chair, and another cry filled the air, sounding louder, closer.

"You know I don't need the gun," Tom said. "You know what I'm capable of." He was still cocky as ever, like he couldn't sweat. No nervousness, no stress. Just pride.

"Which is what, exactly, Tom?"

"You know," he said insistently.

"I think I need to hear you say it."

"Ah, I see. You still need to do the whole procedural thing. You are a man of routine, aren't you? You need to hear that I'm capable of murder. And letting someone else take the fall for it. Is that what you needed? Now, give me the gun, Freddie."

"I'm not giving you my gun. It happens to be valuable. My dad's." Freddie needed to buy himself some time since he hadn't been in a decent fight, or negotiation, in a while.

"Didn't pin you to be the sentimental type."

"We all have our weaknesses."

"Like Veronica."

Freddie wanted to charge at him then, but instead dwelled upon the fact that he didn't bring his phone outside with him to record the conversation or call for reinforcement. He had been too focused on his gun and whiskey.

"Veronica tells me you've got a real problem. And you've been drinking. You shouldn't hold a weapon while intoxicated."

"I'm fine. Sober, in fact. You really shouldn't mention Veronica's name while I'm in possession of a firearm. Not when I'm out here with a killer. At my new home, I might add. There's a room full of people in there, Tom. We can do this calmly and right."

Tom walked closer to Freddie, then stood casually near the pool, Freddie still near his beach chair. *I'm actually going to die in this fucking chair,* he thought.

"You've been drinking," Tom said again. "Everyone in there has seen you with an alcoholic beverage in your hand all evening. And Veronica knows about your drinking habits. Who's to say no one else in there doesn't, or won't find out? One mistake is all it would take for you to disappear like those people Nathan's in prison for, or like Nathan for that matter."

"Did you run Veronica over with your car, Tom?"

"No," Tom said like he was all put out. "I didn't hit Veronica. Come on, Freddie. I thought you were a good cop. You know it's not my M.O. Are you *that* paranoid? She said it's why you two could never work out, you know, romantically."

"Why did you do it? Why did you kill innocent men? *Four* innocent men. You all knew each other?"

"Yeah, I knew them. The first kill was tough. He was a friend, Hudson Ross. Which is why it was sloppy. Well, not *that* sloppy. I didn't have it in me to do anything creative with the body. I let people grieve for him. He deserved that. But that *feel*. It made it easier for the other three. Look, I'll spare you the villainous backstory, Fred. Let's just say they got in my way. It doesn't matter how they got in my way. They just *did*. After the first kill, the others grew suspicious of me. One of them particularly never really liked me, to tell you the truth."

"What about me?" Freddie interrupted Tom's thought. "I came around asking questions."

"Oh, yeah. You fit the description, man. So did Ted Finley, but he moved away and I never had to deal with him again. Lucky him, right? He would've been Victim One. I do wonder if he were, maybe the investigation wouldn't have picked up like this. I like to think it all worked out for the best. You were on my list for a while until I found out you were with—oh, what's her name? Charlie?"

Freddie's brow twitched.

"Ah," Tom said with a grin. "Yeah, Charlie. I'd heard you were growing some cred around town and, I admit, I got wigged out when I'd found out some of it was within the police department. The day I changed my mind about you, though, was that night with you, Charlie, and Nathan on Mystic Place."

Freddie remembered that night well, but not with Tom Coaster. He had even looked for a vehicle hoping to get information on Nathan, but he hadn't seen anything or anyone.

"That's right, Fred. You're not the only one who's been doing some watching. I knew about you when you moved in, but when I saw this other guy trying to get into a fight, I did some research. It was perfect." Tom looked up to the sky as he said it, enjoying his moment. Then back to Freddie: "Nathan was perfect. So really, I guess you can thank him for saving your ass. He really took one for the team going to prison. Poor bastard doesn't even know it."

"Nathan confessed," Freddie said, knowing Tom would let his ego do the talking.

"He did. It was easy to get him to do. After I knew the three of you were linked, I got to know him. He told me how he and Charlie know each other from support groups. He's a deeply unhappy man, Fred, did you know? And part of that was envy for Charlie's freedom. How could she walk around so free and carefree and help him? Nathan never hurt anyone. He was giving people meds they *wanted*. We agreed it would be easy to pin the fall on her."

"Charlotte has never poisoned anyone."

"Nathan lost a job, did time, and had his reputation ruined. He wanted her to know what that felt like."

"So did you. But you failed at that."

Tom smiled like the criminal he was. "I think it all worked well for me."

"What about the note that was left on my property? Was that you?" Freddie asked for good measure.

"I read about that, but Nathan's proven to be the sucker of his own demise for everything."

Freddie didn't know why, but he managed to chuckle. "I think I've had enough, Tom. I've had enough of you the day you walked into that restaurant. Before I met you, even."

Tom also managed to get a chuckle in, another moment of pride. "I don't think so, Freddie. You and me? We're the same. Maybe not *completely*. I'm obviously smarter to get away with a lot more than you have or can. But underneath it all, we're the same. Smart, acute, deep, obsessive. But for all the right reasons. Hell, you've got good taste in women and liquor too," he pointed at the bottle Freddie had set down.

Freddie stood there, somewhere between being paralyzed and full of rage. He had some admiration for this asshole threatening him on his own property. If anything, at least Tom had guts.

Tom said, "I know, I know. You're probably mad about the bodies on your girlfriend's side of the beach, but I had to leave *something* if I wasn't going to do anything else to you two. You probably need some time to process it all. I'll wait."

Tom started to pace near the sliding door, and somewhere in a split second that Tom's back was toward Freddie, Freddie knew that if he didn't act now, it would be too late. And frankly, he was tired of always being too late.

Freddie rushed after Tom from behind, ready to wrap him in a chokehold and turn him around to give him a good punch with something extra on Veronica's behalf. But months of early retirement and drowning in alcohol with minimum exercise had taken a toll on his body. Tom, on the other hand, was the epitome of the fit, L.A. stereotype.

As Freddie lumbered toward him, Tom deftly sidestepped and countered with the coming punch Freddie had been thinking about since the one at the bar. In his shock and pain, all Freddie could do was blink dumbly when his body hit the ground. The impact of the punch and fall would've felt a lot worse if it hadn't been for the whiskey. Maybe the alcohol would save his life after all.

Adrenaline pumping through his veins, Freddie was coming to his senses but struggled to stand. Trying was pointless. He was met with a vicious kick in the gut that caused him to hit the ground again, this time, by the edge of the glowing pool.

The evening chill made little waves, the pool's light shimmering against the house and palm trees around the yard, the sky a deep purple now. His back against the floor, Freddie could see another house's warm lights across the hills overlooking the ranch.

But the gun. It wasn't in his back pocket anymore.

He kept searching the grounds with his eyes burying themselves deeper to the sides of his sockets while Tom's strength felt crushing after a punch to his gut.

This is what that retired life had come to: rolling on the ground, desperate for life, and Tom just had to go for the neck.

A crazed, devilish grin spread across Tom's face as he tightened his grip around Freddie's windpipe. Now was not the time for that neck trigger. His body remembered what to do. With the last of his strength, he was able to use his hips and legs to throw Tom off him. Freddie scrambled away from the pool's edge and greedily gasped for air, each breath the best air his lungs had felt.

Freddie feebly staggered to his feet, unsure of what he would do, but determined not to die in his own backyard, at least not before he got a chance to really enjoy it. He didn't have time to search for the gun, spot it, grab it, then kill a man, probably bloodying the remodeled pool. No blood there. No, no; he had plans for the New Year. Indefinitely, but at least these flexible plans didn't involve him sitting out there alone drinking. He wasn't ready to kill a man; at least, he didn't want to. That would be something to give Detectives Wesley and Acosta something to be right about after all this time. Not in his new house and new life.

Surprisingly, Tom didn't try for the gun and instead charged at Freddie. Where Tom's movements had once been clean and technical, rage made him sloppy and Freddie was just able to dodge out of the way by a matter of inches. He swept up from behind Tom to try to put him in a chokehold again. Tom easily reversed the hold and with a swift, powerful turn, was able to knock Freddie onto his back. And that wasn't all. Tom threw several kicks and stomps all over Freddie's body, still careful not to make the scene a bloodbath.

"Let's try this again," Tom whispered with malignant relish, and dragged Freddie's limp body back to the edge of the pool and knelt down beside him. "Listen, Fred. This is a lot harder for me to do knowing I can't pin this on an idiot like Nathan anymore. But I'll take good care of you, like I did with the others. The truth is, you were, and still are, so far up your own ass, that this will still be enjoyable for me to do." Tom placed a firm hand around Freddie's neck again and leaned in. "And don't worry. I'll make sure to take care of Veronica for you." He pulled Freddie upright by a strong tug on his shirt, took the back of his neck, and plunged his head into the pool. After some long seconds, Freddie's vision began to blur. He didn't have the strength to fight back anymore.

This is how it ends, Freddie thought, aware that this may be his last thought ever. No women, no drink in hand, no heroic last stand. His vision swam and began to fade to black.

It was over. *Bam,* like that.

Freddie had felt a heavy shove to his head again before Tom's grip loosened, which allowed him to muster the last of his energy to throw his head back out of the water. He coughed up a lungful and gulped down the air.

Tom had begun to slowly limp backward toward him until he took another few unbalanced steps forward, like a funny little dance. He was still in close proximity to Freddie before stopping in his tracks. Tom fell to his knees before falling face flat onto the pavement, away from the pool. As Freddie could catch a breath, relieved of this fact, he saw a set of horror-filled eyes in view. Veronica's.

Then the ringing in his ear came. At first it was low and steady until it sounded like a high-pitched alarm. He couldn't even hear himself breathe. For a moment, he thought maybe all the pressure in his head made his eardrum pop. Or was this what dying felt like? Had he been shot? Had Tom been shot?

Freddie looked past the sliding door to see if any of his guests saw or heard anything, to make sure he wasn't having an out-of-body experience. On the other side of the glass, everyone was in the living room, toward the front of the house, but the smell of cigarettes and hash were still poignant. Then he remembered being particularly satisfied about the fact that the ranch's windows were soundproof (and wondered why the villa, closer to the water, didn't have such an amenity).

He glanced at the side gate that led to the front yard. No one was there. Veronica hadn't moved and her eyes were still wide and frozen like the rest of her body. Shock. He must've had it in his eyes too.

"Veronica," he called out, just to make sure he could speak and hear his own voice.

She stood still. Maybe he was inaudible.

"Veronica," he tried again as he walked toward her, feeling his wet chest get colder with the night. This time, he heard his voice, muffled, and his eyes dropped to the revolver, large in her hands, unbecoming. It was then that he noticed the blood splatter on his shirt sleeve. The day he decided to actually dress up, of course.

They both had their eyes stuck on the bloody body by the pool. "When we said we'd kill for each other all those years ago, I didn't think we were serious."

She waited for him to straighten up as he caught his breath.

"Have you killed someone for me, Fred?" she asked, her voice shaky like her hands.

He finally caught an even breath. "I've killed."

When he saw she was still standing in the same position, he lowered her arms nice and slow, her finger still on the trigger. She resisted at first, but he pushed harder until she gave in and her arms finally lowered. He took the gun from her and placed it on the ground a few feet away.

"He's—he's, uh…"

Freddie didn't finish the sentence for her, afraid of what it could do to her mental state. She was strong, yes, but he could be certain she had never killed anyone before, let alone shot anyone, or killed anything but those mosquitos they all hated so much. "Did I—Shit. Shit, shit, shit. I can't talk, Fred. Why can't I talk?"

"You're okay, you're talking."

You have good aim too.

He spared her of this compliment and said, "How did you know you'd hit him and not me?"

She shook her head slowly. "I didn't."

Freddie let out a sigh, more like a whistle.

She said, "When Tom and I ended things…when things between us ended, I started going to an outdoor shooting range here in the canyons. I was good at it, kind of like you are at bowling."

He didn't want to tell her they weren't the same, and he couldn't think of the last time he went bowling. "Don't say that out loud again," he said, wondering if Veronica could be capable of premeditated murder.

They both looked at Tom's body dark before the shimmering pool, the waves starting to calm since Freddie's plunge.

Freddie checked on the people inside again, saw that no one was rushing out. No one had seen anything, heard anything. That would either make a terrible statement for the cops or benefit the two of them.

"I don't even know why I just did that. I mean, I saw you struggling and thought maybe you were drunk, and that I'd come outside to break it up. But then I came out and no one heard me. But I heard him talking about those *horrible* things. Then I saw him throw your head into the water like that—" She was in full sobs now.

"Veronica," he reached for her, but she stepped away fiercely. "You saved me."

"No, I saw the gun there and I—"

"Don't do that. You saved my life. If not, he could still be enjoying this party and that could be me or you on the ground. Worse things could've happened. But they didn't, thanks to you, Ron." He wanted to hold her, but when he moved closer to her again, she flinched and took a step back. He couldn't blame her. He was wet, cold, and bloody. He stood still. Maybe she needed more logic, not support. "We're going to need to call the cops. And this is all self-defense. You don't even need to be involved." She gave him a glance that he hadn't seen since she was flunking out of Russian History. "I can take care of this, Ron. All we need to do is call the cops right now, and I can *arrange* this."

"I can call the cops. Because I did this." It was the shock talking. "I don't know if I can right now, Fred. I mean, I shared a little more than time with this guy, you know? And I...I kil—"

"Ron, listen to me," he said, holding her by the shoulders now so she couldn't look past him at Tom. "You go back inside, wash up, and go back to your hotel. Better yet, just call a car, get your stuff, and go straight there. I was fighting with Tom. The evidence of that is here. I brought the gun out with me, I'll admit, and look"—he picked up the gun and wiped it with his shirt before holding it again— "I have my prints all over it. And it'll have Tom's on it too. I shot him. No one heard because of the windows and music and the drinking. Understand?"

She nodded though she was still in shock. "Why did you have your gun out here?"

More concern filled his heavy heart for her. He gave her the short version of an explanation: "I carry it around with me when I feel nostalgic. Now, Veronica, leave."

"I can't—"

"*Yes,* you can. Go to your hotel, Veronica. You bullshit your way out the door if anyone asks you questions. You're giving your foot a break, can't be standing on it for too long or you'll relapse. I owe you, I love you, I thank you, but get the fuck out of here, because I need to make this call."

He looked at her until he knew she understood. There was a strange feeling between them, like they wanted to hug before they parted, but that would screw up the forensic system he had to stage, and now was simply not the time to mend other affairs. He watched her leave, saw no one was coming outside. He spotted Ben talking to Veronica at the front door as she was making her exit. Freddie worried she'd crack and tell him everything. Just what he needed: a journalist friend to put him in the dumps. He was relieved to see Veronica put on her best fake smile and give Ben a tight hug—she needed it—then leave her old home, scarred like Freddie was.

Everything was quiet again. Freddie twirled the gun around his index finger and returned to his new view. He sat in the chair, which, like Freddie, now had a new home and view set overlooking the hills of brown, red, and green. The chair had been with him for so long that he couldn't stomach leaving it at Mystic Place, among other things. As he sat, he realized he'd had his phone in his pocket all along.

He heard the echoing animal's scream, then another. He clicked open the cylinder and saw it was empty. The one bullet he had loaded was Veronica's lucky shot.

Why *did* he have the gun outside with him? The cops would ask too. He would tell them he had a habit of keeping his dad's revolver on him when he was at home, like it brought some type of comfort the way feng shui did to normal people.

He thought about what he was going to tell his guests, the bunch of whats-your-name-agains, when they would notice the corpse lying on the soon-to-be bloodstained pavers. He pictured the neon yellow tape all around the scene, just when he thought he was done with that. Funny, he thought, how he was always done with things, moving on, only to find them crawling back to him.

Freddie finally pulled out his phone and dialed 9-1-1. He sank into the chair, tired and achy, realizing how uncomfortable the chair actually was. Maybe he had finally outgrown it. His hand hung over the armrest, gun dangling from this index finger. With the phone in his other hand, he kept his thumb hovering over the Call icon.

The wild keened, sounding closer yet again. The animals moved fast in the night, but he didn't see anything in the darkness. He thought maybe he was too frenzied to be so calm. But he was calm, finally ready to execute his plan, because this was the one thing he knew he had to do. The rest was unknown.

The wild keened again. He listened.

For once, he just listened.

Acknowledgments

For starters, I am thankful that I have never encountered any human carcasses thus far in my life. I am by birth and heart a Southern California woman, and have nothing but fond memories at my state of residence. As far as I'm concerned, I know of no murders in Malibu or its beaches except this work of fiction I share with you.

A special thanks to anyone who asked, "How's the book coming along?" To Hourig Mardirossian and Fehbe Meza for the random legal Q&A sessions. To Rudy and Sarah Wohlgemuth for the emails and lengthy texts full of artistic insights. To Matt Fernandez for answering questions on the fly. To Aline and Talish Babaian, Savannah Hernandez, and Lori Olmassakian for sticking to it from inception. To Matthew "Nemo" Niemiec for the agent-style conversations, and Stacey Schepens Niemiec for all the laughs in between. To my Prince: the bravest little guy with the biggest heart. Lastly, to Los Angeles: There's no place like home.